STANDOFF

How the Cold War REALLY Ended

Rick Karlsruher

dixi
books

The Voice of the New Age

Rick Karlsruher

Rick Karlsruher is an American writer living in California. He grew up in Philadelphia drinking in the history, music, art, and stories of the city. His life has taken him around the world to see the good, the bad, the ugly, the silliness and kindness of the people across many continents.

If it has words, Rick has written it. From advertising to poetry, songs, scripts and two books, he has put it on paper or tape. His first book, *A Story Almost Told*, recounts his attempts to get *Standoff* made into a movie. This took him from Los Angeles to Johannesburg to many stops in Europe and North America. *A Story Almost Told* reached #1 on Smashwords and Amazon for the memoir genre. *Standoff* shows why he put his life at risk for his art.

Rick likes to teach by disarming people with laughter and history. Telling stories breaks down walls and brings people together. When not writing, Rick loves sports, movies, art, and music.

Dixi Books

Copyright © 2023 by Rick Karlsruher

Copyright © 2023 Dixi Books

Standoff

Rick Karlsruher

Editor: Andrea Bailey

Designer: Pablo Ulyanov

Cover Design: Yasha Harrari

I. Edition: April 2023

Library of Congress Cataloging-in-Publication Data

Rick Karlsruher - 1st ed.

ISBN: 978-1-913680-58-9

1. Fiction 2. Political Satire 3. Cold War 4. Humor 5. Alternate History

© Dixi Books Publishing

293 Green Lanes, Palmers Green, London, N13 4XS, England

info@dixibooks.com

www.dixibooks.com

Chapter 1:
Miles from Nowhere

The *clickety-clack* of the Trans-Siberia Railway was equally hypnotic and torturous. I woke up half-naked in my compartment, with a throbbing, two-day, drug-induced headache and a note taped inside my briefcase that read, "If I can do this, think of what the FSB and CIA are capable of." My thoughts ran to self-preservation rather than the mind-numbing sounds.

So much of my odyssey had been a living combination of Monty Python meets Dr. Strangelove that I had almost forgotten I was dealing with superpowers, real people, and telling a secret that would change the world. I entertained the notion that if I could concentrate, the migraine would dissipate.

I reached for my backpack and pulled out my notes. I spread them on the bed and tried to make some sense of what I learned on my journey thus far. After sorting through them aimlessly for a while, I decided there had to be a system: put each prong of the story in one pile rather than trying to make a single, convoluted epic from four diverse groups who had no idea about what any of what the others were trying to do. The participants sounded like a bad joke. What if the Soviet Union, the U.S., a small European prince and an angelic African leader were all trying to save their countries at the same time?

The first portion of the story came from the data I had collected about the Russians —Soviets, as they were known at the time. I'd uncovered a lot of information about the inner-circle of the Kremlin. I read it and re-read it, unable to believe what I knew from experience was true. There was no way these megalomaniacal buffoons and paranoid *apparatchiks* could have run an empire that spanned major parts of three continents.

As was always the case, the worker bees were the competent ones, brave and able to work under pressure. Much of my information had come from former KGB operatives who had been involved all those years ago.

Damn, I kept thinking during the five-thousand-mile journey each way from St. Petersburg to Vladivostok, *this can't possibly be true.*

My piles of notes kept shifting with the movement of the train on antiquated tracks. I grumbled and stood, opening the door of my compartment to recapture the ones that had slipped outside.

A beautiful conductor bent over to help pick them up, and her skirt rode up to show spectacular legs. She smiled as she handed me the stack of papers. I struggled to remember my rudimentary Russian, finding her beauty distracting. "Are you writing a book?" she asked me with a brilliant smile.

Oh shit, had she read my notes? I swallowed against the sudden dryness in my throat. "No, I'm helping with some research for a university."

"How interesting." Her eyes sparkled.

The train shimmied, and she fell into me. I wrapped an arm around her to steady her, or so I told myself. Her smile grew to almost feline proportions. Man, this was more of a test than any other I had thus far. I couldn't cheat on my girlfriend. More importantly, no matter how cute she was, I couldn't let this conductor see what I was doing. For all I knew, she could be FSB.

"Th-th-thanks. I need to get back to work," I said, releasing her and clutching the notes to my chest.

"If I see your papers in the corridor again, I'll knock on your door." She smiled and walked away and into the next car.

I closed the door, sat on my small chair, and took a deep breath. Looking in the cabinet for water, I discovered only vodka. I drank it straight from the bottle like a true Russian.

Fortified by the liquor, I returned to my review, starting on the next stack of notes: the scant information referencing the United States. As I read through it, I couldn't help but laugh. Doonesbury wasn't a cartoon. It was a documentary.

I gagged on my next slug of cheap vodka. The idiots in charge of the United States were every bit as crazy as the Soviets.

I found that the American team left a land of Victoria's Secret, Monday Night Football, and shopping malls for Russia, a country of perpetual gray skies, no hot water, and umbrella-wielding babushkas. The KGB was omnipresent, and the Americans could be shipped off to enjoy the Siberian winter if they were caught. Hell, if someone caught them, being sent to Siberia would have been downright lenient. I doubted any of the Americans would have made it to the next street corner. Stealing Soviet national secrets was understandable during the Cold War. But how could anyone have come up with this crazy plan?

I understood why the world's superpowers were so frustrated and willing to try anything, but their plans weren't what *really* ended the Cold War. In the geopolitical world, as in the real world, accidents often create the greatest results. I needed more vodka and sucked down a third of the bottle in one swig.

My notes blurred, and my head spun as I considered the two men central to my journey. The key players in this farce couldn't be more different. No amount of vodka could possibly make this make any sense, but I had met them and knew all of this was real. Insane, wild, crazy — but real.

Of course, I had to change the names of countries other than America and the U.S.S.R. The names of the players had to change, also, for my own safety and the safety of everyone involved.

The next player in this mad story was President Mbangu of Madibu, who has often been considered a living saint. Hell, he's known as The Great Man throughout the world. During a time when Africa suffered through brutal civil wars, dictatorships, corruption, and economic unrest, his idyllic island nation was poor and happy. He was a much better man than I ever could hope to be. However, his nation's successes were waning and he had to come up with a way to turn Madibu's fortunes quickly or chaos could ensue.

Although it was against his better angels, he tricked the U.S. and U.S.S.R., but no one lost, and his people benefitted greatly. How could he ever know that his beaches, hotels, a cargo/cruise ship port, rhesus monkeys and new-found libation production would help end the Cold War?

Mbangu's friend, and polar opposite, was Prince Claude of Luxenstein. All anyone needed to know about him was his nickname: The Pied Piper of Panties. As outrageous as it may sound, it was a gross understatement. Casanova was a virgin compared to the Pied Piper, and the Pied Piper was real. He was a one-man good year for casinos around the world. But this time he had gone too far; he only had a short time to fix it or his fairytale nation would be gobbled up as a province of France or Belgium to protect the public from his excesses. His family's five-century-old principality would be history. He couldn't hold back. If he had to be dangerous and crazy, so be it. Who would take him seriously anyway? So, he jumped in full force, hoping he would succeed against all the odds.

The last notes I organized before putting them back in my briefcase for the evening were the perfect ending point for the night. They came from Petey, an eighty-five-year-old former pit boss in Vegas, who had seen the Pied Piper in his wildest days.

"You gotta promise me one thing," Petey had told me.

"What's that?"

"If you find out the real story before I die, you gotta tell me."

"Absolutely."

A huge smile lit his wrinkled, ancient face. "When you come to tell me, make sure I give you my will first."

"Why?"

"Because when I hear what he did, I'll probably laugh my ass into the big one. It'll be a helluva way to go. Die with a smile on my face. Man, I haven't been this excited since that hooker in '83. You've made this old man very happy. I've got something to look forward to now. Thank the Pied Piper for me."

"You've got it, Petey," I said with a snicker.

Perfect. I let the vodka and *clickety-clack* of the train put me to sleep. I smiled to myself with that one last thought.

When your kid asks, "How did the Cold War *really* end, daddy?" you can tell him, "This is how. Don't believe what you read in the history books. Sit back and read the real story."

Chapter 2
Stumbling into History

A Few Months Earlier

How could I know I was about to change the history of the twentieth century? How could so many people keep such a huge secret for decades, even into the twenty-first century?

I've always believed the crazier a story is, the more likely it is to be true. But this? Let me explain how I stumbled, and I mean stumbled, into history.

I'm Mark Stern. I started writing for *The Philadelphia Inquirer* right after college and was the golden boy at the Inky within a few years. Hell, I was mentioned as one of the *Thirty Under Thirty* to watch in Philadelphia. The general feeling was I was a buttoned-down, serious reporter who looked for the story behind the story. Most people, especially women, found me boring. This, no doubt, prompted Charlie, my boss, to pick me for the biggest interview of my life.

I was on my way to interview UN Secretary General-Elect Mbangu, which would put me into the big leagues of political reporting. I could develop contacts worldwide rather than just in Philly and Harrisburg. I had no idea how big a deal it would be or how little in my life would remain buttoned down. Like one of my favorite singers, Jackson Browne, once said, "I'm just a happy idiot, struggling for the legal tender."

My newspaper's office was a two-block walk to the 30th Street Station in Philadelphia. In a city of parks, rivers and beautiful historical sites, my path to the classic station included an old office building, tacky parking lots and an overhead train trestle. The juxtaposition of the route with the magnificence of the building was not lost on me. People gave me strange looks as I passed, and I had to admit I looked a bit like a hobo juggling an overnight bag, laptop, digital recorder, and a news camera. In bygone years, I'd have an entire crew accompanying me, but with the way newspapers were cutting back, it was now normal to be a one-man production crew. In some ways, I'm grateful. I never would have been chosen to tell this story if I had other people with me.

After fumbling my way through the terminal, I boarded my train and flopped into my seat, grateful my circus act was over. I always found traveling on Amtrak trains relaxing, especially the oversized seats. Even when all the seats were filled there wasn't much noise. It was almost peaceful. I used the time to go over my questions. I must have changed them and the themes a dozen times in the first sixty minutes. It wasn't until we passed Princeton Station that I had settled on which line of inquiry I would use. Who was I kidding? I wasn't sure I'd get any of my questions out in an intelligent manner, since Mbangu was the rock star of political rock stars, and I was just a scrub reporter from Philly. I couldn't believe I'd scored half-an-hour with Secretary General Mbangu. Fifteen minutes was the norm, and then, his time was reserved for re-porters with household names. It never occurred to me that there could be an ulterior motive for this bounty of access.

The reality of meeting the Secretary General of the United Nations hit me after I disembarked, doing a reprise of my juggling act and rid-ing the escalator up to street level at Penn Station. Time felt like it had slowed down, and I became acutely aware of everything and everyone. It was almost as if I knew on an instinctual level something life-changing was about to happen.

I wove my way up the staircase from the platform into the main terminal. Knowing that I had a schedule to keep, I plowed through the throngs of people to the escalator to the street and strode to the curb to hail a cab, puffing my chest out and standing straighter than normal. As usual, lots of cabs passed before one stopped, but there was no way I going to take the subway that day. I wanted to get there in one piece with all my equipment intact and not having been peed on.

"Where to, sir?" the cabbie said with a thick African accent when I piled into the back seat of the car.

"UN Millennium Hotel, please."

"Security is incredibly tight over there today. Might be better to wait." He gave me a politely concerned look in the rear-view mirror.

"I don't have a choice. I have an interview there."

"For a job?"

"No, with the new Secretary General of the UN," I said. I couldn't contain my pride, and my chest puffed out like one of those birds of paradise on National Geographic.

The cabbie kept driving but turned his head to look at me. He managed not to kill us, but I swallowed the lump in my throat, wondering if he had cabbie ESP that somehow kept him in our lane. "You are mighty young to be speaking with The Great Man."

I fished my notepad out of a pocket along with a pen. "I'm older than I look. What do you know about Secretary Mbangu?"

"My home country is very near his. When they had great success, he shared it with our people."

"Why did you leave?"

"The war. It was many years before his marvelous success, but because of Mbangu, my wife and children could join me in America. I owe him everything. I will get you as close as possible." His expression took on the resolution of a soldier, and he looked back at the road. I jotted down what he'd said, thinking it would make a good addition to my article.

My new friend was true to his word. I wasn't entirely sure a couple of the alleys we took were wide enough for the cab – or legal – but he found a way to get me near the building. Definitely ESP.

The cabbie refused payment. When I put the money out again, he pushed it back towards me and looked hurt. I sighed. "I don't want you to have to pay for my fare."

"Please thank His Excellency for me. This is a great honor for me to pass him a message. It's a day I will never forget. Thank you, sir." A tear rolled down his cheek, though he was smiling so wide I was convinced his face might crack apart.

His reaction threw me off. Maybe Mbangu truly was a saint. The cabbie certainly thought so. My thoughts wandered to how I'd bring this encounter up to the Secretary General-Elect. I didn't want to embarrass him, but I felt obliged to deliver the message. I told the cabbie I'd relay his gratitude and stepped out of the cab and onto the street chuckling to myself that I had to be careful or I'd become the part of the story.

I used my foot to open the cab's door as I fumbled to collect all my gear and suitcase. I pushed much of it onto the curb. As I kicked the door to close it, I put the laptop case over my shoulder, strapped the camera around my neck, pulled the suitcase. and started walking.

As I turned the corner, I saw police barricades blocking off the street in front of the hotel in a veritable sea of blue. Cops nearly stood on top of each other. An angry-faced, middle-aged officer approached me as I pushed the barricade to the side. My ebullience faded, tempered with a healthy amount of concern. Was I going to make to my appointment in one piece?

"What the fuck do you think you're doing?" the portly, balding cop barked.

I plastered a smile on my face, not sure how he'd react. "I've got an appointment to interview Secretary General Mbangu. Here's my ID," I said, handing him my press credentials.

"Let me call it in." He gave me a suspicious look, his eyes narrow. He lifted his radio and spoke into it, turning away from me, though he watched me out of the corner of his eye.

It took forever for whoever was at the station to answer him. He glared at me and put a hand on his holstered gun as he waited. I thought he might be fucking with me, but better safe than shot.

When the answer finally came, he nodded and pointed toward the doors. "Go on around front. You will be searched when you enter."

"Thanks." A huge weight lifted off me, and I took a deep breath.

"Next time, ask before you try to go through a police barricade. The next cop you run into may shoot first and ask questions later. I just didn't want to have to fill out the damn paperwork."

We both chuckled, and he patted me on the back as I walked into the hotel. Two more cops and two UN guards waited inside the door. They waved a metal-detector wand over me. Then, they searched my overnight bag, turned my computer on and checked everything I had on me. Finally, they put it all through a metal detector.

After I retrieved my stuff, one of the UN guards took me by the arm, led me to a private elevator, and pressed the only button. We rose and were totally silent. The door opened. I got out.

An elegantly-dressed black man met me at the elevator. "Mr. Stern, I am Jinare. His Excellency President Mbangu is looking forward to meeting you. Please follow me."

"I'm very grateful that he's willing to talk to me." My heart pounded in my ribs as nervous energy washed over me.

We walked down the hallway until we came to a set of twelve-foot-high mahogany doors. Jinare opened one, and we entered a magnificent suite. White marble floors shone with recent polish, and dark wood paneling, matching the mahogany doors, covered the walls. Elegant furniture, artfully arranged into several seating areas, filled the room. Each area was a little different. One had overstuffed leather sofas, chairs and inlaid tables. The next had tasteful, antique cloth-covered furniture. It was elegant and understated. This is where President Mbangu sat on a large sofa. A peaceful aura surrounded him, and I'd never met anyone with a presence like his. He gave me an easy smile, full of confidence and gentle strength. His peace washed over me, and some of the knots in my stomach released. Despite the size of his presence, Mbangu himself was not a large man, maybe 5'10" and one hundred-sixty pounds. In the prime of middle age, he had smile lines around his mouth and eyes that were soft but strong. A smattering of white touched his dark hair.

"Your Excellency, may I present Mr. Mark Stern," Jinare said, bowing to President Mbangu.

Mbangu rose and walked towards me, offering me a hand. "Thank you, Jinare. Mr. Stern, it's a great honor to meet you. I read your series about improving education in Philadelphia. They were excellent. I implemented some of your ideas in our country and I am pleased to say that they worked."

I almost fainted and shook his hand. The soon-to-be Secretary General of the UN had read my work. I understood the cabbie's reverence. Some people are just powerful, but Mbangu fit his moniker, The Great Man. "Thank you, Mr. Secretary General."

"I am not yet Secretary General, but you are most welcome." His eyes glittered with laughter.

Jinare turned to leave the room, and they shared a grin. Mbangu winked. I had the feeling they knew something I didn't, but I wasn't afraid. For some reason, I was more excited than terrified. "Come, let us sit." President Mbangu gestured to one of the clusters of seats.

"Mr. President, the cabbie who drove me here asked me to thank you for helping create peace in his nation, which led to his wife and children being able to come to America."

As we sat down, President Mbangu smiled, his expression almost shy. I could have sworn a tear came to his eyes as he listened. "Mr. Stern, that was very kind of you. I will always remember your kindness. How shall we start?"

I pulled out my notepad, turned on my recorder and took a breath, diving right in. "When did you first decide to get into politics?"

His smile widened and took on a nostalgic note. "My father left our family when I was a young boy. I watched how my mother took care of my brothers and me with so very little. She was a teacher and mother to all in our village. I saw our country and realized that they were all my brothers and sisters, and they had no one to care for them. I decided someone needed to take care of them, so I have."

As I wrote notes, the door swung open. Before I could turn to look, I saw a huge, almost childlike smile on Mbangu's face. He stood and walked over to the man who had entered. They were about the same age, though that's where the similarity ended. The other man was a bit taller, white, and had a regal air. He looked a bit like Cary Grant and the twinkle in his eyes lit up the room. They hugged.

"Mr. Stern, this is one of my oldest and dearest friends, Prince Claude of Luxenstein." Mbangu faced me and gestured to Prince Claude, his grin matching his friend's.

"Any friend of Mbangu is a friend of mine," Prince Claude said, grinning.

"Mr. Stern is here to interview me for the *Philadelphia Inquirer*."

"May I stay?" the Prince asked, looking in my direction with his brows arched and a hopeful expression on his face.

I shrugged. "That is up to President Mbangu."

"Of course, you may stay, Claude. Join us." Mbangu gestured to the seats and returned to the couch.

"This should be fun," Claude strode over to where we sat and flopped carelessly into a chair, slouching a little.

I looked between the two men, struck by how different they were but at the same time, how very much alike. "May I ask Prince Claude a question, sir?"

"Absolutely. We are more than friends. We are brothers."

"Why is that, Your Highness?"

"Mbangu and I met at Harvard," Claude explained. "He took his studies far too seriously. I was way more interested in the local women. My father's influence got me in, not my grades. We couldn't be more different."

"That may be why we got along so famously," Mbangu said with a smile.

I scrawled notes across the page. "Have you stayed close throughout all these years?"

This caught them off guard. They looked puzzled and exchanged uncomfortable looks. Mbangu frowned at me. "That's an interesting question. Why do you ask?"

"Well, I'm still young, but I've already lost contact with many of the college friends I thought would be in my life forever."

"Ah. That makes sense." Prince Claude's shoulders relaxed a little, and a smile covered his face again.

The thirty-minute appointment turned into nearly a sixty-minute marathon, covering a range of topics from politics and the state of the world to Mbangu's plans as Secretary General of the UN. Mbangu was completely open, and he spoke easily and passionately about his country and his plans.

Conversely, Prince Claude was a player, but he looked out for his friend. At times, they finished each other's sentences. They laughed often and shared jokes and memories. It felt more like a family dinner than an interview. Looking back on it, I was lucky to have met them in the time and manner I did. It gave me an insight into two of the most powerful men in the world in ways I never would have received otherwise.

Mbangu was as generous as he was graceful. But I could sense that he and Prince Claude were holding back and not telling me everything. My reporter's sixth sense, a less exotic version of the Spidey Sense, was tingling, but none of the prodding questions I asked breached that gap.

After an hour or so, Jinare opened the door, his expression polite and apologetic. "Your Excellency, it is time for your next meeting…"

"I am sorry Mr. Stern, but my schedule is so tight. I have very much enjoyed speaking with you. It has been a pleasure."

"Mr. President, thank you so much for your openness and wonderful details. Prince Claude, thank you for all your help. You have both given me great insight."

Prince Claude smiled. "Thank you for putting up with this old man."

We all laughed, and I left. I still felt a strong sense something was going on, but had no clue what it was.

I was in heaven. This interview was the most exciting experience of my life. World leaders had treated me like an old friend and given me perfect material for my article. I just about floated home from the hotel and spent the afternoon and evening working on my article over take-out Chinese.

There's no way I slept more than two hours that night. I had already begun writing the column in my head. Hopefully, I could finish it in the morning. Maybe I could convince Charlie into making this a three- or even a five-part story? There was so much more than either of us expected.

Mbangu's swearing-in and inauguration speech was to happen at 6 p.m. the day after the interview, in front of the General Assembly. I wasn't sure if I had enough time to polish my first draft by then. I could feel the words exploding inside me.

My alarm went off at 8 a.m., and I got out of bed and headed into the shower. The hotel had a continental breakfast downstairs with my name on it.

Within seconds of getting out of the shower, the phone in my hotel room rang. A voice on the other end said, "Prince Claude respectfully requests your presence. Can you kindly meet his car in front of the hotel?"

Taken aback, it took me a second to answer. "Certainly, I'll be down in just a few minutes." I hung up the phone and stared at it like it might bite me. Was he afraid of what I might write? Regardless, I had to go. I dressed quickly, grabbed my gear and left my room, heading into the elevator and mashing the down arrow.

I discovered a large man wearing an expensive suit waiting for me in the lobby. "Mr. Stern, please come with me to His Highness car."

I followed him to a stretch Rolls Royce. Boy, did this ride stand out! The car glided away from the curb, heading uptown to stop in front of a magnificent brownstone. The home looked like the others around it. Nothing marked it as different or unusual, yet there was a perimeter of security that encompassed more than an entire square block. This didn't smell like it belonged to a playboy prince from a second-tier country.

One of the security people opened the limo door and gestured to me. I picked up my computer, pads and camera and prepared to step out.

"Please leave everything in the car. It will be safe," he said, shaking his head.

"But, how will I do my interview?"

"Everything you need will be provided for you by His Highness. Please go inside."

I was dumbfounded. Why the cloak-and-dagger routine? They'd been so open with me yesterday. What had changed? Had I somehow offended them?

I took a deep breath, climbed out of the limo, and went inside. A sleekly-dressed butler ushered me into a classic European-style library. The Prince sat behind his desk. The fun-loving, amused attitude had shifted into a cool, serious expression. I almost didn't recognize him. "Please sit down, Mr. Stern."

I swallowed hard and took my place across from him. "Your Highness, is everything okay? Did I do something wrong?"

The silence in the air between us deafened me. I was about ready to speak again when Prince Claude spoke, his eyes assessing as he watched my face. "Can we trust you?"

"Of course," I hesitated. "But who is we?" Despite my worry, my mind started preparing to write an addendum to the column I'd been working on since yesterday.

"If we tell you a story —" the Prince started to say.

At that moment, President Mbangu entered the room through a hidden door, disguised in the wood paneling and bookcases. "If we tell you this, we must control all your notes until we are ready for you to make it public. Is that agreeable to you?" Mbangu asked.

"Uh, I guess so. But I confess, I'm more than a little confused. What story?" I asked.

"Mbangu and I have about sixty percent of the greatest story of the past fifty years. However, we don't know everything. That's where you come in."

I didn't know if I should run for my life or listen. Damn my reporter's heart. I stayed. "Alright. Well... what's the story?"

"Can we trust you?" Claude asked again.

Mbangu walked over to my chair and put his arm around my shoulders in a companionable manner. "Mr. Stern can be trusted."

Bolstered by Mbangu's faith in me, I nodded. "You have my word."

"Do you trust *us?*" The Prince said, the mischievous sparkle he'd worn when we first met returning to his eyes.

"Of course, Your Highness," I said.

"If I hadn't lived the story we are about to tell, I wouldn't believe it. It is how my old friend Prince Claude and I ended the Cold War without realizing it until the war was almost over," Mbangu interjected.

"*What?*" My jaw dropped.

Mbangu looked me in the eyes. "For nearly three decades, we couldn't tell anyone. But now that I am in the public eye, we are afraid it will come out on its own. We need to know the entire story before that happens; we must control how that information makes its way into the world. In the wrong hands, the information could ruin us."

"We just want you to find and tell the truth, wherever it happens to take you," Prince Claude said with a chuckle.

"I wouldn't do anything less." I couldn't say no. Journalism was in my DNA, and there was no way I could let a story like this prance on by without leaping on it.

"We will give you the pieces we have and protect you as best we can," Mbangu said, patting my back.

"First, you must quit your job. We'll set you up an account in one of my country's private banks," Claude said, his tone businesslike. He poured three glasses of an amber-colored liquor. It smelled strong, and strong was just what I needed.

I reached for my glass, taking a sip of the scotch within. My head spun. Was I about to become an unholy melding of Bob Woodward, Inspector Clouseau and James Bond?

"Second, you must believe whatever we tell you, no matter how outrageous it may sound. I promise, you will find proof of our tale, but when we begin, you must simply trust us," Mbangu repeated. His voice struck me as being worried and reassuring at the same time.

Prince Claude smiled. "By the way, before you go, it wasn't *seven* super models naked in my plane two months before my wedding. It was nine. It was an off night."

I nearly choked on the drink Prince Claude had just poured for me. The grin on Claude's face told me he enjoyed my reaction.

Mbangu smiled as well. "I think he's ready to know the truth."

Jinare entered the room. Horror crossed his face when he saw me, and he stopped dead in his tracks. Claude smiled broadly. Mbangu walked over and stood with his trusted aide.

"He knows," Jinare said, his voice flat.

Claude's amusement showed in his huge smile and twinkling eye. "He was told. I'm not sure he believes us."

Mbangu put a fatherly arm around my shoulder. "We've given him more than enough to think about. Now, it's up to him."

Chapter 3
So It Begins

Jinare led me to the car. He was totally silent and conspicuously wary. As he turned to walk into the townhouse his stride had shortened and become choppy. The past few moments had a visible impact on him. I was becoming scared of him.

The driver tried to carry on a conversation with me on the way back to my hotel. He asked me about the Phillies, movies and I can't remember what else. It's doubtful I said anything coherent, but he acted like I was insightful and funny.

What the hell had just happened? Did I have "sucker" tattooed to my forehead?

Could what they were saying be true? There's nothing in history that would lead anyone to believe them. How had it been kept from the public for two entire decades? There had to have been *hundreds* of people involved.

What if it *were*? If it were true, what did the Prince and Mbangu have on the U.S. and Russian governments that kept them alive for all these years? Nothing made any sense whatsoever.

My mind was racing so much that I didn't notice the car had stopped until I heard the driver say, "We're at your hotel, sir."

I nodded and said "thanks" as I grabbed my stuff, got out of the car and walked towards the hotel's revolving door. I may have been talking to myself as I rode the escalator to the bank of elevators. I had to show my room card to the security guard. Luckily, no one got into the elevator with me. I got out and walked to my room, opened the door and flopped onto the chair thinking.

We're talking about pissing off ex-KGB, CIA, NSA agents and lots of other people with guns, not to mention all types of exotic poisons and ways to create "accidents." Not that it was making me paranoid or anything. This was shaping up like an average Tuesday at my Inky office. Yeah, right.

I was thinking like a four-year-old who just learned how to ask questions. The problem was, I didn't know who to ask. Could Prince Claude and Mbangu be having one last college prank before giving Mbangu to the world? And, in any case, who would believe my word against theirs? It couldn't be true, but maybe it had to be.

Sweat poured out of every inch of my body. I opened my laptop to memorialize what had just happened, but my hands were shaking uncontrollably. All I could think was, if my body was acting like this in the privacy of my hotel room, what in the world would happen in a room filled with foreign dignitaries and the international press? I figured it was at least even money I'd pee my pants tonight. That is, if I didn't have a heart attack.

I changed into jeans and a sweater before leaving my room to take a walk outside. It felt like I was running a marathon at sprinting speed in midtown, although I was hardly moving at all. Every few steps I felt myself looking over my shoulder for spies or killers.

I found a Blarney Stone bar and had two drinks. I left and I got a hot dog and a pretzel from a vendor. There's something about a New York street dog. Between the drinks and the food, I started calming down.

Soon I was in front of the Milford Plaza, my hotel. I went through the revolving door and up the escalator to the mezzanine. I think I took four steps at a time. I couldn't imagine what I must have looked like.

"How's your trip going?" the security guard asked me as I showed him my key and pressed the elevator button.

"If I told you the truth you wouldn't believe me."

He chuckled. "There seems to be a lot of that going around."

In my room, I checked every drawer, lamp, light fixture and under the bed for bugs. Someone had to be watching me. I was a little buzzed, exhausted and frightened as I flopped on the bed. Every breath had a life of its own. Hell, I could even feel a pulse from my eyelids.

The next thing I remember was being in the shower, the water splattering and bouncing over me. Each drop echoed. I tried to pump myself up by convincing myself how great I looked in my classic black suit and red tie. Of course, the other part of me was thinking I looked like I was just a bad embalming job.

Calm down, keep calm. Did I have all my ID and passes? Check. My cell phone rang. It was a blocked call. What the fuck was this? Who had this number? Was it a threat?

"Hello?"

"Mark, I think it would be much easier if we went together tonight. We should be in front of your hotel in about five minutes." Prince Claude sounded downright ecstatic.

"Thank you, Prince Claude. I'll be waiting."

His car pulled up. The driver got out and opened the door for me. One of the most elegant and beautiful women I had ever seen was sitting next to Prince Claude. She was tall, slender and looked many years younger than her true age of about sixty.

"Ah Mark, glad you could make it tonight. This is my wife, Lauren," Claude said.

I tried to bow as I shook her hand. "Your Highness, it's an honor to meet you."

"Please, I'm just Lauren, and the pleasure is all mine."

"Yes, of course," I stammered.

"Are you ready for tonight, Mark?" Prince Claude asked.

"I don't know how you do it. This is the most remarkable night of my life," I said haltingly.

The Prince smiled. "It's just another day at the office for us, and it's just the beginning for you."

I remember being insanely nervous, scratching my neck, as I gazed at him and they started chuckling in unison.

"He is exactly as you described him. It's okay, darling," Lauren said, patting Claude on the arm. "You can breathe again, Mark."

"Your Highness?" I paused. "What do you mean?"

"He's good," Lauren said as she held my hand. "Mbangu never misses when it comes to judging people."

"Yes, he seems to have a sixth sense about everyone," the Prince said with a smirk.

I mustered up some courage. "She knows President Mbangu?"

"Of course, I do." Lauren said as she fixed my hair with her hands.

"Mark, you should know up front that Lauren was an integral part of everything."

"But Mark, Mbangu's wife doesn't know anything, nor should she, until your book is finished."

"Look at him; he's whiter than the sand on Mbangu's beaches. Don't worry sweetie, we take care of our friends," Laruen calmly said as she kissed my shaking hand.

The car wound its way from midtown across to the UN building, an imposing and hopeful structure. Ever since I was in New York on a fifth-grade class trip, the UN building has given me shivers. I hoped these feelings were of anticipation and marvel – not abject, overwhelming terror.

Suddenly, we stopped. The driver opened the door and motioned for me to exit first. I waited for the Prince and Lauren on the red carpet. I let them pass me and kept several steps behind them. Before I moved I put my press lanyard over my coat.

There were world leaders everywhere, many dressed in traditional clothing from their country. It was like I had walked onto a movie set. What the fuck was I doing here?

A security team approached. "Your Highness, please follow me," the lead person said.

We were led to the front row of the balcony of the main hall. Caroline Kennedy, Bono and the Cardinal of New York were several rows behind me. Everyone in the room seemed so calm. Just another day at the office. On the other hand, my head was on a swivel, and I was drowning in a pool of my own sweat.

The ceremony was remarkable. Leaders from around the world spoke of their love and respect for Mbangu. The room was electric as Mbangu walked to the podium; the standing ovation was long and thunderous. I could see the pride and tears welling up in his eyes. Three times, he tried to get the audience to sit down. They refused the first two and seemed to get louder.

Finally, they sat and he began speaking. It was mesmerizing. His eloquence lifted everyone's heart and mind. Unlike many politicians, he was eminently believable. He spoke of how easy it would be for the peoples of the world to work together. There were no problems that couldn't be solved. This was what he believed. This was what he wanted to do for the world and all he needed was their help. It calmed me greatly.

World leaders were weeping as Mbangu spoke. I looked over and Prince Claude had a couple of tears running down his face. His love of his friend was so evident. Lauren grasped each of our hands, a tower of wisdom and strength.

The Prince gazed into her eyes. Their bond was unbreakable. At that moment, I understood she was his equal. They were partners in life. What they had was far deeper than any love I had ever seen. She was a formidable woman as well as a beautiful one.

When Mbangu finished, the audience rose as one. He only paused for a moment before leaving the stage. He seemed self-conscious about all the adulation. When the crowd realized he wasn't coming back, they turned to each other. Handshakes turned into perfect strangers hugging. It was exactly what Mbangu would have wanted them to do.

I was now a believer. It was my duty to try to find and tell this story. What was the worst that could happen? Well, if everything went to shit, I'd be a lock for a posthumous Nobel Prize for Literature or be dismembered in an unmarked grave in Siberia.

Before the audience had a chance to exit, our security team came to get us. Silently, we were led through the crowd. The dignitaries looked at us with obvious curiosity.

There were three levels of security between the lobby and the private reception room. We were ushered through that room to another one. There were two more security guards covering the next set of doors. Our crew nodded and the doors were opened. Our phalanx waited outside.

As we entered the room, only Mbangu, his wife, and Jinare were there. Leather chairs as well as a wet bar and two sets of sofas, love seats, chairs and tables were in opposite corners. In the center was a ten-foot European-style fabric sofa with six chairs and a carved wood table. As they met, the women embraced. Mbangu and Prince Claude hugged for a very long time.

Lauren took my hand and led me to Madame Mbangu, "This is our friend Mark Stern. Our husbands have chosen Mark to write a story of their lifelong friendship."

She put out her hand. I shook it. "I hope you don't have to listen to their college stories. They keep growing greater over the years."

"I'll keep that in mind, Ma'am. It's such an honor to meet you."

Prince Claude opened two bottles of champagne and poured each of us a glass. "My brother now belongs to the world. They are so lucky to have him."

We touched glasses and drank. There was a different look in their eyes. I was now a member of the family.

After a few moments, Jinare nodded. "I think it's time to join the crowd, Excellency."

"I think you're correct, Jinare, but frankly, I'm not sure I'm ready for this."

Lauren smiled. "You were born for this, Mbangu."

"So true," said Prince Claude.

Jinare and I were led out of the room first and shown to the ballroom by security. The Prince and Lauren followed a few steps behind us. After a slight pause, Mbangu and his wife followed them. Everyone in the room stopped what they were doing and joined in applause.

It was wonderful and uncomfortable at the same time. I believed I was being told the truth. How crazy could this get? I had read several articles about Prince Claude and was getting the distinct impression that he was certifiably insane.

I made my way to the bar and got a double bourbon. As I took my first sip, I felt someone tugging at my elbow. Jinare. I followed him to a distant corner of the room.

"His Excellency is a Great Man. Do not harm him." He was as serious as a heart attack.

"Why would I dream of doing that?"

"There will be many times you won't believe what you see." He drank his champagne in one gulp. "I lived it, and I still don't believe it."

Jinare grabbed another glass of champagne and chugged it in one gulp. Then grabbed another. Was he acting out of relief or fear? He was the one person in this group who was impossible to read.

"Are you okay?" I asked as he did the same again and again.

"We had nothing to lose. We were young. Claude was crazy." He set his glass down. "Monkeys, vodka and more. Excuse me, please, I must attend to Madame Mbangu."

He left. What a way to leave me. The world knew Claude was crazy, and now Jinare was telling me that monkeys and vodka were part of the story. I knew I was getting drunk, but now I was trying to wrap my head around the idea that the Russians and Americans had to deal with Prince Claude and monkeys.

Lauren walked over with another a drink for me. "Jinare has been looking for someone to talk to for thirty years. Everything he and Mbangu say is recorded. He will be your friend and protector."

"May I ask you a question here?"

She smiled broadly. "You may not like the answer, but of course you can."

"What did he mean by monkeys and vodka and more?"

She leaned in to whisper to me. "That's only the beginning. There's pretend sex and money too."

"What?"

"We were young and Claude was Claude. Life was a game and he played it every second."

The Prince came over and took Lauren to work the room. It was about sex, vodka, nuclear weapons and monkeys. Oh yes, and Prince Claude playing games. But Mbangu had always been serious. Was his insanity intentional or accidental? If the U.S. and U.S.S.R. were involved, then the CIA and KGB had to play major parts. I'm sure they'd be happy to answer my questions with no repercussions. Maybe I could ride that unicorn home rather than the limo.

I thought to myself that I should start drinking like Jinare. Either I'd get too drunk and pass out, or I could develop the calm craziness of Prince Claude. It was a no-lose choice.

Chapter 4
Through the Looking Glass

The potential of being involved in changing history was mind-blowing, but I had to give my notice at the Inky. I had no choice, as I had already become part of the story. I'd have to man up and tell Charlie Bryant the news face-to-face.

I owed everything to Charlie. He gave me my first job out of college. Over the past ten years, he had mentored me, groomed me, and helped me move up the ladder in the crazy business called journalism. Now I was going to tell him I'd be leaving in two weeks to write a book about Mbangu. Hell, he was the one who sent me to do the column on the Secretary General in the first place.

I got out of the local train on the upper platform at 30th Street Station and took the escalator to the main floor. For some reason, I was drawn to stroll around the great hall of the classic station. It was probably a way to say goodbye to an old friend of a place. I finally left the building and headed to the Inky office. Rather than walking, it felt like I was trudging up to see Charlie. I don't think I lifted my feet a single time. I closed the door behind me, which caught Charlie off guard.

"Mark, this is the best damn column you have ever written."

"Thanks, man." I coughed and played with my pen.

"What's wrong?" Charlie put the sheets he was reading down on his desk, sat up straight in his chair and looked me directly in the eyes.

"I got an offer to write a book and need to give my notice."

"Fuck, after that column, I was planning to ride you like a $3 mule all the way to the big job here. What's the book about?"

"Mbangu."

"Figures. Did they see this column before they hired you?"

"No."

"Who's paying you?"

"His government. They want to play it up. The funny thing is, he just asked me to tell his real story. He said no fluff at all or he'll throw it in the trash."

"Sounds like a great gig. How long do you think it'll take?"

"They want to keep me around for a year or so."

"I'll call upstairs and see if they'll keep your job open if you let us debut it in the U.S."

"You're amazing, Charlie. I'll ask his people about that."

"When do you need to leave?" Charlie asked.

"I was going to give you two weeks," I said hesitatingly.

"Mark, if they want you now, don't make them wait."

Charlie reached into his desk, pulled out a bottle of scotch and poured us huge drinks. He had the look of a beaming, proud father. I sighed deeply.

"Thanks Charlie, I owe you everything, everything." My voice was trailing off.

We drank that one and he poured a bigger one for our second drink. It was 11:30 in the morning and I was smashed. Being old school, he poured us a short one for the road. We chugged our shots and slammed the glasses on the desk.

"Don't forget us, buddy."

We hugged. I staggered out of his office and left the building I'd called home for ten years. I gave it up for sex, vodka, monkeys, nukes and who the hell knew what else. Of course, I should go into it totally blind drunk. After all, it was only my entire life that was on the line.

I left the office, looked around for a last time, and started walking – well, staggering would be more accurate – towards the 30th Street Station to get on the commuter train to go home. I felt a presence closing in on me. Who was it? Was I becoming paranoid? At least I'd die drunk on great scotch.

A Cadillac pulled alongside me. The window went down slowly. The driver was a bearded man who looked to be in his late fifties. He eyed me up and down. Then he cleared his throat. I wasn't sure if I should run or pass out.

"You look like you could use a ride?"

"I'm not into that sir, but thanks anyway." I was drunk and he was creepy.

Suddenly there was a bellowing chortle from inside the car. "My accent is pretty good, eh Mark?"

I looked again. How did this guy know me? I looked at his eyes, his smile. I was still puzzled.

"Are you usually this drunk so early in the day?"

"I'm buzzed. I don't know you."

"Oh, yes you do. Didn't Lauren tell you I like to play games?" The man could hardly conceal his joy. He was a teenager in a late middle-aged body.

I almost shit my pants. I opened the door and got inside. "Prince Claude? What the hell are you doing here? Why the costume?"

"From now on, please call me Claude. I'm here so we can get started on our project. How much longer will you be working there?"

"Charlie said I could start today if we let him do the American debut of Mbangu's official biography."

He chuckled. "Nice choice. Of course, he can. You need some food. I saw a dark pub with a great name. I'll drive."

"What place?"

"Professor Moriarty's Pub. Sherlock would probably wet his pants at the mystery you are about to discover."

"Claude, that place is a dive."

"I surely hope so."

We careened around the narrow streets of Center City. He went the wrong way down one alley. Then he backed into a big blue dumpster, which attached itself to the bumper. Claude stopped so I could pull it away from the car. We merrily hit another trash can. Claude was loving every second. I pointed for him to turn at the corner. Luckily, I convinced him that the streets were alternatingly one way each, and somehow, he got us to our destination. We found a parking place about half a block from the bar. I'm not sure what was scarier, Claude's driving or the way he was trying to insert a twelve-foot-long car into a nine-foot space. As I jumped out of the car, he bellowed in amusement.

"You aren't going to vomit, are you?"

"Not if you don't drive anymore."

He bellowed again. "I like playing a character. It's a lot of fun."

Moriarty's was dark inside, slightly above a dive bar. A mural of Sherlock Holmes chasing Moriarty covered two side walls. There were about three dozen bottles of decent booze behind the bar and ten or twelve large pitchers for beer in front of them. Claude stopped by the bar to get us each a scotch and menus. We sat in the corner. As drunk as I was, I was still acutely aware of my surroundings. My eyes darted around the slimy bar. This amused Prince Claude greatly.

"Until a few months ago, around the corner from here was Dr. Watson's Pub. Only in Philly can Dr. Watson and Professor Moriarty serve drinks a few hundred yards from each other," I said.

"Then it's the perfect place to start. The most serious reality is often composed of dire need and uncontrollable hilarity. If you think I'm being bad today..." Claude stopped himself from cackling at his own words and at my overt paranoia.

The bartender screamed to ask us if we wanted some food. Claude had to have a cheesesteak. His family had run a country for centuries, and he wanted a frickin' cheesesteak. A few minutes later our food arrived, and Claude immediately inhaled it. With each bite his pleasure grew. I loved him for that but remained very scared at the wide swath of life he grabbed.

"Cheesesteak may be the perfect food. My chef will start making it for me all the time. Well, at least whenever Lauren's out shopping. She won't let me have as much fun as I like to anymore. She claims it's something crazy, like she wants to keep me alive a little longer."

"But you are the Prince."

"And she's the Queen." He wiped his mouth and sighed happily. "Are you ready to get started?"

I chugged my drink. "Maybe." I hesitated. "I think so."

"Think is a good word for this. Keep an open mind, my friend. The more outrageous something is, the more likely it is to be true. This story is no different. Stupid luck has changed many historical events. Fear keeps more secrets than you can comprehend."

"How should we start?"

"I would say somewhere near the beginning, but there is no real beginning. We figure at least four major stories exist. You'll have to research each one. I only know mine and bits and pieces of the others."

"How am I supposed to find out the others?"

"You're a reporter, aren't you?"

"You make that sound ominous."

"Are you good with languages?"

"I speak German and a little Spanish."

"You'll need to learn Russian."

"Okay, will do. What are the four stories?"

"They are mine, Mbangu's, the Soviets', and the Americans'."

"I bet this will be easy." I got us another round of drinks. Claude was like a kid on Christmas morning. I don't think he understood the word fear – maybe he was the world's greatest optimist or the luckiest bastard. Either way, the results would be the same.

"The Russians and the Americans won't like you telling their stories. You'd better be careful. We do have some names for you to find, but some will be hard to interview, if you know, uh, what I mean."

I almost pissed my pants. "Dead?" I finished my drink and chugged his.

"Calm down, Mark. It was thirty years or so ago. Lots of people involved were already old. Back then to get power, you had to be in your 50s or 60s. In the U.S.S.R., you had to be even older."

I gasped.

He looked up. "Hey, only a few people were killed in the name of national security."

"What?" I gasped. It pissed me off that he chuckled.

"We're going to need more drinks." Claude was smiling and motioning to the bartender.

"How – how did you get involved?" I stammered from a combination of fear and scotch.

"No one knew I was until it was too late." Claude's voice temporarily got serious.

"Why didn't they kill you?" I asked, feeling sweat on my brow.

"I've got insurance. So, do you."

"Are you sure?" I said, trying not to throw up.

"Yes, it comes from the top. For both of us." Claude become almost jovial.

"How about the bottom?" I said with hesitance.

"You can't predict crazy. Just ask Lauren, but let me put it this way; what you think happened didn't, and what you can't imagine, did. And you will explain it all to the world."

There was a long pause. Claude continued. "Mark, I can tell you now that sex, vodka and monkeys are some of the more serious parts of the story you are about to tell."

Come on. Was he toying with me or being serious?

"Think about it. I bankrupted my country in Monte Carlo before I started my part of ending the Cold War."

"Was all of this your idea?" I asked.

"Nope, just not getting hanged by my subjects was my idea." He laughed loudly.

"What?"

"Mark, I had lost the entire national treasury in Monte Carlo, Las Vegas, and on women. Of course, there was some of it I wasted on silly things other than women and debauchery."

"No way."

"My young friend, I'll send you to the people who knew about my true life. I was the world's greatest optimist and the world's craziest person. But to get to where the world is today, someone had to be certifiably insane. Why not me? And why shouldn't you be the person to tell the story?"

He reached into his pocket and threw some keys to me. "I think you'll find your new apartment in Manhattan satisfactory. By the way, both the doorman and the guy at the reception desk have been through high-level security training. Their jobs are a cover for their real purpose."

He chuckled when I choked on my drink.

Aw, let's get started. Why the hell not me? But first, I needed more scotch.

Chapter 5
On My Own

When I returned to New York City the next afternoon, I used the keys Claude had given me at Moriarty's to get into the new apartment. It was amazing, with two bedrooms and great views of Central Park from the floor-to-ceiling windows in the living room/dining room. Berlitz, Rosetta Stone and other Russian language study courses were on the living room table. I opened a large manila envelope that contained several credit cards and a safe deposit box key. A note said there was $250,000 in dollars with more in Euros and rubles waiting for me there. Not too shabby.

Claude left me password-protected and encrypted files on a high-end laptop. Curiosity got the best of me and I had to glance at a few. I turned it and read some. Holy shit! What I was seeing couldn't possibly be true.

Claude left me a note saying to learn as much as I could and then I was to report to him and Lauren in sixty days at their castle. A little Jew-boy from the suburbs was going to be staying in a castle in Europe. Yep, it made perfect sense.

One of the first people I decided to meet was a guy named Scott. He ran with Claude's crowd in the 60s and 70s. He suggested we meet in a semi-dive bar in Tribeca called Mudville Nine. That was a perfect name for a place where the first pitch in the game was going to be thrown. I wondered if Mighty Casey would be part of my story. Everyone else seemed to be.

I took the R Train downtown and got off at Chambers Street. I found the bar. Over in the corner was a man in his late 60s with a ponytail, with a leather jacket and a few empty shot glasses in front of him.

"Are you Scott?"

"Yep. Hi, Mark." He waved me to sit across from him. "What would you like to know about the scene in the late 60s and 70s?"

"I'd like to know a little bit about Prince Claude."

He smiled broadly. "The Pied Piper of Panties… now there's a real legend."

"The Pied Piper of Panties?" I said incredulously.

"That's how everyone knew him back in the day. Man, he had the best of everything and I mean everything. But he was a very cool cat. He was a prince, but he was great to everyone."

"Why did you call him that?"

"Because that's what he was. Once the word got out that Claude was in town, every beautiful woman on the East Coast would be hanging out waiting for him. Hell, Mick took his castoffs."

"Mick?" I asked.

"Jagger treated Claude like a god. He learned from the Pied Piper."

This took me a minute to absorb.

"Were you ever at Claude's parties?" I asked.

"He'd rent an entire fucking hotel and have parties on every floor. My favorite ones were his flying parties." Scott was smiling broadly.

"What?" I was puzzled.

"He'd get wasted. Then call airlines until he found a plane he could rent. He'd hire bunches of cabs and limos to take us to LaGuardia or JFK. Then we'd fly to LA, Hawaii, the Bahamas. But by far the best was Vegas."

I waited for him to continue.

"All the way there, there'd be an orgy. They had to kick us out of the plane. Limos took us all to the casinos. Back then, you didn't have all those giant hotels run by corporations. The boys ran Vegas back then."

"The *boys*?"

"How naïve can you *be*? The Mob. If you had enough money, they didn't give a shit what you did in *their* town. It got even crazier when Claude would go on a losing binge, and drop $5-10 million. When that happened, they'd fly in movie stars to fuck all of us. There'd be bundles of pot, piles of cocaine and all sorts of acid."

"Claude was part of it?"

"*Part* of it? You're *kidding*. No one could keep up with him. He seemed to have more fun when he lost, and he lost a *lot*. When he won, he'd give everyone stacks of hundreds. They were nothing more than party favors to him."

Scott had the waitress bring over a bottle of Patron and I poured us each a glass.

He raised his glass. "To the Pied Piper of Panties, may he live *forever!* Thanks, bro."

We finished that entire bottle. Scott kept regaling me with tales of night after night of unmitigated hedonism and debauchery. I was amazed anyone lived through such madness. But as things turned out, it was just the prelude. Without his madness, Claude couldn't have pulled it all off. Or did the madness make him believe anything was possible?

"About ten years ago, Michelle got sick. Claude flew her to the Mayo Clinic. He chartered a plane to take her family to Minneapolis and rented a floor at the best hotel in town so they could be near her," Scott said wistfully.

"Who the hell is Michelle?" My speech was slurring from the Patron.

"She worked at one of the bars where we hung out."

"Was she his girlfriend?"

"No, she was just a waitress and not even that good at her job. Someone dropped Claude an email that her granddaughter wanted to go to college but didn't have the money. Magically, a scholarship appeared. That's just the way he is. The Pied Piper is a wild man, *the* wild man. He's out of his frickin' mind. A lot of people are called "prince," but Claude is one through and through. If you're his friend and ever need anything, he'll give it to you. Thousands of people would give you the shirt off their backs if they know he picked you to tell his story."

I was floored. Claude wasn't just wild, he was a soft touch. Of course, as soon as Scott finished his monologue, he went face down on the table. I figured I was about to join him.

The waitress came over shaking her head and smiling. This wasn't her first rodeo with Scott.

"Don't worry about him, hon; Scott is family here. We'll get him home. I'm Marci, by the way."

"Thanks, Marci."

"I've heard stories about the Pied Piper. Is he your dad?"

"No, just a friend," I said, smiling at her.

"He's gotta be old. I'd bet he's still that crazy?"

"He just might be, but in other ways."

She snickered. "That's a nice way to say Viagra."

"Oh no, his wife is amazing."

"How come I'm not surprised? Can I get you a car service? You're from out of town and way too drunk to take the subway," Marci said, smiling at me.

"That's very nice of you."

"I hope you stop in again. If you don't have the cash right now, it'll be on your tab next time."

A Lincoln town car took me back to my apartment. What a night. I remember thinking I hoped I could remember all, or most of it in the morning. The truth is, what I wanted to remember was Marci.

The next day I staggered out of bed and into the shower. When I dried off I went to the living room. As I am addicted to email, I sat by my computer in a towel. There was one from LSE Stone. Who? I opened it.

It said: "Mark. If you are a friend of the Pied Piper and need to know anything, call me. Mick."

Holy crap! If the good stuff was this good, what about the scary stuff? The secret stuff? I wasn't sure if I should be excited or very, very scared. How did Jagger find out? If he knew, did the CIA know? How about the FSB (Russia's new KGB)?

Claude spent like a drunken Congressman and lost tons of money gambling. Did he owe the boys? Was he in too deep? Did it get him in trouble?

I made a few calls and found a casino manager from The Dunes who was still alive at eighty-five. He could put the stories of the Pied Piper in perspective. Could it all be true? The only way to find out for sure was to go to Vegas.

***

Unfortunately, there was no orgy on the plane. I wanted to feel like being in Vegas in the 70s, so I got a reservation at Caesar's Palace. For many years, Caesar's was the living image of hedonism. After taking a shower, I jumped in a cab and went to meet Petey, the casino manager, at a diner off the strip.

I saw an old guy dressed like it was still the 70s in the back booth, sitting with his back to the wall. It felt like 70s gangster movies. I chuckled to myself. He motioned for me to sit down.

"Just so you know, we don't talk bad about our friends. I'm old school." Petey stared at me as he said this. Although he was an old man, his glare scared the shit out of me.

I handed Petey an old key card. He looked at me. "You must be close to him. Only the real big hitters had this card. If he gave it to you, he must trust you."

"I hear he lost a lot of money in Vegas," I said, hoping to get a number.

"He could afford it. He never got in over his head and man, did he have the broads." Petey's smile covered his entire face.

"Did he play anywhere else?" I asked.

"He wouldn't play in the off-the-record games. He was smart. He knew he wouldn't be safe if he left one of our joints. He's royalty. There were classless bastards who would have loved to have taken him and we always took care of him. There were lots of crazies around him. But they loved him."

"Did you know about other losses?" I was intrigued.

"The rumors back then were he lost nine figures in Monte Carlo. Then, he went legit and lost more in the stock markets. There were guys who would bet the opposite of every one of his trades."

"He was that bad?"

"Sonny, your boy couldn't pick a winner in a one-horse race for about ten years. Then he got it all back and then some. I'm glad. He's good people. Maybe karma does exist."

"Thanks."

"I don't know how he got it back, but I bet he had more fun doing that than losing it."

"Yeah."

"And no one – and I mean no one – ever had more fun in Vegas than Prince Claude. The Rat Pack and everyone else were the '62 Mets to his '27 Yankees... You gotta promise me one thing."

"What's that?"

"If you find out the rest of the real story before I die, you gotta tell me."

"You got it, Petey."

He was wrinkled and old but a huge smile lit up his face, "When you come to tell me, make sure I give you my will first." Petey snorted loudly.

"Why?"

"Because I know when I hear what he did, I'll probably laugh my ass off so much that I'll give myself the big one. It'll be a helluva way to go. I'll die with a smile on my face. Man, I haven't been this excited since that hooker in '83. You've made an old man happy."

"Any time, Petey."

So far everything seemed harmless enough, but I had a deep foreboding that there was no way it could continue. We're talking about ending the Cold War, bringing the U.S. and U.S.S.R. to their knees.

Chapter 6
Digging

Back in New York, I knew I had a lot of work to do. The more I dug into the past the less I knew. So many of the leads I thought I had didn't pan out at all. Add to this that so many of the people I thought might be involved were dead. The stress was building. The uncertainty of whether my questions rattled the wrong cages was disconcerting. How could I know?

I started watching old Rockford and Monk DVDs. I was preparing for the inevitable metamorphosis that would require me to become a detective. Hopefully, I'd be somewhere between the manic perfectionist and the glib semi-action hero. The biggest difference would be that I'd be going this alone. It couldn't work any other way. I was likely to stick out too much to bring anyone else on board.

It would be like being a spy behind enemy lines. I couldn't help but wonder what would happen if I ever get caught. Would I be left hanging out to dry? Who would ever believe that the Secretary General of the UN and the Pied Piper of Panties put me up to it? I'm sure any court in the world would believe me and Charlie would do a multi-part series in the Inky defending me. If you believe that last sentence, I've got a bridge for sale. Claude had infected me. I had to know.

Okay, so I'd turned into a detective and a spy. With all the bodies being buried and clues being in the dust, I guess now I'd be an archeologist as well. My thoughts were that I'd have to be Indiana Jones on steroids with a little James Bond and Bob Woodward thrown in for good measure. Seriously, half the people were dead. Those who were alive wanted the past to stay in the past and I had the distinct impression that some might be certifiable, not to mention dangerous. After a while, I might start talking to the dead.

Claude had given me a few names, a couple of dates, and told me that the outcome was that he and Mbangu had won the Cold War. I wonder if Charlie Wilson was around to give me insights on how to break the government without it realizing that it's happening. At least with Charlie and Claude. I'd get to fuck some smoking hot women and do a lot of blow.

So far, all I knew was about the Pied Piper's orgies and excesses and that he'd outlived them all. I had to get deeper. I could access almost everything from anywhere, but it might be better to do it from different locations and on different computers. I told myself I was being smart or maybe I was simply experiencing unabated paranoia.

As I thought more deeply about what to look for I began to worry if I might be failing. Was I the right guy? More importantly, would I get caught as I looked for the smoking gun leading to the Cold War ending with a whimper rather than a bang? How did the Soviets and Americans let this happen? And why?

The next morning, I went to the main branch of the New York Library. The lions in front fit right in with the insane megalomania I was investigating. Why didn't they just tell me what I was supposed to look for or what they did? I was a pro. Help me find the damn story and let me write it. Whatever happens, happens.

Maybe they didn't know the whole story. I was buck naked, alone and blind in the world.

Where should I start? I decided the time I should search would be 1977 until the alleged end of the Cold War. Earlier than that and the Cold War would have ended sooner. Any later and it would have left us electronic tracks.

My basic premise was whatever happened to end hostilities left time enough to arrange a smooth transition to cover the mayhem that led to history being changed. Also, was it one-sided? Or did events balance each other out? Was one a reaction to the other? How did they pick what their attack would be? And most of all, why Mbangu and Claude? Did they just luck out?

I planned to do a search of front pages, business sections, and obituaries. I guesstimated that I could go through six to nine months of news per day, so it would take me about two weeks to cover that time span. Hell, there was, of course, no guarantee that I'd I ever find anything.

That first day of reading all that old newsprint nearly killed me. My eyes were moving independently by about 7:30 p.m. I had a few notes but nothing jumped out at me. There was an ominous air around my efforts as I left the library. A lot of strange people were there, any one of whom could be a spy tailing me. I decided that I'd wear a disguise the next day. I was sure I could find something suitable on the way home. Jesus, Claude had infected me.

I stopped at a little store and bought three wigs, some make-up, and some cold cuts. What you can find in some of these New York bodegas is amazing. I put the costume stuff on my desk and headed to the kitchen. When I opened the fridge, it was obvious that I hadn't shopped in a while. Shopping in Manhattan sucked. Everything was very expensive and you either had to find parking or take a cab. You might as well eat out.

I decided to go back to Mudville for a bite to eat. The internet said their ribs were great. Who the hell was I trying to fool? I wanted to see Marci. She wasn't wearing an engagement or wedding ring, so maybe I had a shot. James Bond had Bond girls. Maybe I could have Sternettes.

I took the R Train downtown, and when it stopped at Chambers, I started feeling like a fifteen-year-old trying to ask out the captain of the cheerleaders, not cool for a newly minted international spy and changer of history. I started running up the steps to the street. No, I had to be cool. I slowed down. It was literally only ten steps from the subway stop to Mudville. I saw Marci through the window. I went in and sat at one of her tables. She came right over. Her smile melted me.

"Hi, Mark. How've you been?" Marci said to me with a huge grin.

"Good. I'm surprised you remembered me," I replied.

"Of course, I did, you were so nice to Scott. Some people are rude to him."

"They're crazy. He may have left a few brain cells in the 60s and 70s, but he's the kind of guy you dream about meeting in a bar. What great stories!" I was trying not to talk as fast as my heart was beating.

She smiled at me. "Would you like a Patron?"

"You know, I've heard your ribs are great."

"They're my favorite thing to eat here," she said, licking her fingers.

"I love it! A woman who doesn't just eat salads!" I was smiling.

"Thanks." She was flirting and I was in heaven.

"How about some ribs and a Sam?" I stammered.

"Man! That sounds great. I'll be right back with your Sam."

The ribs were great and I had a few more beers. I was about to ask Marci for her number when she handed the bill with a note that had her number on it and a note saying "I'm off tomorrow night." I looked up. We both grinned.

"I'll call you about noon. Is that too early?"

"No, that's perfect."

"I'm new to the city. I bet you know the perfect places to do everything."

She leaned over and kissed me. "I think I just might."

The beer had given me a little buzz, but the kiss set me off. She turned to grab something at the bar. As I left Mudville I couldn't help looking back at her. I grabbed the railing as I went down to the subway; I didn't want to fall and break a leg – not before we could go on a date. It seemed like the ride took two seconds. I floated back to my apartment.

I went back to the library the next day and got into a rhythm. I got through about two years of history and took a ton of notes. I had no idea what I was finding out, but I kept plugging away. I figured that after I got back to the apartment I'd read all my notes and find a thread that would lead me to a major breakthrough. Fuck that, not tonight. I was going out with Marci.

I was like a teenager waiting for my first date. What would I say if Marci asked more than a basic question about what I was doing for a living and why I was living in New York? It would be a very good test of my spy chops. Forget waterboarding, her tongue was far more threatening.

***

Marci lived just above Canal Street and suggested we go to Little Italy. She had her own apartment, so I guess her tips were good. Even tiny apartments in Chinatown were very expensive, but it's a cool place to live. The building had a detective story vibe.

I buzzed her, she rang me up, and I trudged up the three flights of stairs to her floor. She was waiting with a glass of wine and looked great. I was mush.

I took my glass and we kissed. She shut the door behind us. I told myself to keep my shit together. Man, that was going to be tough.

"I hope you don't mind. I decided I'd rather make Italian food for you rather than going out. I'm guessing you haven't had a real home-cooked meal in a while."

"You'd be right. But you didn't need to go to all this trouble."

"I like cooking," she said.

We put our glasses down and made out on the couch. A bell rang in the kitchen. I had no intentions of stopping, but she got up.

"Damn, our food is ready." She kissed me one more time. "Sit at the table and I'll be right there."

She brought out salad and penne and I brought the wine to the table. She filled our plates.

"This is fabulous," I said as I wiped tomato sauce off my cheek.

She blushed a little. "Thanks. Can I ask you something?"

"Sure."

"Are you working with the Prince?" she said, looking away a little.

"Sort of," I replied.

"Sort of." She wanted a real answer. Every guy knows this look. It's in her eyes and the way she stands and looks at you.

"I'm researching a book on Secretary General Mbangu. They went to college together. It's sort of a present to the Secretary General."

"So, a puff piece," she said, making a face.

"I've been told to write whatever I find out, regardless."

"What would you like to find out tonight?" she said as she reached for my hand.

"If you'll still be smiling that much in the morning."

"I think I will be."

We leaned in and kissed deeply and didn't even finish dinner. I carried Marci off to bed and made love as if we'd been together for years. Becoming James Bond was a great thing; there's no way she would have slept with me before I became a spy.

She looked wonderful in the morning. She leaned over and kissed me, and rested her head on my chest.

"What are you doing today?" I asked.

"I'm taking a Bar Association class."

"You didn't tell me you graduated from law school."

"For some reason, we didn't get around to that last night." We giggled and kissed. "It only took me nine years," she said laughing.

"You'll be a great lawyer," I said, kissing the top of her head.

We kissed some more. I didn't want to stop. Lots of me didn't want to stop.

"Not if I don't get to class." She pulled away from me and sighed.

"Can I see you later this week?" I begged.

"You bet. What are you going to do today?"

"More boring research," I said, pulling her towards the bathroom.

We jumped in the shower, had great sex and then went our separate ways for the day. This almost never happened to me, certainly not with someone so hot and so smart.

Over the next few days I found a few things that might help lead me to the story Claude and Mbangu wanted to tell. I wasn't sure, but they felt promising. What was becoming difficult was that Marci and I were growing tighter and I realized I was going to have to travel to follow up on my leads.

How was Marci going to react? How would I tell her? What if she got pissed?

She had worked early on Sunday. We went to a movie and had ordered some food from a Chinese place. I was in the bathroom when the doorbell rang.

"I'll get it," Marci said.

"Do you have cash?" I asked.

"Yep."

She opened the door as I entered the living room.

"Oh my, am I intruding?" Claude said with a not-so-innocent smile.

"Mark, it's not the food." Marci said.

"Who is it?" I asked.

"I'm not sure."

"Yes, you are, my darling. You know perfectly well who I am. Mark, come out, come out wherever you are," Prince Claude said. I was fucked. On the other hand, Claude was beaming. He loved making me uncomfortable.

Marci had opened a bottle of wine before I got to the living room. They were on the couch chatting.

"She's gorgeous and smart. You're good at keeping secrets," Claude said playfully.

"You don't know the half of it, Claude, but that's a decent start." I leaned over to kiss Marci's cheek.

"My darling, since you work at the bar where Mark met Scott, I bet you're dying to ask me *the* question." He was beaming.

For the first time, I saw Marci both blush and recoil. Claude's posture, tone and his tailor-made, pure cashmere suit made him look and sound regal.

"How did you find us?" I asked.

"You are far too valuable to be completely alone in the world."

Marci looked puzzled. Claude's smile showed how much fun he was having.

"Since you have far too much class to ask, I will come right out and tell you. Yes indeed, I was the Pied Piper of Panties. But since Lauren became the singular love in my life the Piper has played his last tune."

We all chuckled. The Chinese delivery guy arrived. Claude answered the door and paid the bill.

"Chinese will be excellent for breakfast. Please allow me to take us all out for dinner."

When Marci went to put the bag in the refrigerator, Claude whispered to me, "We'll need to talk in the morning, but I wouldn't dream of interrupting tonight. Except for dinner."

We walked to a local steak place and had a fabulous meal. After two or three bottles of wine, Claude picked up the check and left. His timing was impeccable. He was always one step ahead of me.

Marci was speechless until we got back to my apartment. She was positively bursting at the seams to ask tons and tons of questions. She would start to say something, then stop and start again.

"What did..." Marci stopped mid-sentence. "Did I..."

"What do you want to know?" I put my arm around her.

"Do you think he's angry with me?"

"Why?"

"Pied Piper."

"He loved saying that again." I chuckled.

"Did I keep you two from doing something important tonight?" For the first time since we met, Marci was outwardly nervous with a bead of sweat on her brow.

"We're supposed to get together tomorrow. I'm not sure if I'll be able to be with you."

"Don't worry. I understand." She paused. "Do you think he approved of me?"

"I approve of you."

We started kissing and made love all night. For the first time after we spent the night together, Marci awoke before I did. She was lying there looking at me when I woke up. I couldn't tell if she was scared, impressed or just puzzled.

"What's wrong?" I asked

"Nothing, I'm just happy. And impressed."

"By me?" I was almost snickering.

"Yes, silly, by you," she said, kissing my neck.

"Why?"

"You're doing something important. I want to help if I can."

"I was worried about that. You see, I'll probably do some travelling to do more research. I don't want to be away from you, but I'll have to be," I said, voice quivering.

"If you always come back, I'll understand," she said, wrapping herself around me and kissing my neck.

"You are amazing."

I started to kiss her. She smiled. "I've got class and Claude needs you to have your energy."

We kissed. "Okay," I moaned, and sighed as she left.

About an hour later Claude arrived at the apartment. "She's wonderful. Don't mess this one up."

"I'll try not to. All she knows, by the way, is that you're paying me to write a book about Mbangu."

"How did you get around Scott?" Claude asked, peering at me.

"Marci thinks I'm doing background on you to cover my butt."

"I must say, she's doing a very good job of that."

We laughed. I took out some notes. I fumbled through them, trying to put everything in some sort of logical order. It was basically hopeless.

"I think I might have found something."

"What?" Claude said lurching towards me.

"While I was doing background at the library, I found some data that makes it seem like there was some odd stuff happening in North Carolina and Virginia at the right time. I couldn't find much, but there was also a huge problem in the tobacco markets. It seems there was a mysterious disease destroying the crops and someone almost cornered the market."

"You're reading way too many spy novels. Don't you think if one person nearly cornered a market there'd be a serious paper trail?" His bluff was amazing.

I remember thinking at that point I was onto something. Why did he say "one person"? It was a curious choice of words. Were there two people? Did he and Lauren literally corner the market?

"You're probably right. I'm going to Washington, DC, then North Carolina." I gave him the basics of my itinerary.

"That sounds like a good plan. Be careful, I've heard they don't much trust outsiders down there."

"I know. Some friends went to school down there. Everyone is related to everyone. I'll be careful." I was trying to put him at ease.

"And don't be stupid. Send Marci flowers at least once a week." Claude looked me in the eye to give this advice about keeping a woman happy.

"I'll remember to send flowers and I'll also remember to call my favorite Uncle Claude."

"Good." He gave me a grin that was either reassuring or threatening, I couldn't tell which.

Chapter 7
The First Pieces Fall into Place

At first, I didn't think I was on the right track with the tobacco angle, but Claude's reaction indicated otherwise. I think he needed me to find out for myself and learn details he didn't know.

Claude had something to do with the commodities hijinks, but how? Further, Petey and others said Claude had been flat broke. How did he come up with so much money? Plus, there wasn't computer trading back then. How do you pull off a worldwide coup like this without computers?

I didn't see Claude being in on anything nefarious like espionage. Was he simply the luckiest bastard on the planet? Or did he do something insane out of panic? Or was it both and more?

Who was on the other side? What did they do? How? I had more questions now than when I started. I started thinking, the more I learned the less I'd know.

Finding out I was on the right track created more questions than I had when I knew nothing. I decided to first go to DC to do some searching about problems in the tobacco industry and to look up SEC documents to see if there were any investigations into Claude or anyone else from Luxenstein. I also would go to the Departments of Agriculture and Commerce.

What would my cover story be? I decided I was going to do a story about the ups and downs of farm products and I picked tobacco as the product. Luckily, I hadn't written anything about tobacco in my ten years at the Inky. But this wasn't anything like the industry lying to the people or lying to Congress. This would be much more involved and much less obvious.

***

I was in DC for about a week. For an outsider, it was a strangely incestuous place. More than once it seemed like everyone knew everyone and each other's business. Part of the week I spent learning about the maze of departments and agencies. Other days I discovered how these groups were intertwined to the point of madness. I learned a lot but realized the answers wouldn't be found there, because most of the bureaucrats were far more interested in protecting their territories than helping outsiders.

The heart of tobacco growing in the U.S. is in North Carolina and Virginia. So, I decided to take the five-hour drive down to Raleigh to sift through archives. Maybe there'd be something there to lead me to the *smoking* gun.

When I got to Raleigh I sent Marci a bouquet of chocolate flowers. She loved them and it worked for me in a very important way. She called me immediately after receiving them, which bought me more time on the road. I couldn't believe how understanding she was. I decided to go to the NC Department of Agriculture the next morning. Maybe I'd find something there.

As I looked through crop reports, pricing trends and other data provided for me in the archives department, a fiftyish woman named Molly came over to my table looking puzzled. She was squinting to see what I was reading. I guess I'd dropped the receipt for Marci's chocolate flowers near my pile of reading materials. She saw it and smiled.

"I wish my husband would send me chocolate flowers. Heck, I'd be happy if he picked some dandelions off the lawn and brought them to me. The documentation you have selected makes it look like you are looking for weird things that happened a long time ago."

"I'm just doing a history of commodities and how prices/availability changed over the years, but it looks like some odd things happened here about thirty years ago," I said.

"My daddy might be able to help you. He's eighty-two. He used to be an Ag Extension Agent and knew everything there was to know about tobacco. When I was getting out of college, he kept telling us stories about crops all over the state failing. What was also odd is that a few months earlier, daddy and three other agents all won trips to Hawaii at the same time. Lots of strange things happened. Would you like to talk to him?"

"Would it be okay?" I thought about how lucky I had gotten. Maybe Claude was rubbing off on me. Plus, I was becoming smooth.

"He loves to tell stories about the good old days. Be warned, though if he asks you if you'd like a Coke, that means when you turn your head he'll slip some Jack Daniels in it," she said with a chuckle.

"I think I can deal with that. Thanks, Molly."

***

The next day I drove about fifty miles into the country to meet with Molly's dad. His was a classic southern home, two stories and a covered porch, easily one hundred-fifty years old. He was sitting on the porch when I drove my car up the quarter-mile long driveway. I parked and got out of the car.

"Mr. Roberts, I'm Mark Stern. Molly said it was okay to come and talk with you," I said with a smile.

"Come on and sit for a while with this old man. Call me Bobby, son. Mr. Roberts was my daddy." His voice was friendly. And loud.

"Thank you, Bobby," I said.

"When I saw you comin' up the road, I got you a Coke."

I smiled and took a gulp. It was at least 50/50 with Jack Daniels. "Thank you. Molly told me that once you won a trip to Hawaii."

"Damnedest thing ever. Carter, Joey, Billy and I all won the same trip at the same time. We didn't get notified until a month before we had to go." Bobby shook his head.

"That's strange. Did you get to go to Hawaii?"

"You bet your ass we did. That's the great thing about government jobs. We got lots of time off. It was almost like they knew we could do it."

"That was mighty convenient," I said as I drank more of my "Coke."

"Neither Carter nor Billy remembered a damn thing about entering a contest to go to Hawaii, but they got drunk on the plane just the same," Bobby said with a huge cackle while taking a huge gulp of his drink.

"Do you remember entering the contest?"

"Do I look like the kind of guy to ask how I won a free trip to Hawaii?" He chortled heartily.

"No sir, I don't think you do." I gagged a little. That sip was almost all Jack Daniels.

"When we got back, my Millie tried to send a thank-you note to the company that gave us that trip and it was returned to her like the company had gone out of business. She was genuinely upset at not being able to say thanks. That's my Millie. So much nicer than I am."

I finished the rest of my "Coke" in one gulp. Why would a company spend tens of thousands of dollars on paying out a contest if they were going out of business? I couldn't go back and check the company out. Most states didn't have computers back then. Plus, the company could have faked everything anyway.

Bobby poured us a couple more "Cokes," glasses of Jack with a splash of Coke. Jesus, I might not make it back to Raleigh after this one. Hell, I might not make it out of the driveway.

"Something even stranger happened while we were away," Bobby said, scratching his head.

"What was that?" I asked.

"The state sent four guys to take our places."

"Why is that so strange?"

"We were only going to be away for a couple of weeks. Nothing was that urgent. The Ag Department knew that, and they were way too cheap to pay for subs. Everyone knew that. Never did it before or after," he said, shaking his head and wiping his brow with a big blue napkin.

"Did you ever find out why they did?"

Bobby took a long sip from his drink. "Nope, and no one ever heard of those people before or after our trip. There's a rumor that good-time BJ ran off with one of them."

"One of them was gay?" I asked. My head started spinning from all the Jack Daniels, since all the people I knew called BJ were guys.

He snorted. "Hell no, BJ was the barmaid. She was everyone's favorite, if you know what I mean. Just don't tell Millie, although these days, she might not mind me finding a girl like that." He roared with laughter.

"Anyone know where she went?"

"No, but all the Connors died off or moved away. Bobbie Jean Connor was her name. I may not remember fifteen minutes ago, but I damn sure remember BJ. Hell, everyone in these here parts remember BJ."

We talked about baseball and that North Carolina/Philadelphia religion, basketball, for a while, and I was gaining a strong sense that something had happened here. Then I went back to Raleigh. I was sweating, thinking about the power the people who could have pulled this off had. As I sobered up, I realized that keeping this secret was far more difficult than pulling it off. Did they kill the lackeys who'd posed as agents? Where did BJ and her guy go and how the hell have they stayed hidden? Damn, this shit was starting to get real.

I began to realize that Claude and Mbangu had benefited by whatever happened, but they only found out about the madness when it was too late to change it. Or did they embrace it? Was I their guinea pig and bird dog? Or was I the bait?

Was I in danger? As crazy as Claude was, I had to believe he'd cover my ass if things got too deep. Had I already turned over a rock that would be used to bash my head in before I could see it coming?

A few weeks ago, I naively thought I'd be writing an historical book about how the Cold War *really* ended. I'd find out the deep causes and events that led to explaining the inside story about how this monumental change occurred. It may have been a little silly and purely accidental, but the story had to have some logic to it. However, with every new piece of information I discovered, it seemed more and more likely that somewhere north of four stories were going on at once in parallel and may have been crazier than the others.

After talking to Bobby, I wasn't sure people on the same side knew anything more than their most immediate role. This wasn't one story. It was many.

The most logical way for me to report on what happened all those years ago, is to tell each part through the individual stories. I think – no, I am certain – no one is going to believe me. This is going to get crazier than the Pied Piper of Panties's flights to Vegas.

Before I decided if this was going to be a written version of a Steven Soderbergh story or a classic Doris Kearns Goodwin historical representation, I'd have to track down BJ. I thought I needed to go to Luxenstein soon. I had to ask Claude and Lauren a bunch of gnarly questions.

***

Somehow, I managed to get back to Raleigh after visiting Bobby. It was terribly wrong to have tried to drive that afternoon. I was intrigued by Bobby's story and decided to do a little homework from my hotel room in the state capitol.

The Internet age makes a lot of investigation much easier. The converse is, no one has real privacy unless they go completely off the grid. Since these events happened before the Internet existed, the participants may have had natural cover. Forgery was much easier then as well. I found that Bobbie Jean Connor got married in Las Vegas to a Peter Martin. What was odd was, this so-called Peter Martin didn't have a shred of a paper trail six months prior to getting married. It was like he dropped out of the sky. It looked like his Social Security Card was issued less than a year before he showed up in North Carolina. His driver's license was weird too. He was about thirty but hadn't had a license before then. I didn't want to think about who could have had the power to give him papers that perfect.

I followed the lives of BJ and Peter for about twenty years, even though they moved multiple times and worked a lot of different jobs. They had one son named Alexander. In about 1993 the entire family disappeared off the face of the Earth. Maybe they realized that several years after the Berlin Wall came down and the Cold War ended that the superpowers might be getting nervous about leaks of their stories. Peter Martin, whoever he was, might have figured that someone would come looking for him. I doubt he would have guessed that it would be someone like me.

I found a cousin of BJ's who said no one in the family had heard from her for close to twenty years. Unless you go into witness protection, why would you leave your own family hanging? Did she find out Peter's real identity and get scared? But back to the story.

Crops on farms in and around the areas the substitute agents visited failed quickly and horrifically. The pseudo-agents seemed to get into the biggest farms the most readily. A few of the farmers were still alive, but none had any idea of why their crops had failed. No one had thought about the strangers when it was happening. What mattered to them at the time was saving their farms, many of which had been in their families for generations.

The fear of contamination killed the market. Many of the problems continued through the next crop, but disappeared the following year as mysteriously at it arrived. Technology wasn't what it is today. No one thought of keeping samples for posterity. Crops just failed, and sometimes you didn't know why.

The North Carolina Department of Agriculture said they hadn't sent anyone to those farms while the agents were surprisingly on vacation in Hawaii. Someone or some group had to have planned these acts. Was this my smoking gun? Who could have done this?

Or was it an invisible gun, as the only possible lead disappeared in 1993? All dead ends so far.

I did get a notebook full of bizarre stories about those apparently fake agents. These guys acted like they were from Mars. Their accents were hilarious, and colorful would be a gross understatement. Where were they from? Why didn't anyone say anything at the time?

Chapter 8
Hitting the Road

I went back to New York for about a month to put together my notes and to plan my next steps. Marci and I were inseparable. We went for a weekend in Vermont. She was completely understanding about my upcoming trip. What was more amazing was she didn't ask any questions about what I had learned on my previous trip, nor about what I was looking for in Europe. It was weird and exhilarating at the same time. What woman would act like this?

We were at her place two nights before I was scheduled to leave. Everything was great. When she asked, "Do you think I could come to Luxenstein with you after you do your research? I have some time off coming."

I thought about it for a minute and did my best to be diplomatic. "I hope so. I'll try. It'd be loads of fun."

I had to know that was coming, but she blindsided me with her timing. I knew Lauren would love Marci. It was disconcerting that I trusted Marci so quickly and so completely, which struck me as either a great move on my part or my potential downfall. I was also worried that harm might come to her. Why should anything make sense or be easy here? Women were more mysterious and confusing to me than anything in this story. I had come to accept this fact; it made life so much simpler.

I was also scared about what I might find out when I was in Europe. Who, in fact, was Peter Martin? How were he and his crew able to enter and leave the United States without leaving a trace? What happened to BJ? Would I find this out in Europe or would I have to go someplace else? Were they still together? Were they still alive? Were they still, or ever, spies? What were they doing now?

Thus far, Claude seemed almost innocent, but it seemed like he wanted me to tell his story, so what might he do if I found something out that made him look bad? Or harm Lauren? Or Mbangu? The info I had found so far created many more questions than answers.

I kept getting the feeling that this was more *The Russians Are Coming, The Russians Are Coming,* than it was a Tom Clancy novel. The obvious downside was the Russians or the Americans or Claude could want the story to die with me. Would they think Marci was involved? Was I putting her in danger?

Let's stop and take a second to look at the notes about the people involved so far:

Prince Claude – By any rational definition, Claude was a madman at the time of the end of the Cold War. There was literally nothing he would consider out of bounds. In fact, the crazier something might have been, the more likely he was to try it.

Mbangu – He was a competent, honest leader in a country that had been going backwards. Almost overnight he became a legend in Africa. How do you do that? But he wouldn't have planned anything too crazy. He has always believed in the system.

Lauren – She played a part. Who was she before she met Claude? How did she get into this mess?

Peter Martin – Who was he? Where did he come from? Where did he go? He must know something.

Peter's Team – Who are they? Where are they? Can I find them? Do I *want* to find them?

Jinare – He knew everything about parts of the story. He wanted to tell me what happened but didn't dare do so until Mbangu allowed him.

How did so many people keep these secrets for so many years?

For some reason, we were much more comfortable at Marci's third floor walk-up than at my high-end condo. She took off from work to be waiting for me when the car service dropped me off in Chinatown. I ran up the steps and knocked on the door. She opened it immediately, holding a key for me and wearing only a smile. Oh, yeah!

We lost it for a couple of hours. It was wild, passionate and crazy sex. How the hell did I do that? She looked spent. I jumped up, took a quick shower, and put some clothes on.

"Honey, I'll go get us a pizza. Should I stop next door and get some wine?"

"That sounds good," she said surprisingly calmly.

"Be back in a few."

First, I stopped at the liquor store to get the wine. As I was paying, a well-dressed man brushed my shoulder. When I got to the pizza place, I reached into my pocket for some cash. As I pulled it out, a scrap of paper fell to the floor.

I quickly picked it up. It said "Café du Pain – Luxenstein, 3 p.m. every day until success. Look for cell phone number taped under third table from front on the left."

When I got back to Marci's apartment, she had a robe on. "You look like you saw a ghost."

"Nah, I was just thinking I wished I could stay a little longer. I'm going to miss you."

She smiled at me. "I know that's not what you were thinking, but it's such a great answer I'll give you a pass."

We alternated eating the pizza and making out. That night may have been the best sex I'd ever had. I stayed all night. It was memorable in a bizarre sort of way.

I had barely gotten out of the shower when the car service rang the bell. Marci helped me get dressed and made sure I wasn't leaving anything behind.

"Be careful, you won't be in the U.S. on this trip," she warned.

That was a weird statement. What else did she know? We started kissing again. The driver rang the bell again. It was as if she was too scared to let go of me.

"Call me from the castle. No one has ever called me from a castle," she said with a wry smile.

"My castle is wherever we are together." Man, I was becoming smoother than I'd ever been.

"You can't leave after saying that, babe, but you gotta go."

We kissed once more. She patted me on the butt as she shoved me out the door.

The drive to JFK was slow and uneventful. The limo pulled up to the curb and the driver took my bags to a sky cap. Claude had booked me a first-class ticket. The line was short and being in first class gave me a special entrance at security. I was through in a couple of minutes and went to the airline club.

Soon, they called our flight. I got on and had a couple of drinks. Part of me wanted more. The rest of me was almost shaking too much to drink. I didn't dare get sloshed.

About halfway there I smiled and chuckled a little. In my head, I'd been organizing all the pieces. There were superpowers, spies, a crazy prince and more. I realized the story behind this story might be totally insane. Claude had figured this out, but he didn't know how or why. Maybe he thought the reason the story hadn't come out yet was that it was so insane that everyone involved would be way too embarrassed? He was protecting his friend. This was the moment many things started to truly sink in. I was on a plane, in first class. There was only one thing to do.

I ordered a double and thought to myself, the Pied Piper of Panties wants to leave a legacy for the world to see. My other thought was, could I say anything that didn't help or protect them? Who would believe me when I was sober, much less if I were drunk?

"You look like you're having a good time," said the lady sitting next to me.

"I think I might be." I had to be careful. I did have a bit of a buzz.

"Are you going to stay in Luxenstein?" she asked.

"Part of the time," I said, trying to be vague.

"Where else are you going?"

Suddenly, I wasn't sure who this woman was. Did she know the person who slipped me the note? "I'll probably head to Venice to meet my girlfriend for a few days."

I thought that might diffuse the two paths she might take. First, she could be pumping me for information. If so, it would throw her off. If she was flirting, I'd covered myself.

"She's a lucky lady. Venice is so romantic."

"I'm the lucky one." Whew, maybe I'd dodged this one.

We chatted for the last two hours of the flight. When I got off the plane, a man in a black suit took my arm.

"Come this way Mr. Stern. His Highness is waiting."

I followed him to a stretch Maybach. I had heard about these cars but had never seen one. Rather than typical limos, the back seats were equipped with Swedish massage units with an ice bucket next to it. Claude and Lauren were waiting inside.

Lauren leaned over to kiss me and asked, "How was your flight?"

"Excellent."

"You're spoken for. Don't you dare, Mark," Claude said with a smile on his face.

"Don't worry, Claude. He did the right thing."

"How did you know that, Lauren?" I was puzzled.

"I know you, Mark. You aren't the young Pied Piper."

"Two months ago, I wouldn't have minded trying to be the Pied Piper for a while."

They chuckled. Lauren kissed us on the cheek.

"So, what have you learned?" Claude asked.

"I've found some leads, but they all seem crazy."

They looked at each other and laughed. Lauren reached for Claude's hand and said, "As they say in America, you ain't seen nothin' yet."

This only confirmed what I was thinking. "What would you think if I didn't report what happened overall, but told the stories from the point of view of the people who lived it?"

Claude smiled broadly, "That sounds perfect."

"The only problem is, I'm not close to having even one of the stories complete."

Lauren nodded, "In a few days, you'll have our fifth of the story and a good idea of where to go for more."

That was the first real encouragement I'd received. Of course, knowing for sure that the story was going to be crazy was nerve-wracking. Crazy usually meant dangerous. When you add crazy to governments, I was looking at sheer terror. And who the hell would I be meeting at the Café du Pain?

***

The castle was right out of a fairy tale, with magnificent paintings every-where. The ceilings rivaled anything you ever saw from the Italian Re-naissance. The furnishings made museum pieces look like thrift shop offerings. I wasn't sure if next I'd be seeing King Arthur or a leprechaun.

The butler ushered me to my quarters. Jesus, the main bedroom alone had to be at least two thousand square feet. The bureaus could have been at Buckingham Palace. Correction: this stuff was nicer than anything I had seen in Buckingham Palace picture books. The handles in the bathroom were solid gold. I was living in a fairy tale. You know what? I could get used to this.

I slept late – jet lag. I got showered and dressed. Claude and Lauren were reading papers on the portico. It was right out of a Cary Grant/Grace Kelly movie. The sun was brilliant. The breeze gently swayed the trees. They were above the world and in one of their own.

"How nice of you to finally join us," Claude said with a smirk.

"Jet lag and six scotches can do that to you."

Lauren asked, "What would you like to do today?"

"Would it be alright if I just walked around town to learn a little about your country? Then we could do some work after dinner." I didn't want to give away my real plans.

Claude looked puzzled. "By yourself?"

"I'd love for you and Lauren to show me around, but I like dive bars and little bookstores. Could I do that with you two?"

Lauren smiled. "I don't think so."

"I don't mean to be rude or not appreciate your hospitality, but I think today may turn into a long night."

"Don't be silly, and don't forget to get something nice for Marci." Lauren seemed to know Marci very well.

"I got chocolate flowers for her when I was in North Carolina."

"That was a nice touch. There may be hope for you yet," Claude said with a chuckle.

"Claude, please call for the driver."

"Can I be a little less conspicuous than the Maybach this time, please?"

Claude said, "I think that can be arranged."

They guffawed. A stock Audi pulled around to the front of the castle. When I got inside, the driver handed me a cell phone.

"When you are ready to return, please dial hash 1, and I will be right there for you, sir."

"Thank you. Would you drop me by the fountain, please? That looks like a good place to start."

"Of course, sir, it's a fine place to start your journey."

He dropped me off. I walked all over the lovely little capital. At about 2:45 p.m., I sauntered over to the Café du Pain. I got there almost exactly at three. After looking around, I went to the prescribed table. A few people were drinking coffee and eating. None looked like the man at the pizza place or like someone who would be involved in this caper. My palms were getting sweaty. At least I didn't have a sniper's red dot on me... yet.

After ordering a coffee and a pastry, I reached under the table, and sure enough, there was an envelope with a small bulge in it. I kept it under the table and slid it into my pants pocket. After I had the waitress refill my coffee, I went to the bathroom. I locked the door and took the envelope out of my pocket.

It said:

*Call me when you are free. Hit *1.*

Lucy Diamond

Gabe Stein

Ken Peters

Tim Richards

That's all. I folded it into tiny pieces and put it into my wallet and flushed the envelope in the toilet. Then I went back into the café. I finished my coffee, paid, and left. I called for the driver. He picked me up about thirty minutes later.

We had dinner at 8 p.m. Then we went into the grand library for drinks. The opulence of the castle and "no big deal" attitude of Claude and Lauren were kind of freaking me out. I dreamed of being rich and having a giant house, but this was completely out of hand.

"I stopped at one of the amazing shops across from the train station and got Marci a scarf that the shop owner had made himself and a small silk bag. I thought Marci would like that better than something from Hermes or one of those fancy stores you can find almost anywhere."

I showed it to Lauren and Claude. Lauren smiled and kissed me on the cheek.

"She'll love it. I can't wait to meet her," Lauren said with a sigh.

"Just before I left she asked if she could come over."

"Of course, she can, and the sooner the better," Claude said. "Did you know that Lauren was an up-and-coming actress before she decided to reform me?"

"Please, darling, it was nothing like that."

Lauren lounged back in the oversized chair. Claude took a more relaxed position. She had been a young actress and he was still the Pied Piper when their story began. They started offering a wealth of details that made much of what I had found make sense.

My jaw dropped so often and so deeply that I thought I'd dislocated it a couple of times. As Lauren beamed, she had more than a little bit of player inside her. There was no question that these were the only two people on the planet that could have pulled this plan off.

This was batshit crazy and totally dangerous. Without question, Prince Claude reveled in every moment and fully expected it to work from Day One. But there were points that he seemed a little worried about. If this was what he was doing, what were the others thinking?

I was also correct in assuming Claude didn't know many of the other details and that he had stumbled into history rather than having designed it. What he wouldn't tell me was Mbangu's story. I'd need to go to Madibu.

As Claude took out the two-hundred-year-old cognac and the fifty-year-old Cuban cigars, Lauren leaned over to kiss me on the cheek and Claude on the lips.

"*Bon soir, chérie*," he said. "You are my life."

She smiled and reached to hold his hand. She had taken him hook, line and sinker all those years ago. He may have thought it was his idea, but it wasn't. Once she got on the inside, she owned him. That was very lucky for them... and for the world.

A few moments after she left, Claude took a long drag on his cigar and eyed me. "You were contacted today, weren't you?"

I gagged on my cognac. "Yes. Were you following me?"

"I wouldn't do that – not yet, anyway. But you wouldn't be a very good poker player. You need to work on that as we go forward since some people will try to pump you more seriously for information."

"What exactly do you mean by *not yet?*"

"It's not dangerous yet, but it may get to be. If it does, I will protect you."

"After hearing your story and some of what I've learned, I think the people involved are afraid of looking stupid."

He snickered and poured us a huge drink. "I do believe you're right. Could you imagine if it hadn't been Mbangu and me? The body count would've been much higher. The Cold War might still be raging. But I have a great ego." He put the bottle down.

"I don't think anyone other than you could have pulled this off."

He smiled again. "Necessity is the mother of pure insanity."

We laughed, smoked and drank. "Do you think the person who contacted you is real?"

"At one time, I think he was. I'm surprised you aren't asking more."

"It's not time for me to know. Would you like to use the Audi without Jacques?"

"That might be a good idea."

"Did you get a card for Marci?"

"Yes."

"Bring everything to breakfast. I'll send it by diplomatic courier. In fact, let's have some fun. I'll send her a diplomatic passport."

"I'm not sure if that would make her chuckle or scare the daylights out of her."

"Either way, she'll have a great story to tell. There is no downside. You're fast becoming part of the fun that is my life. Many times, it's the little things that are the most fun. I think I'll instruct the courier to wear the pouch handcuffed to his wrist. That should get you a call." He couldn't control his pure glee at this idea. I think he liked rubbing America's and the U.S.S.R.'s noses in their own arrogance. For Claude, it was a game. The superpowers took it a bit more seriously. That was to his advantage.

We drank and laughed for a few more hours. I stumbled through the maze of hallways before I got back to my "chamber" that night. The fact that Claude and Lauren had opened with so many details led me to believe this was a turning point. But I was so drunk that I barely believed I could breathe at 4 a.m.

***

Somehow, we had breakfast at 10 a.m. Lauren made fun of Claude and me. I brought Lauren my package for Marci. She added a beautiful blouse, skirt and pair of shoes.

"Girls like to know what other girls think of them. Be careful, Mark, everything is riding on you."

She was truly taking care of me. I couldn't believe it. A couple of months ago, I was a schlep reporter in Philly. Now I could be changing world history. Maybe Claude was right. Life chooses you. You don't choose life. I still don't understand how Marci chose me.

We had become family. Lauren was the mom. Claude was the big brother. I was the kid who tried too hard but couldn't get out of my own way. We parted ways and I drove into town.

I parked the car near the train station and dialed *1.

"Yes."

"You said to call."

"Were you followed?" The voice was unsuccessfully trying to be mysterious. It was all I could not to laugh out loud. When did I grow these brass balls? Whoa!

"No."

"Take the train to Thionville, France. Go across the street to the bar. Then call me again."

"Who are you?"

"One of the names on the list."

"I'll call you when I get to the station."

"Fine."

I bought the ticket and got on the train. The trip involved one connection and took about two hours. The entire way I wondered if the owner of the voice was on the train with me. I got up and walked to the dining car, looking for anyone who seemed out of place.

My guess was the voice was Gabe Stein, since it sounded like something a Gabe Stein would do. I was pissed at myself for getting too drunk the previous night to Google all four names. I should have also bought the service to find background data on them.

I love riding on trains, especially in Europe, where there is camaraderie; people seem to chat more than in the U.S. What is weird in that in about 80-100 miles I will have gone through three countries. But there weren't any stops to check papers or passports. There was a sense of security.

Soon we arrived in Thionville, a quaint, old small town in the heart of farming country. The buildings were from the early 20th century if not a hundred years earlier. It looked like WWII had missed this town. I was relieved; so many of these little towns were nothing but cannon fodder.

I felt strangely invigorated as I left the train station. It was time to dial my cell phone buddy. It rang twice. I was listening to see if I could locate the other party. Strangely, I thought I had the upper hand here. This guy seemed clownish and over-paranoid.

"Good, you weren't followed."

"Gabe, why are you acting like a spy afraid of his shadow?"

"Why did you call me Gabe?"

"You sure as hell aren't Lucy. I didn't think you were Tim. I guessed Gabe. So, Gabe, why do you want to go to these extremes to speak to me?"

"Have you done any homework?"

"Nope, I got too drunk last night. What would I have found?"

"Everyone on that list has a central role in the history you are investigating."

At the bar, there was a man trying to look like he was in his forties but wasn't pulling it off. He had dyed hair and a bad fake beard. I walked directly to his table.

"Hi Gabe, I'm Mark. May I sit with you?" I said quietly.

"Sure, but be careful." Gabe kept looking all around the bar. It was creepy and funny at the same time.

"We are in a tiny town in France. How much more careful can we get?"

"All of the people I listed are a part of your story." His finger-tapping was uber-annoying.

"How about you?" I asked.

"You can find out about me. It goes much higher and broader than me. No one knows all the players. I was a new guy at the time." Gabe kept looking around.

"Is everyone as squirrelly as you?"

"Look at how well I've stayed hidden. I am in control. No one has ever gotten close to me."

"You are thousands of miles from home trying to look twenty years younger than you are. To me, that's the definition of squirrelly."

"What?" He also twitched from time to time. He scared me.

"Oh, my God, you want me to find answers for you so that you can cover your own ass. Jesus, this is going to be wild."

"You need to keep me in the loop."

I snickered. "Find something more for me and I'll give you a heads-up. You seem to need me more than I need you."

At that point I understood I owned him. He would jump through hoops if I asked him. I figured he could be my bait if I needed it. Bond and Bourne were pussies compared to the great Mark Stern.

I thought to myself that he might be willing to do my leg work in the

U.S. when I eventually got to Russia and Madibu. Hell, maybe I could use him as a decoy. Who would ever believe this bozo?

***

Claude was listening to music when I got back to the castle that night. He looked cocky drinking a huge cognac, knowing I wouldn't take such a big slug after last night. He does love to play.

"You knew I'd have to go to Russia, didn't you?" I asked.

"I didn't know for sure, but it was a good bet," Claude said, looking me directly in the eyes.

"How much more do you know than what you've told me?"

"Only enough to know that it could become dangerous and more insane than my Vegas trips. I don't know the entire cast of characters. Even when I was at the Piper's apex, people had my back. That might not exist in Russia," he said with a snort. "From what you and I have learned, Lauren and I might be the sanest people you'll meet for a while. What you are about to do might scare Bram Stoker and Wes Craven enough to wet their pants in terror."

"What?" I was puzzled and had to ask.

"I only started out to be Robin Hood for our nation," Claude said, looking at the walls.

"But..." I stammered.

He chuckled. "But... we got a bit carried away. I don't want to carry your body away afterwards."

"Should I go to Russia or Madibu?"

"How did you do on Rosetta Stone?" he asked, ignoring my question.

"Hopefully well enough not to get killed."

"They never kill the joker. Sometimes acting the fool works. I am looking forward to proving to you that I was the voice of reason."

"I'm starting to get scared... I think I believe you.'

"Always remember, the crazier something sounds, the more likely it is to be true," Claude said impishly.

"You're starting to convince me."

And I was more afraid than ever.

Chapter 9
Learning About the Eastern Front

I still had to prepare to go to Russia as it was still a very dangerous place. You can't know who is on your side. These days it's not just who's being paid by the FSB, but who's being paid by the Mafia. Add to this the generations of fear of outsiders that millions of Russians exhibit readily and warily. This trip would be as easy as walking through Gorky Park eating an ice cream cone.

Part of my homework was to get a Russian language laptop, since Googling people in English would have inherent problems. Allegedly Russians keep to themselves, fearing everyone might be a spy, but I couldn't run the chance that a few weren't like this. Regardless of where I was, I tried to spend six hours a day for the past month practicing my Russian. It was very helpful indeed in my searches in trying to locate some of the people I was trying to find.

One thing everyone in the world understands is that many of the world's best hackers are in Eastern Europe. Another good thing about them is if you pay them well enough, they won't ask any questions. I took the train to Mannheim, Germany to meet a Polish "computer consultant," who called himself "Stan."

We met at a Turkish-owned bar. Stan was blond and blue-eyed and I was dressed like a semi-tourist. Because we stuck out, I suggested we go to another place by the university. It was an interesting bar, crowded at 8 p.m. There were very active conversations going on at many of the tables. It was very different from U.S. college bars with chugging contests and shot girls.

We sat at a corner table. After our beers came, the smoke girl came by and we got a couple Cuban cigars. I lit our Montecristos. We took long puffs and sipped the beer. It seemed like the ultra-spy cliché we see in so many movies. I loved it!

"How can I help you?" Stan finally asked, looking directly at me.

"I need everything you can find about a few names I have. Follow them everywhere you can. If it goes to multiple countries, I need to know where and when. I've got pictures of three of them. The others are ghosts."

"That will be good. I can use facial recognition software to cross-check against passports and driver's licenses in the U.S., E.U., and other places."

"Are these databases accessible?"

"If you are willing to pay, they are. You didn't like comparative religions class much at university, did you?"

I gulped my beer. How could he have located my college transcripts from my first name and a burner phone number? Jesus, he was good!

"Are you going to stay in Mannheim?"

"No. I'll call you on this phone and tell you where we should meet," he said, handing me a different burner phone.

"How long will it take for you get me the information I need?"

"I should have a good amount of data within forty-eight hours."

I slipped him an envelope. "Here's one thousand Euros. Is that a reasonable down payment?"

"Will three thousand more be a problem in two days' time?"

"Not if you get me some excellent intel."

He smiled, took a big drag off his cigar and chugged his beer. "If that's the criteria, maybe you should bring five."

"Three thousand is fine."

I got up and left. It was still weird to me that nearly all the taxis were Mercedes. I headed back to the train station, where the next train would arrive in about half an hour. The stories about how regularly German trains run are completely accurate. These were more commuter vehicles than the touring cars I had been on over the past few days, but they were still comfortable.

The Audi was waiting for me at the train station. It was fun being catered to at the castle. I tried to rationalize about getting spoiled by thinking it protected the others from potential danger. I told myself it was best not to introduce potentially sketchy people to Claude and Lauren. The reality was, I liked being the cool guy for a change.

***

Claude had a sly grin as he poured everyone a beer and motioned for Paleau to join us at the table. That caught Lauren's attention. The chef rolled in a cart full of covered dishes. Claude was getting excited and thanked the chef. He started by serving Lauren, then Paleau, then he put a dish at his place and finally I got mine. The aroma was a dead giveaway. Claude was almost giddy.

His smile lit up the room. *"Bon appétit!* Everyone, you may now take the covers off your dinners."

Paleau and Lauren looked completely baffled.

"My darling, this smells wonderful. But what on earth is it?"

"This is the namesake delicacy of Mark's hometown. It's called a cheesesteak. I fell in love with it after my first bite when I visited Mark. I didn't want him to be homesick."

Paleau took a bite and grinned like a Cheshire Cat. Lauren went next. She tried to put every hair in place. Then she let out a deep, almost erotic sigh. Her eyes opened wide.

"Oh, my God. This is heaven." She tried to eat it in a classy fashion but it was way too messy and way too good. She inhaled it. "Are there any more?"

"Yes, my love, I had the chef make more. Mark, would these be considered good in Philadelphia?"

"They are amazing. How did you get the rolls so perfect? What kind of meat did you use?"

"I called Amoroso's and offered the baker a vacation in Luxentstein for his recipe. The steak is Luxenstein's version of Kobe beef. We never export even a kilo of it. I keep it for our people."

"Jesus, this is like a $300 cheesesteak."

Lauren smiled, "Honey, it's only money. This tastes better than a stack of soaked bills."

I think the best part of the meal was how much fun Paleau was having. It was great to see Paleau just being Jacques. The old friends played cards as Lauren and I relaxed. A perfect dinner. All that was missing was Marci.

Soon, Claude went off to bed. I was in the main library practicing reading and speaking Russian. About 12:30 a.m. the doors opened. It was Lauren.

"How's your studying going?" she asked.

"I'm not sure."

"You'll be fine. Do you have a minute?" Her tone was quiet and serious.

"Of course, is something wrong?" I was becoming a little worried.

"Claude wants to protect his friend, but if what happened in the rest of the world was as silly as what we did, nobody will be able to stand the embarrassment."

"Come on." I didn't know if I should be frightened or reassuring to Lauren.

"What I did sounded like a lot of sex, but there wasn't any at all. Well, other than with Claude." She smiled broadly and nodded.

"Huh?"

"Well, all those men thought they had sex with me, but none of them did." Lauren was almost giddy, after all these years.

"How did you pull that off?" I was intrigued and wanted to know what her tricks were.

"Lots of drinks. Lots of sleeping pills and lots of dirty pictures." She let out a belly laugh.

"No way."

Lauren howled. "But they did get to see naked pictures of me."

I joined her with a whoop.

"I was beautiful then."

"You are beautiful now."

She kissed me on the forehead. "Marci is a lucky lady. Please, be careful, Mark."

"I'll try."

"Oh God, that's exactly what Claude said and look where we are now," she said. Her voice had an ominous tone to it.

***

The next morning the cell phone Stan gave me rang. I answered and he said he wanted to meet me for lunch the following day. Hackers are notoriously cool. They exist in a world that is somewhere between reality and a place that only they inhabit. Few see the light of day. They create master mazes to conceal everything about their lives. His voice wasn't as certain as it was when we first met. It quivered a couple of times before he gave me the instructions for our meeting.

I got on the train and headed to Metz, France. It was a small station. I was surprised he wanted to meet in a place with so few people. Stan was smoking a cigarette as he approached me.

"I think you're getting a big bargain."

"If so, you'll be making a lot more money later."

We walked across the street to a bar. We took an inside table and ordered some beers. I leaned back against the wall as he reached into his pocket for a flat envelope.

"What a crew of people you gave me. Can I ask what they have in common?"

"Nope..."

"Let's get rid of the sort of powerful empty suit. Gabe Stein was a White House insider during the Cold War. He was NSA or intelligence. Right before the end of the Cold War he went underground. He's got family money in several countries and at least four passports."

Since Stein was a White House insider, he was likely a top player in the story. Other than being a desk soldier, it was weird that he was a pain in the ass. I thought he would be more cautious, wanting to know how I was going to paint him. But he was a paranoid goofball. I wanted to take him seriously, but I liked having a lot of fun making him squirm.

"Good stuff," I took the envelope with the money out of my pocket and put it on the table. I kept my hand on top of it.

"Peter Martin was born just outside of Moscow as Georgi Malkinovich. He went into the Red Army and KGB. He is an expert in linguistics. It looks like he got a Canadian passport and a Belgian one. He married a lady named Bobbie Jean Connor. She got a Canadian passport as well. They have a son, William Connor. He's twenty-one and goes to Penn State."

"What are they doing now?"

"They went dark a few years ago, but I'll keep looking."

"OK, how about the others?"

"Peter Andreev died in 2002 under his own name. He was also KGB. Sergei Popov was a professor of American Studies at Moscow State University. He is now an actor in St. Petersburg under the name of Fyodor

Lasky. Alexi Sakharov is a government worker in Siberia. Were they a team?"

I pushed the envelope to Stan. He put it inside his jacket. We nodded. He gave me the portfolio with all the data printed out. I went back to the train station. For the first time, I was acutely aware of all my surroundings.

Then I started laughing. How did Sergei go from professor and KGB to being an actor? He went from spy to side show. I knew I had to meet him. He had to be in Claude's story. Was Sergei the Soviet Claude? Why did Georgi disappear off the grid?

Suddenly, everything seemed so serious. The people were becoming real to me. The players had real life stories before and after the event. This was a truly bizarre team.

I had to get to St. Petersburg and off to Siberia. This was going to take a lot of time. I wasn't sure which place would be more dangerous. There were cops, informants and Mafia throughout St. Petersburg. But I'd stand out in Siberia no matter how understated I tried to be.

If Lauren and Claude used naked pictures and fake sex to get their power, what did the others do? How could their actions have been the sanest of all? Maybe they had truly planned their actions and the others fell into the rabbit hole of history.

Unlike the Russians, Lauren, Claude and Paleau understood that they were acting crazy. The Pied Piper was used to it. An actress is trained to take her work beyond the limits. However, bureaucrats and, especially, spies need everything fit neatly into the plans or the contingencies. They could end up in jail if found out. They had everything from money to enforcers to threat of jail or even death for the non-connected as aces up their sleeves.

What would happen if everything fell apart? What would happen if everything fell apart multiple times? We know no hot war got started. Could everyone have screwed up so badly that they couldn't come clean? Could I be in danger just for knowing?

My mind was rushing so quickly the trip seemed like it took ten minutes, not two hours. The Maybach was waiting at the train station. I got inside. Claude and Lauren were glowing. It was the first time I had seen that type of excitement in Lauren's eyes.

"Are you getting more confused?" she asked.

"I'm not sure. I'm learning more. There's someone you may have to protect. Stan doesn't know what he's getting himself into. He knows some of the pieces, but not why."

"Give me his information and I'll take care of the rest. It sounds like this info means you will be leaving again," Claude said.

"Probably tomorrow or the next day."

"Remember, we knew what we were doing."

"Claude, please be honest. We didn't know most of what we were doing, only some, only our part."

"Well, we *thought* we knew what we were doing."

They both chuckled. Was it cute or a Stephen King level of terror?

A part of reality just sunk in. "Oh shit, I'll be gone for a few weeks. What can I tell Marci?"

Lauren put her arms around my shoulders, "Don't worry about Marci, sweetheart. I'll take care of her. You need to keep your head clear."

"Just don't drink too much vodka, it could be dangerous," Claude said with a twinkle in his eyes.

We all split up and went to bed. I didn't sleep very well. What was stranger was that I dreamed in Russian. At least my psyche was getting into character. *Dasvidaniya* safety, comfort and decent food.

Chapter 10
On the Road Again

I took a commercial flight to St. Petersburg. Security at customs was tight. It looked like there were government agents and goons looking over the shoulders of the legit people. It was a first glimpse into the new Russia. After waiting about an hour in line, I started thinking I should have used my diplomatic passport; but it would have raised way too many red flags. I would have had a target on my back and a phalanx of police following my every step. It was bad enough just being an ordinary Joe.

Boy, did my life change 180 degrees in a day. A castle, an Audi, a Maybach versus a 70s-era jalopy driven by someone who smelled like a mix of borscht and vodka. He miraculously dropped me off at the hotel. I checked in. The bellman was totally indifferent to me until, of course, it was time for his tip. I got changed and headed out to see the sights.

The Hermitage was amazing. Every nook and cranny were crammed with treasures. The wealth of respect the janitors had for the museum was evident in their every move. St. Petersburg was trying to be a modern town while celebrating its past at the same time. Boulevards formed spokes of a wheel. There was also a network of alleys running into the boulevards.

I went back to the hotel to get changed. Then, I took a cab to the theater district. My research said specific troupes hung out in their own cafes. There seemed to be a pecking order of where actors were seen in public. My research, however, added another chilling aspect: it was organized as self-protection for gay actors. Russians thought nothing about beating them up just for being gay. Homophobia was almost celebrated. It was sickening.

I sat outside at a table belonging to the café where I figured I could find Sergei/Fyodor. I doubted he would see my passport. It said I was from Philadelphia, but I thought having a North Carolina accent might be valuable. I felt lucky enough to try to wing it.

As I sipped my coffee, I read a copy of the International Gazette. I was trying to look above it while remaining eminently accessible. I was starting into my second cup of coffee when Sergei/Fyodor approached me. His smile was unexpectedly electric in a city of down-looking denizens. I thought to myself that his old KGB training had kicked in and he must have spotted me as someone who didn't fit in.

"Are you American?" Fyodor asked.

"Yes, I am."

"Your accent, I know it. Are you from North Carolina?"

"I grew up there but now I live in Philadelphia. I'm Mark." I was having fun being a spy.

"Hello, Mark. I'm Fyodor."

This is when I noticed something: Sergei/Fyodor was gay. Not just a little, rather proudly, but out to the entire world. How did he fool the KGB to get his posting?

"Have you been to America?" I asked.

"Maybe in another lifetime, y'all. What brings you to St. Petersburg?" He was prodding me.

"I was in Europe and hadn't ever seen The Hermitage."

"A handsome young man like you wouldn't normally travel alone." His eyes twinkled.

"My trip to Germany was business."

"You found your way from the museum. I bet you didn't find this place by accident."

"You might lose that bet. Where's good place near the Grand Hotel Europe to have a drink after dinner?" I tried to deflect his question.

"There's a place called Peter the Great's on a small alley. It gets busy around 22:00 hours. If you want a seat you need to arrive earlier."

"That sounds good, thanks. I think I'll rest a little and go there."

Using military time is not something actors normally do; he was giving me a hint. I decided I couldn't buy Marci anything that would show her I was in Russia. Wait, she'd see my passport and find out. It was damned if I do, damned if I don't. I'd tell her the whole truth… someday.

I took a short nap. When I got out of the shower, Fyodor was waiting in my room. He was smiling, looking proud of doing something he hadn't done in many years.

"Don't worry, Mark. You're too young for me. I'm guessing you know my name is Sergei. By the way, I only found four listening devices in your room. Here they are," he said smiling.

He handed them to me. "Holy shit," I gasped.

"Don't worry. They do that to all foreign rooms. Are you CIA? NSA? MI5?"

"Nope, just a writer."

He started cackling. "I've been hiding for twenty-five years and get found by a writer. As you say in America, holy shit! What do you know? You must know something or you wouldn't have been looking for me."

"Not much." I was trying to decide if I was scared or relieved.

"Imagine a gay Russian professor KGB agent sent to rural North Carolina as one of the cornerstones of the USSR's most important act of Cold War espionage."

"Cornerstone?" I asked, feeling I had struck gold.

"Peter was the leader, but I was the one who knew about the people and language of North Carolina. The others trusted me and leaned on me more. I was the one who did the ongoing training," he told me.

"Did the KGB know you were gay?"

"No way, I'd have been killed or put in a gulag. It was a great way to put myself above suspicion and see America." His voice was serious.

"Why didn't you go back home as a hero?" I asked.

"We figured that there could be no loose ends. Georgi had fake papers for me." His upright sitting position became more relaxed.

"Why haven't you said anything?"

"I've got family and I'm a gay actor. Who the hell would believe me?"

"I will," I said, reaching to pat him on the shoulder.

"I took Peter's death as a hint. I've got some insurance, but it will be better if you tell the world."

"I'll try."

"I only know what we did. The craziest of us all was Georgi. That girl BJ gave him more sex in two weeks than he had his entire life before coming to America. Peter was supposed to kill him before he took off. Are they OK?"

"They dropped off the grid a few years ago. He's making it much harder to find him than you."

"If you keep going on this story, he'll find you. You know where Alexi is, don't you?"

"Are you going to follow me?" I thought his KGB past might be roaring back to life.

"Absolutely not! If they think I'm trying to find him, we're both dead. Before I got here, were you on the phone?"

"No."

"Good. They don't know why you're here, but you should leave in the morning and buy your ticket to see Alexi with cash. You shouldn't leave a paper trail."

He pulled a bottle of vodka out of his satchel. We started drinking it like water. The drunker we got, the more outrageous the story became. To him the strangest part of the story and what made him love America the most was how the farmers and locals treated them like family almost instantaneously. In the Soviet Union (and in today's Russia), you don't trust your neighbors or friends even if you've known them for years.

He seemed incredibly relieved to share his bizarre story. Much of it contradicted the outside world's concept of how cold and calculating the KGB was. For decades, the world thought the KGB was nothing but robotic killers and spectacular spies.

Boy, was the world wrong about them. The Russians did come. The Russians did come. Barney Fife met James Bond and Liberace. The KGB thought there would be resistance. They were prepared for everything. Well, other than being welcomed as friends and *much more*. They became brothers. In some ways, it was amazing they didn't get caught due to all the peripheral events, but they had fun.

I woke up the next morning and gathered my things before going to the front desk and checking out. It was a short walk to the train station. My Russian worked well as I ordered and paid for my ticket to Siberia.

Now, I was on my way. I had to figure out where it all started. That wasn't going to be easy, more like playing Jeopardy than putting together a puzzle. I knew some of the story, but not how or why. Add to this, the person I was relying on had changed his identity and literally moved to the end of the world to obscure his very existence. Why would he trust me? Why wouldn't he just take me into a field and kill me? What great thoughts to have while being stuck on a train for thousands of miles!

Putting my paranoia on the back burner, I had to snicker. It sounded like a Jewish comic's Vegas lounge act: a KGB assassin, a scientist, and an actor walk into a bar in North Carolina...

The problem is, it wasn't a joke. In hindsight, maybe John Cleese should have been Prime Minister of England and Chris Rock POTUS. It couldn't be any worse than what we had.

I was worried about this trip after learning my room in St. Petersburg had been bugged. How did they know I was there? Did they have cameras to catch what I typed into my computer? So, I booked a single sleeper-room on the Trans-Siberian Railway. It sounded luxurious, but it was barely better than a commuter train with a couple of sleeper cars and dining cars – most assuredly not the Orient Express. Many cars smelled like they hadn't been cleaned since Khrushchev was in office.

You can have no real understanding of how big Russia is until you take the train across it. There's every kind of geography you can imagine in its vastness: mountains, valleys and forests. To me, the most amazing thing was the astounding amount of emptiness. For thousands of miles, there was nothing. Day after day the train rumbled through empty countryside until I reached Alexi's new hometown.

Why there was a city of a million people five hundred kilometers from anywhere positively baffled me. I walked across the street from the station to a small hotel. My Russian was good enough that the desk clerk started telling me about the problems he was having with his girlfriend. I had pulled it off for this tiny moment! I told myself not to get cocky. I couldn't let my guard down. It wasn't just Alexi I had to fear. *All* outsiders were threats in Russia, it was even truer in the outskirts of Siberia.

There was no shower in the room, but I took a bath and a nap. It was great to be on firm ground. It was about 9 p.m. when I awakened. I used clothes I bought in Germany to dress like a Russian and went to the bar a block away. Damn, it was cold. No one seemed to care except me.

Man, it was depressing. It was dark, dank, and cold. The people looked like a bad country and western song. The guys at the first table looked like they had all just lost their jobs. The next group was talking about their evil girlfriends. All we needed was a group talking about someone stealing their trucks. You could barely see the people next to you due to the thick veil of smoke. Until you come to a place like this, you don't truly appreciate the no smoking in bars back home.

After a while, a man walked over to my table. He stared right through me and said in Russian, "You aren't Russian. What are you doing in this godforsaken place?"

I answered in Russian that I was. He shook his head. You can take the man out of the KGB, but you can't take the KGB out of the man. It had to be Alexi. Who else would care, or who else would notice? I was happy and scared shitless at the same time. Now this was the epitome of what we thought KGB agents were.

In Russian, I asked him where he thought I was from. He looked at me and said I was American. I smiled.

"What are you looking for in Siberia?" he asked.

"I'm looking for you, Alexi."

"How do you know who I am?" He glared at me and took a step back.

"Sergei hopes you are well." I hoped this would give me credibility, or it might get me knifed.

This confused him. "We should take a walk? It's not good to speak English here."

I put my coat on and we started outside. He looked in every direction to see if we had caught anyone's eye. He leaned over and whispered to leave slowly and quietly.

He pulled me into an alley and pushed me up against the wall. "Who the hell are you? What do you want with stirring up the past? It's over. Leave it alone."

"I'm a writer. I was hired to write a book about what happened before the Cold War ended."

"Do you have half a clue about what you are doing?" Alexi grabbed me by the neck.

"I'm learning." I tried my best to be tough.

"In America, you would call it a clusterfuck. Even that doesn't go far enough. I'm not sure if we were the smartest and bravest people ever, or the craziest and luckiest. You couldn't possibly understand without being there. I was and don't believe ninety percent of it myself." Alexi was almost opening up.

"That's what I'm learning. How did your team work?" I asked, looking him in the eyes.

"I was the team leader. Sergei was the sanest and most organized member of our crew. I couldn't believe what they asked us to do. Have you found Peter or Georgi?" he asked softly.

"Peter is dead. Georgi has dropped off the face of the Earth."

"That's too bad about Peter. Was Georgi with that crazy girl when you lost track of him?" He was sad then amused.

"Yep, they got married."

He howled. "Everyone was afraid that while he was drinking and screwing her and her sister he'd start talking. Peter was supposed to kill him, but Georgi left too quickly."

"He was having sex with both?" I was surprised at this turn, but I felt like it meant Alexi was starting to trust me.

"Oh yeah! I was surprised he could stand up after all that fucking. Hell, I had to drag him out of their bed several times to get the job done." Alexi laughed.

"I bet that didn't go over too well in Moscow."

Alexi started laughing more. "Are you kidding? No one was crazy enough to tell them anything. His sex life was the least of our worries. The people in the Kremlin were much worse. Remember, it was their idea. Nitvik was certifiable. Petrov wasn't much better."

"How do you know all this? No one on any side seems to know as much about their own part as you do."

"Who knows about what you are doing?" he almost stammered.

"No one knows everything I do, nor will anyone until I am finished. Tell me how to reach out to you before I go public so you can do whatever you need to do," I said looking him directly in the eyes.

"Thank you. I was the team leader. I had to deal with the suits in Moscow. Tell me where you're going and I'll send you documents about our training."

"Why not give them to me now?"

"Anything can happen in Russia. I'll give you a simple code. Memorize it. Do not write it down under any circumstances." He stared directly into my eyes to let me know he was completely serious and I needed to pay attention to him.

"How will you get the materials to me?"

"Don't worry about that. Just don't use any of our real names. I don't know what the Americans did, but we made Inspector Clouseau look super-competent."

I chortled. "Thanks."

"Can you tell me anything about the prince who ended up so rich?" He smiled – and it was clear he knew a good bit more than he'd told me.

"I can tell you what people who knew him call him."

"What?"

"The Pied Piper of Panties."

We both roared. "He sounds more rational than our side. By the way, Petrov's son is in London. I think you might find some good information there. Be ready for surprises, though. If I were looking for Georgi, I'd see if there were any drive-in movie theaters left in America. He loved drive-in movies. They changed his life... well, at least his sex life." He couldn't help himself from a deep, guttural guffaw. It was the first time he'd let his guard down at all.

"Thanks," I said. "Good tip."

"You should leave in the morning. It will make you look like you came to do business and went home. The police will think you are a cheap Russian." His fear of being found out was being transformed into worrying about my well-being and wanting the story to finally come out.

I took his advice and decided to take the train at 10 a.m. I packed and then looked in the closet and drawers to make sure I wasn't leaving anything behind. I saw nothing. When closing my suitcase, I found a dozen pages of notes under my shirts. How did he do it? I understood why he was the team leader. He knew what had to be done and got it done.

I started reading them and couldn't believe what they said. In true KGB fashion, Alexi had kept voluminous notes.

What was most amazing and telling is that the people who were trained and carried out the plan were the most competent and sane. Theirs was a special kind of loyalty that was unbreakable even in situations they thought were irrational.

So far, I'd seen parts of three sections of those in the trenches. Mbangu and Jinare knew whatever it was that they did was necessary and were totally devoted to the other. The same was true about Claude, Paleau and Lauren. I was genuinely surprised at how close Sergei and Alexi were. After all, theirs was a society that rewarded turning in your neighbor. They would never do that to each other. They had true honor but weren't above doing completely crazy things.

It is very apparent the world truly needed crazy. Think of the other alternative. There were large numbers of "experts" on both sides who thought a nuclear war was winnable. *They* were the crazy ones!

Chapter 11
This is the Sane Part?

It took another week, but I made it back to the castle in Luxenstein. God-damn, Russia is big! It's barren and gross as well. There's nothing for a thousand miles at a time and it grated on me. Travelling back to civilization, the depth and importance of what I was doing sunk in for the first time. The pressure was becoming oppressive though it had been totally unseen. My mind was racing. Fear and humor lived side by side. I was ready to take a small break from what was appearing to lose all touch with reality. No matter how crazy, I had to remember this was history, not fiction.

Claude may have lived in his own little world, but at least he knew what that world was and how to control most of it. He might look like a lunatic to those who don't know him, but he was far from it. What separated him from other world leaders was his big heart. He truly loved his people. Every one of them was his cousin. Yes, he was an unabashed hedonist, but in the end, Claude cared.

Life is often about limitations. That's where Claude began his life, not stopped. He understood the power of freedom more than anyone I have ever met. But this was one time when he didn't have control of the answers, so he asked for help.

Claude was strong enough to know freedom is gained through working with others. Some think freedom can come from oneself and can be a solitary event. It can't. Freedom doesn't exist if it is singular. It must be shared.

Holy shit, I was becoming a philosopher. Yes, I wanted desperately to tell the story. But it had been almost three weeks of living in crap.

I need my castle again. I wanted to be pampered before I had to start dodging the Americans and Russians. Gimme! Gimme!

Claude and Lauren came into the living room. He sauntered in with studied casualness. The Claude I had seen was like a kid on Christmas morning when he was going to learn something. It had always been a game to him. Maybe I was still exhibiting my Russian level of concern in wondering why he wasn't much more animated wanting to hear what happened.

"Did you like Siberia?" Claude asked nonchalantly.

"There was a lot of it. Man, was it boring," I answered.

"Lots of beautiful women in Russia, aren't there?" Lauren asked, not as nonchalantly.

"I was busy and I was scared. I don't remember any."

Claude looked puzzled. "Why were you scared?"

"Sergei found four bugs in my room in St. Petersburg."

Lauren's eyes opened wide. "Are you sure?"

"Yes, he showed them to me. Then we flushed them."

Claude started snickering. "The actor played you. He couldn't give up his KGB past."

"Yep, Mark, you were a sucker." Lauren's grin widened.

Suddenly, I heard a very familiar voice. "I can't believe how gullible you are."

I looked over my shoulder and it took a second to realize that the angel standing there was Marci. We hugged and kissed. "How much did you hear?"

"A lot more from Claude and Lauren than from you."

"Uh oh, Mark. You'd better start groveling. It usually works for me when Lauren catches me."

"A book about Mbangu, eh?" Marci said, putting her arm around my waist.

"He *is* in the book," I said, tickling her.

Claude raised his eyebrows. "He's got you there... ouch."

Marci and Lauren slapped Claude's arms at the same time. They were exerting the power only beautiful women have.

"I take it Marci knows everything?"

Lauren poured us some cognac. "As much as we know, which is less than you do."

They all roared. For a moment, there was silence. All three looked at me like kids watching a clown at a birthday party. I looked down. Hmm, I did have size 24 shoes on. Whew!

Claude said, "Mbangu will be in New York next week."

"Before we go back to New York, how about if we all go see a play or two in the West End?" I said with a smirk.

"But the food and weather are so dreary in London," Claude said.

"Hush, Claude! Let's show Marci our home and go to London the day after tomorrow. There's another reason Mark wants to go to London." As usual, Lauren was right on target. I would never, ever be stupid enough to play poker with her.

Marci smiled. "That sounds perfect."

Claude and Lauren left the room. Marci and I started making out on the huge leather couch. I carried her back to our room. Wow! What a night that became.

***

In the morning, Marci rolled over and kissed me. "So, Mr. Cloak-and-Dagger, how did Claude save the world?"

"I haven't figured out how everything got started or ended. The middle is Barney Fife meets Inspector Clouseau with a little Austin Powers for good measure. And the entire world was doing mushrooms and acid for a few months."

She slapped my naked butt. "I'm insulted that you'd expect me to believe that."

"I spent two weeks in a tiny train compartment going back and forth across Siberia. A gay KGB agent was sitting in my hotel room when I got out of the shower in St. Petersburg. I found out Lauren took naked pictures with drugged, dirty old men who were commodities brokers. And you're calling what I just told you a fib?"

Marci's eyes rolled back in her head. She looked me dead in the eyes. "Now, you're telling me the truth."

"I am."

"Oh, my God! This sounds like it could be outrageously dangerous. Is it one story or a bunch?"

"It seems to have four prongs that were going on without knowing what the others were doing."

"Do you have any prong finished?"

"Claude needs to fess up a bit for us to have at least one full prong."

Marci stood up and grabbed my hand. "Well, let's take a shower and then ask him?"

Marci lost total control. She was primeval. It was the best shower sex ever. She was getting into being part of changing the world. We got dressed and headed out to the patio. Claude and Lauren were having juice and pastries.

Marci kissed Claude on the cheek and hugged Lauren. The princess' face almost exploded from pure glee and anticipation. "I think she came for you, Claude."

"I did. You turned Mark into Marco Polo and you haven't told him your story? That ends *now*."

Everyone snickered. Claude studied Marci for a moment. "Well my darling, our nation was broke. I couldn't exactly sell the palace. I had to figure out a way to save our country. So, I tried the best way I could."

He stopped right there and sipped his coffee. I laughed, knowing that Claude was done for the day. He loved knowing how that was frustrating to Marci. It was the poker player in him. She had no shot at getting at more information until either she backed off or until Claude stopped having fun playing with her.

"Honey, let's go into town."

"But Claude hasn't finished telling us the story."

Claude just smiled.

"Hey Marci, let me show you where I got that purse. We'll be back in plenty of time to get on the plane for London."

We left the castle. On the way into town in the Audi, Marci asked, "Why won't Claude tell me anything?"

"He will when you stop begging," I said with a chuckle, knowing it would piss her off.

"Wait a second. It's his plane. Let's go to London now."

"Oh, Jesus, you're going to get into a pissing contest with him, aren't you?"

She unbuttoned her blouse. "I wouldn't exactly call it a pissing contest."

"You think you can change the mind of the Pied Piper of Panties with tits? Well at least, you'll make him feel young again." My guffaw was an appreciation of her boobs.

She laughed and asked the driver to take us back to the castle.

***

We went to London. I hadn't been in the royal plane before, but, of course, it was pure Claude. There was a small gourmet kitchen and a great bar, with seats almost like leather thrones and a formal dining table. Of course, the back third was a bedroom that was almost all bed. Some of the Pied Piper still lived, or maybe he just enjoyed having his guests think about what may have happened in bygone days and that it could possibly still happen today.

The flight took less than two hours. It was a bit strange landing on a runway with no other planes on it. We came to a smooth stop and the flight attendant moved to open the exit door.

A Rolls limo came onto the tarmac to pick us up as well as another car to take our bags to the townhouse. London's traffic was awful. We were taken to a boutique where Lauren and Marci bought way too many dresses and shoes. Claude was amused by my toe tapping and watch checking, but Lauren had taken Marci completely under her wing. She wouldn't let anything happen to my lady.

Claude was like the proud papa. He was watching from above as we stopped a few other places before reaching the opulent townhouse. It must have been fifteen thousand square feet. We got changed. Claude and Lauren toned their lives down, as if we were just an ordinary group of friends going out for dinner and drinks in a stretch Rolls limo.

That night was a lot of fun, but from time to time it seemed like Claude's temperament was changing. He was looking around more, probably because he couldn't control everything in London.

At one point, I went into the bathroom. As I opened the door to leave, a very proper English gentleman bumped into me and excused himself. At the time, I didn't think anything about it.

When getting undressed that night, I found a small, creased envelope in my inside jacket pocket. Alexi had gotten that guy in the restaurant to put that letter in my pocket. What the fuck? How did he do that all the way from Siberia? The letter in my pocket contained Petrov's son's address.

The next morning, I made an excuse about going for a walk to get outside. Then, I took a cab to his mansion in St. John's Wood. How was I going to get in? In addition to the address, Alexi had included a picture of Anton Petrov and his schedule. Alexi had it dead-on. Alexi was walking towards me in just a few seconds. I decided to speak Russian to him.

He looked at me. "You aren't Russian, but you know me. Who are you?"

"Mr. Petrov, I am a journalist. I'm doing a story on the fall of the Soviet Union," I offered.

"Buy Gorbachev's book. It's quite good."

"Yes, indeed, but there's nothing about North Carolina in it."

This struck a nerve. He tensed up like he'd been tasered. Then he turned and smiled. "If you know about North Carolina, you will enjoy coming into my home. Please join me."

He unlocked the gate and we went inside. We put our jackets on the hooks. He motioned for me to sit in the living room. In a few moments, he returned with a twenty-something Russian woman.

"I don't know your name, but I'd like to introduce my wife, Natasha Nitvik Petrov."

I almost peed my pants. The Field Marshall's son had married the daughter of the Director of the KGB. He was totally amused by this situation.

Natasha smiled, "North Carolina, eh? How is Sergei? Or, I mean Fyodor?"

Had I fallen into another dimension? How did all these people know all this and kept it quiet?

"He is well and loving his new life."

They sat on the couch. Anton smiled. "I'm glad he is happy, or should we say, gay?

This was a game to them. They chuckled. Of course, they'd grown up with intrigue and power.

"You know who we are. But we don't know you." Natasha sounded just like the daughter of Nitvik. The apple doesn't fall far from the tree.

"My name is Mark Stein. I'm from Philadelphia."

"If you've seen Sergei, you've probably seen Alexi. You know Peter is dead. Who is paying you, Mr. Stern?"

"I can't tell you yet."

They nodded knowingly. Natasha looked at Anton. "If you are keeping that confidential, will you keep our identities secret? It's tough enough being the daughter of the last Director of the KGB and the son of the Defense Minister without becoming part of what you are about to do."

"I will."

Anton looked playful. "Mark, coming to England has been wonderful. It has allowed me to learn all the colloquialisms of your native language. By the time you finish this story, you will realize no family in modern political history has been more appropriately named than my lovely wife's."

I was puzzled. "What?"

"You are bright enough to think about Nitvik... come on, do some extrapolating."

Natasha looked at him. "Extrapolating is all Anton will be doing for many months to come."

Then, we all got the joke and he understood his wife's threat about it being Siberia-type cold in their bedroom if he didn't listen.

We spent the rest of the afternoon talking about history and drinking. The more they talked about what they knew about the past, the more I understood the only way to talk about this event was for everyone to be completely wasted. If you weren't, you'd start thinking about what you were saying and stop. No one could believe this story if they were sober.

Nothing either of them said could possibly not be true, but it was as true as my love for Marci. What the hell had I gotten her into? She hadn't seen these parts but wanted to jump right in and do this type of background work.

The time had passed so quickly. In no time, dinner was being served.

I headed back to Claude's home. I opened the door and wasn't surprised I had a welcoming committee in the study. The stares were ominous. The fear was thick. The excitement was palpable. I had to come up with something to avoid a barrage of questions.

I stretched as I saw them. "I'm starving. Are you guys hungry? I think I'm going to order some food. Marci, what would you like?"

She got up, "It's not going to be that easy. You saw someone. You learned something."

Claude looked at us. "It can't be that good."

I shrugged knowing there was no way I was getting out of the room alive without giving up some information. How much and what could I get out answering were the questions.

"He's going to tell me or else..." Marci said, poking me in the stomach.

The way Lauren looked at me she knew I'd learned something big. "Oh, my God, it's so good that even sex won't work. In fact, Mark will get whatever he wants as a bribe for the tiny morsels he gives up."

"I envy you, Mark. Even in my Pied Piper days, I never had this amount of power."

"Who would've ever thought the Pied Piper of Panties would have been the voice of reason? Who would've thought his plan to save his country would be mayonnaise on white bread boring?" I said with a huge smile.

Claude and Lauren started clapping loudly. Marci looked frustrated.

"When did my Mark grow such a big pair?"

"Honey, I would've thought you knew that by now?"

We all laughed and hugged. We felt closer than the embraces.

We stayed in London two more nights, but it was purely rest and relaxation. The girls went shopping. Claude and I went to casinos. He loved his poker. Every evening, we went to a play in the West End. I knew Marci and I would never be as close to Claude as Lauren or Mbangu or Paleau, but now I understood what Scott, Petey and other were saying about Claude.

Chapter 12
America the Bizarre

Marci and I took British Airways first class back to New York. Because she was with me, it didn't seem like I had been gone for almost a month. I had strangely become more secure in our relationship and had an appreciably increased self-confidence. I'm not sure either was rational but it was what it was. Maybe I had grown a pair after all.

As we took the cab back to my apartment, I began wondering if she was going to become the Grand Inquisitor about what I had learned. Surprisingly, that never materialized. We unpacked and got undressed. I think the unspoken stress led us to simply pass out when we got home.

The next morning Marci went to class and I went to the library to do some research on drive-in theaters per Alexi's suggestion. I'd been there about two hours when my phone rang. Jinare wanted to meet for a late lunch.

He asked me to meet him at TBar, which is at about 74th and 3rd, far enough away from the UN to be discreet. He was truly Mbangu's gatekeeper. I wondered how much he knew about my travels and my progress.

I arrived first and got us a table in the back. Every time I had seen him he had been in impeccable suits and overcoats. That day he was almost casual, which surprised me. He came to the table and sat. In some ways, he seemed to have a peaceful air around him.

"How was your trip?"

"It was eye-opening. I got to see more of Russia than I ever need or want to. I met several of the other players. Some of the story is taking shape."

He smiled. I hadn't seen a smile like that from Jinare. "Your eyes are still closed. You've only heard part of the story. I don't know it all, but you haven't got a clue yet about the depth and breadth of what we did."

His openness caught me off-guard. "I am cautiously optimistic. But, how will I get the information from your side?"

"I'll give you a good bit of it, but you will have time with him as well. You and I should meet away from my work. The other meetings have to be structured to be careful." He was being diplomatic but firm as he set the ground rules.

"Of course."

"They are brothers because they are so different but so similar."

"Isn't it ironic this brought them back together?"

"I'm not sure it was irony or coincidence. It was something much bigger than that, unless the entire universe was created to make platypuses feel less self-conscious."

I chuckled out loud. He smiled broadly. His demeanor and smiles were a lot less formal and friendlier than before.

"I think you were sandbagging me before with your oh-so-proper-façade."

"Someone has to appear as such." He nodded in agreement and smiled.

We chuckled. He cautiously chose his words for the next two hours. Of course, that didn't do much to keep my mind from racing. This was a transformative meeting. Jinare's trust was hard to earn, but it was completely critical to our ultimate success.

I headed over to Marci's apartment. I decided to pick up a pizza and some wine on the way there.

When she saw me, she smirked, "*Oh*, now that we're in New York, we eat pizza. You could have stopped to get caviar or osso buco, but now that we aren't staying in a palace, you get pizza."

"But it's good wine and you New Yorkers always say it's the best pizza in the world."

We hugged. She brought out plates and glasses.

"I guess you aren't going to tell me anything, are you?"

I thought for a moment and drank some wine. "I'll do my best, Michael Corleone. I'll let you ask this once."

She kissed me, then giggled. "What did you learn today?"

"I can tell you that Russian workers seem to like rhesus monkeys and American construction workers don't ask questions if they get paid on time and have plenty of beer."

I had never seen a look that blank on Marci's face. I had succeeded! "What in the hell does that mean?" I couldn't tell if she was pissed or amused. She was great at confusing me. Without all this mess, she would have already passed the Bar and become a great lawyer.

"You asked a question. I answered it."

"Just because you think you have all the cards because I love you doesn't mean you do."

I paused and thought about all the women I had dated and smiled the biggest smile I ever had smiled around a woman. For once in my life I held some cards against a woman. YEAH!

"Where did that smile come from? You can't be *that* happy."

"Oh, I am, for sure, and I have to savor this moment."

"Why?"

"Because I'm winning a big one for all men."

"Did you stop at Mudville on the way home?" She thought my balls were created by Patron.

"I'm stone-cold sober. Throughout all of history, men have sought out this moment. I am the first man in history to truly have puzzled his woman and to have her not know what's going on in our life together... I actually did it!"

"That's big talk, mister."

"It's damn well true and you know it. It may never happen again but it is happening now. Forget about my book. I am now a hero to all men. I am the greatest!" I thought about jumping up and acting like a boxer who just knocked someone out to win the world championship. But I came to my senses and realized what the long-term repercussions might be if I took a victory lap.

We giggled, started kissing and made love right there on the couch. It was weird. We laughed during sex. Usually it was women laughing *at* me and not *with* me during sex.

She was naked and looked up at me. "Now tell me."

My face almost broke. "Nope."

She posed seductively. "Russians like rhesus monkeys."

"Yes."

We watched some TV and fell asleep on the couch. Our hearts seemed to beat in unison. We breathed at the same time. It seemed that there was complete peace with us.

Marci left the next morning. I stayed in her apartment trying to organize some notes and do some internet spying. Stein, as nutty as he has been, had given me a few names. Hopefully, there would be a lot of data.

I started looking them up using a couple of tricks Stan had shown me in Mannheim. Some of them were easy. I was surprised as the information popped up for me. It was an effective Tracking 101 course.

There were about a dozen Lucy Diamonds who would have been about the right age. Five were waitresses or stay-at-home moms. One was born and lived in Wyoming on a farm; two were dead but they didn't seem like plausible candidates. That left four.

Lucy Diamond Matthews was a social studies teacher in Ohio and she still lived there. She was a stretch. Dr. Lucy Diamond was a pediatrician in Boston. She'd be Number 3. I decided to track down the other two, who both lived near DC One was an international lawyer. The other was an organic chemist. Either one could be the Lucy I needed to find.

Marci was going to kill me for traveling again. Maybe I would be away just on a night that Marci worked at Mudville. She couldn't get too angry if she wasn't going to be home anyway. But I had to tell her. I heard the door open.

"I have to go to DC to find a woman," I said chuckling.

"What?" Marci said punching me on the arm.

"There's a name I have to track down."

"She'd better not be too cute."

"She's got to be 50-60 by now," I said smiling.

"Well, it's still going to cost you big-time when you get back," she said with a wink.

Very early the next morning, I took Amtrak to DC and traced their cell numbers. Thanks, Stan, for Tracking 101.

Like many powerful law firms, Lucy the lawyer's office was a few blocks from the White House on K Street. I called her telling her I was doing an article on international legal business red tape and we met for about an hour. Her answers showed she had nothing to do with anything other than business. It had to be the chemist.

I waited until late in the day to call her on her cell. "Dr. Lucy Diamond?"

"Yes, who – who is this?" she stammered.

"I'm Mark Stern, Gabe Stein suggested I call you."

I heard a gasp and the sound of her phone falling onto a desk and her fumbling to pick it up.

She whispered. "Meet me at the Old Ebbet Restaurant. I'm leaving now."

"Thanks. I'll get a table in the bar."

The place was getting packed when she arrived about fifteen minutes later. I figured she had to be in her late fifties, but she sure didn't look it. Wow! They sure don't make chemistry teachers like they used to. She sat at the table but didn't take off her jacket right away. Lucy looked around the bar and restaurant and tapped her fingers on the table like she was afraid of me.

"What do you know about Gabe Stein?" she asked, glaring at me.

"He's the one who found me."

"Why?" Her eyebrows raised while asking this question.

"Somehow he learned I was doing a book about Secretary General Mbangu."

"But that's not what your book is really about, is it?"

"Not entirely," I said, looking her in the eyes.

"Are you *that* brave or are you *that* stupid?" she said with great conviction.

"Funny you should put it that way. I've been told both." I hoped using self-effacing humor would ease the tension.

"If I tell you anything, you can't use my name."

"No problem." Every person said the same thing. They all wanted to share what they knew but didn't want anyone in their current lives to know they were part of it.

"I thought I was working for the Department of Defense to create a drug to greatly enhance GI performance."

"But as things turned out, that's not what it was about, was it?"

"No. It changed as soon as I got to the site."

We talked for about thirty minutes. Sometimes she rambled. Other times, she was laser-perfect with her details. As she was about to finish, Lucy directed me on how to find a Bernie Schwartz who had changed his name from Sol Levin. He was the next step after her part of the puzzle. She didn't want to hear from me again until I was ultimately finished with the entire story.

We parted. I caught a cab over to the Smithsonian and went to the gift shop to get the perfect present for Marci. I got another cab to Union Station and a train back to New York. While on the train I called Bernie/Sol to set up a meeting.

When the train reached New York, I jumped off and traversed Penn Station to find the subway entrance. I got on the R Train and went straight to Mudville. Marci was very surprised to see me.

"I thought you were staying over," she said as she hugged me.

"Didn't have to and I've got something for you." I was trying to save a little face and protect myself just a bit.

"Oh, my God! It's the rock club from the Smithsonian like I had when I was eight! You do pay attention." A tear dripped down her cheek. I did very well with that $10 present.

She gave me a huge kiss. "You are amazing."

What better place for a Bernie Schwartz to hide than New York? It's like the adage – when you want to hide a tree, put it in the forest. Thank God Lucy had his number. How did she get it? Why had they kept in touch? Even with these concerns, I called him the next day. He said we should meet at Union Square.

"Stern?"

"Should I call you Bernie or Sol?"

"It doesn't matter. How the hell could you find us?"

"It hasn't been easy."

"How much of the story do you know?" He squinted and a few beads of sweat formed on his forehead. He had been in hiding for over a quarter of a century and wanted to come out of the shadows. It was time.

"I'm getting there." I couldn't show any of my cards; it might spook him. "I know the U.S. and Soviets attacked the other in weird ways using spies like you."

"I can't wait to read your book to find out what I don't know. I lived it and don't know what the fuck else happened. But it was a trip. It was the one assignment for which I had no outs, no cover. I wondered why."

"How long were you there?"

"Several months. The old U.S.S.R. was a shit hole so bad that you couldn't believe it. Tim was nearly beaten to death by an old lady for cutting a line to take a leak. He'd been in Nam and said this old woman was tougher than any Viet Cong he ever saw."

"Weren't they super-secret and scary?" Now I was curious.

"Russians thought everyone else was KGB. No one trusted anyone. Hell, the hookers checked you for recording devices, but we did what we had to do. Nothing in training prepared us for the reality that was the U.S.S.R."

"What was it like?"

"It got crazy, man. When we thought we had it under control, something odd always happened."

We talked for about an hour and a half. By the time we finished discussing the dark, sad, hard place to live that Moscow was, I couldn't believe the suicide rate in the U.S.S.R. wasn't 90%. There was nothing worth living for in those days and no hope for the future. But somehow, they put up with it.

What was becoming weirder was that so many people knew they were a part of something bigger but never tried to find out the rest of the story. There was one consistent feeling from all of them – relief. Everyone had been borderline paranoid and completely alone. They seemed to find some peace when they unburdened themselves. They wanted to know the rest of the story. Then they didn't. Finally, they sought out just a morsel. I came to believe it was sort of a validation that what they went through happened. No matter how much they saw or did, each questioned if it was real. Where was the story? Why didn't anything come for them?

I decided to walk over to Marci's place. I was passing an alley when I got yanked into it. My muscles tensed and I felt sweat on the back of my neck.

I got spun around and saw him. Holy Christ! It was that little bastard Stein. I had to convince myself not to cold cock the asshole.

"Stein, what the fuck is the matter with you?" I said pulling away from him.

"We can't be seen together."

"You've grown a beard. You dyed your hair and have had plastic surgery. Who in the hell is going to recognize you?" I said snidely.

"Many powerful people out there want me dead." Stein was trying to keep his voice down.

"If they really wanted you dead, you'd have been dead twenty years ago," I said.

"That's what they want you to think. They're all fuck-ups," Stein countered.

"Didn't you use to be a big one of them?" I said with a smirk.

"Well, yes I was. Wait a second."

"What do you want?"

"Tell me what you know," Stein demanded.

"Not yet," I said quietly, but forcefully.

"When?"

"When I'm good and ready. I've gotta go."

He left quickly and stealthily like Robin Williams on acid. He looked back after every step. At the same time, it was hilarious and pathetic. As crazy as everything had been, Stein has been the only truly wild card. His actions were the only ones that were erratic like the phone under the table and meeting histrionics I had gone through. Everyone else I had met was simply living their lives as if nothing had happened.

Chapter 13
The Beginning of the End of the Beginning

The plan was starting to make sense, if what you meant was taking a chance on starting a thermonuclear war based on a bunch of crazy people telling relatively sane people to act like blithering idiots. Hell, all that made more sense that than what the U.S. and U.S.S.R. did to try to end the Cold War.

Let me rephrase that. The pieces of the puzzle were starting to fit together, but there were still a lot missing. I knew I would never get all of them. This was going to be history with a bit of educated guessing. It was amusing that millions of people would believe the truth was my conjecture.

The little I knew already would have driven Rube Goldberg into a catatonic state.

A tiny mistake, an auto mechanic, a farmer with a question or any one of a thousand others could have derailed any of the four stories. Rather than the Marx Brothers and the Ten Stooges creating world peace, we could have easily had a long nuclear winter.

As enjoyable as Anton and Natasha were as people and sources of what was going on in the U.S.S.R., it sucked big time that my U.S. source would have to be Gabe Stein. Could his participation in changing the world have made him this nutty?

Nah, I bet his innate craziness came naturally, during and after making history. After talking with Lucy and others, I got the impression that Stein was discarded early on and then did his ghost act. I think he was trying to get back in the game and feel important again.

I met with Jinare two or three more times. He had some good insights about how he and Mbangu had acted but it was very matter-of-fact. Their part of the story was logical. It made sense. Well, it made sense until the warp drives were turned on, and they left this galaxy. In some ways, I think Mbangu and Jinare enjoyed the events more than the others. Other than during that short period, their lives have been very successful. However, they didn't take too many chances. This was like the one crazy woman every guy dates sooner or later. It was fun, but you don't want to go back or do it again.

Thinking about everything, I was pacing and sweating in Marci's apartment. Marci asked, "Are you okay, baby? Is all of this getting to you?"

"I'm trying to figure out how to tell the story."

"That will be easy once you have it all," she said, putting her hand on my shoulder.

"What if I don't get it all?" I asked, continuing to pace.

"You will."

"Can you get a couple of weeks off?" I asked.

"Why?" She smiled and her eyes opened wide.

"It may take that long to find the last two links I'm looking for. One dropped off the face of the planet about fifteen years ago."

"You know where he is?"

"Not exactly," I said slowly.

"What do you mean, not exactly?"

"I have about half a dozen places to look. I think you'd be a big help." I smiled.

"Do you actually want me to come with you?" She sounded excited.

"You're already part of this. I want to share it with you."

"I'll follow your lead. What do I need to know?" She held my hand.

"We are looking for a couple. They are in their late 50s to mid-60s."

"If they've been off the grid for fifteen years, how do you expect to find them?" She squinted.

"Well, I found them in Siberia."

She snickered. "Of course, you did. That fits perfectly. Where are we going?"

"Bumfuck nowhere Canada, Minnesota, North Dakota, and maybe a few other thrilling places."

***

Two days later we hit the road. We had created directions for about eight stops. Although they were spread out, they were in a similar geographic area. Our first stop was in Ontario, a reasonably short drive, not even an entire day. We got there mid-afternoon. The people who owned the drive-in theater in Barrie knew nothing. We took some pictures and got on the road the next morning.

I thought she might think this was easy, but our first stop was of no use. All she knew was that I found a gay, ex-KGB agent and a KGB killer on my first tries. This could take some time and effort. Or maybe she just trusted me that much. Wow!

"Out of all the drive-in theaters in North America, why these?" Marci asked after about an hour.

"A lot of guessing, but these are rural enough for somebody trying to hide."

"And anything else?"

"And they turned over ownership at around the right time." I couldn't tell if she was probing or was trying find my pattern.

"Who exactly are you looking for?

"A Russian spy and a horny North Carolinian bar fly."

She snorted. "That makes perfect sense." This loosened her up. "Who else could it be? What if they aren't at any of these places?"

"We'll have to keep looking."

"Okay."

We headed across Canada and dipped into Minnesota. Crossing the U.S./Canadian border is still very simple and it was the first time I wasn't worrying about being followed. I'm not sure if that was smart or not, but we could see for miles in every direction.

The reason I chose this exact route was because the drive-in was still open, and because I wanted Marci to get some detective action. We drove up to the gate and walked over to the concession stand. A couple was working there like so many do in small businesses. Even though they were doing menial tasks, you could see how happy they were from the shared smiles and pats on the butt.

"Hi, can we help you?" the man said.

This was clearly not Georgi. He was too young. I had to think on my feet.

"Hi, I'm Mark and this is my wife, Marci."

"Hi, Mark. Hi, Marci. I'm Tom and this is my wife Helen. What brings you to Lake Elmo? Are you lost?" He roared.

"Maybe a little. We're trying to put together a book about drive-in theaters – the ones that are still open – and take pictures of some of the ones that are closed."

"We're one of the last ones in Minnesota. It's tough to make money, but we have a lot of fun," Tom said.

"When we were in Canada we found out that a couple of the ones that are still open in Quebec were owned by people from Europe. They said they loved owning their places. It was like a dream to them. I thought that was cool. Do you know of any other immigrants who own drive-ins?"

Mary looked at me. "You know, I've heard someone from Sweden or someplace owned one in Flin Flon."

"Come to think of it, I heard that too," said Tom. "And there was a nice enough guy and his wife who owned a place in western North Dakota. She was American. He was from someplace else. Can't remember where."

"Thanks. I love the difference in how you look at this as fun and helping your community and people from other countries see it as the American dream," Marci said with a twinkle in her eyes.

Mary smiled. "You know, that's a nice way to put things. I bet lots of people will like that story."

"Mary, I hope you don't get too angry with me. Marci, would you and Mark like to stay for the show tonight and bunk in with us for the night? There aren't many hotels on the way to where you're going. You could get a fresh start in the morning."

Marci put her arm around me. "That sounds wonderful. Thanks so much."

We watched the movie, went to the local pub and stayed the night. Tom and Mary were so gracious. Half the people in the pub must have stopped over to say hi and introduce themselves. The next morning Mary fixed enough pancakes and sausage to feed at least twenty people.

"Which one are you going to first?" Tom asked.

"I think we should head to Williston first. I found several in Canada we can visit afterwards."

"That's a long drive," Mary said.

Marci was ready. "I did a MapQuest last night. It's a little less than 700 miles."

Tom chuckled. "Mark, you can drive ninety most of the way if Marci isn't too squeamish."

"Hey, Tom, he's the one who drives like an old lady. If a guy can drive ninety, I bet a semi-cute girl can get away with 100."

I knew I'd better say something fast. "You're far more than semi-cute."

"Come on Mark, stand up for yourself," Mary said with a chuckle.

"It's not like I drive like an old woman. She drives like a New York cabbie with a drag racer and booster rockets thrown in for good measure."

Everyone roared. As we turned to leave, Mary handed us a basket with some food in it. When Tom saw that he went into the cupboard and got us a twelve pack.

"If she drives like that, you may need this," he said, handing me an old airline barf bag.

We took their gifts. "Thanks for everything."

Mary kissed Marci on the cheek. "Don't forget to send us a copy of the book."

"I can't wait to read it," Tom said. "I hope drive-ins don't become extinct too soon."

"I promise to send both of you a signed copy."

"Thanks," Tom said. "It was nice meeting you folks."

We got into the car with Marci driving, waved at them and took off.

"You are so bad. They were wonderful to us. Why did you promise them *that* book?"

"I said I'd send them a copy of my book. I know Mary will love it. She said *Three Days of the Condor* and *Dr. Strangelove* were in her Top 10 movies of all time. Mine will be the bastard child of those two."

"I bet it will. I'd read both books," she said, poking me.

It didn't take long to get to the Interstate. When we did, Marci punched it hard. She did drive about 100. North Dakota was beautiful, at least when were in the hills, but the vast flatlands were almost as boring as Siberia. Soon, we neared the western border where Williston is. I thought we should get our story straight. We had done okay with Tom and Mary, but we could have done better.

"Okay, the drive-in movie book story worked pretty well. Why don't we start that way?"

"That sounds good. I'm your wife, huh?" Marci said. "You sort of like that."

I was waiting for this moment. I had lucked out for longer than I thought. "Well, you're still here."

"Not the best answer, but not the worst."

I had dodged that bullet for the moment.

***

We found Williston, a college town with a few small businesses sprinkled along the main drag. A perfect place to hide. It was late in the afternoon when we got to the drive-in.

"Hi, I'm Mark."

We were surprised to see a thirtyish woman in the office. "What's up, Mark? I'm Sandi."

"This is my wife Marci. She and I are doing a book on drive-in theaters."

"Cool. I love doing this. Everyone who comes here is happy. It's like having a block party every night." Sandi never stopped moving or stopped smiling.

"How long have you managed this place?"

"I started working here in college. About five years ago, Tommy and Sarah decided to open the bookstore, coffee shop, and film shop in town. So, they sold it to me."

"Is it true that Tommy was from somewhere overseas?"

"Yep, from Finland. Sarah's from the south. Why?" she asked, somewhat defensively.

"We found out something very interesting doing this book. Americans and Canadians who run drive-ins have done so as a business and a bridge to their towns. We found a few from overseas who saw owning a drive-in as helping them become real Americans."

"You know something? Tommy has talked about that. I bet he'd have some great stories for you. He loves to talk about movies. His store is right down the street from the school."

"Thanks so much. Do you mind if Marci takes some pictures?"

"Not a bit, that would be great."

Marci did a good job playing her part. Then we drove into town looking for Tommy. Williston is like thousands of other small towns in America, because everyone immediately noticed the strangers with out-of-state plates. Several stopped to look at us and then said "Hi."

We parked right in front of *Tommy and Sarah's Place*. Yep, that was the name. What else could it be? I bet they were celebrities in town. How many kids were conceived at their theater? Hell, how many lost their virginity there?

As we entered, Sarah/BJ was cleaning the tables. "How are you? I'm Sarah. You two are new in these parts."

Marci smiled. "I'm Marci. This is my husband, Mark."

She still had a bit of her North Carolina accent. "Tommy, come on out. We have some new friends."

Tommy/Georgi came out from the back of the store. "Hi, I'm Tommy. What are you guys doing in the fine metropolis of Williston?" His accent was almost gone.

"We're writing a book about drive-in theaters."

Sarah smiled. "We used to own the one here."

"That's what Sandi told us," I said.

Tommy broke in. "She worked for us. Then we sold it to her. Can't she help you?"

Marci was smooth. "What we found out is people from the U.S. who own theaters either worked there as kids or their parents owned the theaters. But they had special meaning to people who moved to the U.S. from other countries."

Sarah/BJ smiled. "Tommy's from Finland. We're about to close. Would you like to come to our house and see some pictures of when we owned the theater?"

Marci beamed. "That would be great."

They closed the store. The four of us walked about a mile to their house on the outskirts of town. At least six people stopped us to say hi and chat with Tommy or Sarah. They were holding court and loving it. It made the short walk take over half an hour. Would two people in deep hiding for over twenty years be so open with everyone?

Sarah/BJ opened the door. "Please come in and sit."

Tommy/Georgi took out some snacks and some beer. I noticed there was some Stoli in the cupboard. When he got glasses, he turned the bottle around. Old habits die hard. He wanted to be Tommy, but Georgi was always with him.

"Thanks," I said, "these are great pictures."

In a heartbeat, Tommy/Georgi looked serious. "Are you here really about a book?"

Busted! His training was kicking in. "I am *really* doing a book and was hoping for your help, Georgi."

Sarah/BJ dropped the box of pictures she had in her hands. "His name is Tommy."

"How do you know my name?" Georgi said with piercing eyes. They were cold and he was serious. Georgi was KGB again.

"Alex... Alexi gave me a hint of how to find you. It took me a few tries." I tried to keep my cool, but I stammered.

Sarah/BJ almost collapsed. "Why can't you just leave us alone?"

"No one will ever know who you are or where you are, I promise. Sergei hoped you two were still alive and happy together."

Sarah/BJ had a tear in her eye. "How is Sergei? He is such a sweet man."

"He is happy and has become an actor," Marci jumped in, thinking this piece of news would soothe the waters.

Sarah/BJ continued. "Is he married?"

Tommy/Georgi chuckled. "I don't think so."

"You knew?" I asked.

"Yes. It never mattered. He saved my life."

"Knew what?" BJ asked.

"Sergei is gay."

Sarah/BJ chuckled. "Oh, good for him."

Tommy/Georgi asked, "What do you know?" He paused and looked concerned. "Is anyone protecting you?"

Once he got started, Georgi's guard came down. He sat back in his chair and drank as he started telling us his story. His demeanor made it seem he had been waiting decades to get his part of the story off his chest. He told us about being chosen for the mission and the training. He told us about meeting Sarah/BJ. His memory was incredible. The girls fell asleep about midnight. For the next three hours Georgi and I talked. He fell asleep in his chair a few minutes before I dropped off on the couch.

Sarah/BJ came in and poked Georgi. "Guys, wake up, people will be waiting for their coffee."

Marci had a huge smile. "Our tough guys here talked like a couple of old hens, eh?"

We tried to wake up. "BJ, would you like me to get your family a note? They miss you terribly and are scared."

"Is it safe?"

"I'll make sure it is. Don't tell them too much yet."

"Y'all are right. Can you wait to leave for a couple of hours?"

"Absolutely, thanks for everything, Georgi. Your location is safe, but the rest of your story will change and amuse the world."

"Do you think anyone will believe it?" Georgi asked with a huge smile. He was finally getting into it.

"Some will come after me, but it's up to me to make them believe it."

We left that afternoon. It took us four and a half days to get back. We weren't in a hurry and wanted to make it look like the trip was about drive-in theaters. So, we made a couple of other stops. We couldn't leave anything to chance.

Marci was beaming. Her smile and confidence gave me strength. She was driving this morning and we were making great time. I had called Jinare from the road. He gave me directions to a meeting at a rural New York estate. There were security guards behind the gate. I parked the car and knocked on the door. Why so far out of the city? Wouldn't there be questions? Wouldn't paparazzi follow?

Jinare answered himself. "How was your drive?"

"It was long. Jinare, this is my girlfriend, Marci."

"My honor, Marci." He reached for and kissed her hand.

"Thank you. Why can't you act gallant like that?" she chided me.

Jinare just smiled. We walked into the study where Mbangu was sitting on the couch. He stood up. "You must be Marci. It's a pleasure to finally meet you."

"Mr. Secretary General, it's an honor to meet you," she curtsied and was a bit self-conscious.

They shook hands.

From a distance, we heard Claude's bellowing voice. "A handshake with a beautiful woman? I thought I had taught you better than that all those years ago."

Everyone laughed. Mbangu grinned sheepishly and hugged Marci after being prompted by his old friend. Lauren entered the room just after Claude. Jinare motioned to a mahogany table in the middle of the room.

Lauren and Marci were sitting together. "How was your first trip?"

"I think it went very well," Marci said beaming.

"Did you find him?" Claude asked.

"Yes."

"The four of us need to spend tonight going over as much as we can."

"I was a part of that," Lauren interjected. "You can't get rid of me that easily."

"Yes, you were, my darling, but tonight, Mark needs to focus on what happened that only we knew. Tomorrow we will need both your and Marci's input."

That worked. Claude, Jinare, Mbangu and I were up until 4 a.m. It was amazing how smoothly we went from source to source. Whenever it seemed we were getting too serious, something outrageous would pop up. The parts were beginning to fit together!

One thing that became evident was that I had one more stop to make. We all knew it was going to be weird. I had to spend some real time with Gabe Stein. He was going to try my patience and would make me crazy. This made Jinare very happy. For once, someone had to suck it up beside him. Like we often said, you need to watch out for the quiet ones like Jinare.

"I would love for you to take a video of your meeting with Stein," Jinare said with a big smile. Mbangu chuckled with him.

"Yes, Mark, I think we'd all like to see that. Of course, Stein might come dressed as Goofy and want to meet you at Disney World," Claude said, exploding with laughter.

They all guffawed and hugged. Time to break for the evening.

The next morning, we all talked over a breakfast of juices, coffee, strawberry preserves and croissants.

"Marci, can you take your classes after this is finished?" Mbangu asked.

"It's taken me ten years to get to where I am, but it's taken all of you almost three times as long. If it's best for all of us for me to delay taking the state bar another year, I'm sure I can."

Claude applauded. "Thank you."

"I have to go see Stein myself. He would freak out if anyone else showed up. He's basically a wacko. Two days before we left to find Georgi I was walking back to Marci's place when Stein grabbed me and pulled me into an alley and tried to grill me."

Claude started giggling. Mbangu looked perplexed. Everyone shook their heads.

I was watching the TV that was mounted on the far wall when a picture of Gabe Stein appeared with a caption, "Homeless man found in New York City alley found bleeding and with a gun."

I spat my coffee and yelled, "Holy shit!"

Claude chortled. "Is your coffee too hot?"

"Look at the screen!" I yelled.

Everyone gasped. Well. Everyone but Claude. He reached for a phone.

Mbangu glared at me. "What does he know?"

"Only his part, but he's a loose cannon," I said.

Jinare shook his head. "Jesus Christ, after all these years."

This was the first real emotion I had seen from Jinare. Claude waved at us and put a finger over his lips to get us to talk lower.

"James, it's Claude. I'm fine. I need a favor, old friend." There was a pause. Claude continued. "Your vagrant is an unfortunate relative of an old family friend. Could you get him out of the news?" He paused again. "Wonderful, thank you. Please keep him away from staff and other prisoners. I'll send my good friend and associate, Mark Stern, to pick him up." Another pause. Claude smiled. "Thank you, James, tell me when I can bring you, Mary and the kids to Luxenstein. After flying on the royal jet, the kids might listen to you for a day or two." Claude cackled and hung up the phone. His smile was as big as I had ever seen.

"That's how it's done, Mark. Get in your car and go get Stein."

"Am I supposed to bring him back here?"

Marci slapped me on the back of my head. "Are you crazy?"

Mbangu smiled, "Keep her, Mark. She's not only wise but is also beautiful."

Marci pushed me. "Get out of here and scare the shit out of him!"

Everyone laughed as I trotted out to my car. I drove about ninety all the way to New York City. It took me longer to get across town to the precinct than it did to travel the hundred miles to the city. Like everyone else, I double parked. A cop snarled as I showed him my press credentials.

I went to the desk and asked the sergeant how to find the captain. The captain came out in less than a minute.

"You must be Mark, I'm James. Let's go get Claude's buddy."

"Thanks, captain. Has he said anything?"

"If he did, no one could hear him," he said with a smile.

We weaved around the precinct until we found an isolated holding cell. "We don't use this cell very often anymore. It's very private."

He unlocked the door and led Gabe out of the cell. James led us to a door that led to an alley and left us alone.

"Are you fucking crazy?"

"I was following a lead."

"You're lucky I saw you on CNN before the CIA did. How did you fool the fingerprinting?"

"I had my old ones washed away with acid."

"You are one crazy fuck. Stay out of the way or a bunch of good people will get hurt! I'll find you when it's time."

Chapter 14
It Started How?

The day that started everything was when President Truman ordered nuking Hiroshima and Nagasaki. During the 1950s, the U.S. and U.S.S.R. tested and built nuclear warheads like it was going out of style. This insanity reached its peak at the Cuban Missile Crisis. In those days, people truly believed you could win a nuclear war.

Since then the two superpowers were becoming increasingly more frustrated at the *standoff*. In both countries were people who believed that nuking the other was unthinkable, due to the minor problem that the world would cease to exist. Others blithely thought that a hundred million dead and farms destroyed for decades was an acceptable price to pay to beat their enemy.

The acronym of MAD, Mutually Assured Destruction, became a mantra for those trying to avoid a nuclear war. Unfortunately, the madness of a manageable nuclear war was becoming normal and acceptable. How could it be avoided? Something had to be done. It was now time for action.

For years in Washington, there had been infighting between those who thought war with the Soviet Union was inevitable versus those who thought it is unthinkable. Then, there were nuances between the ones who were in favor of land forces and those who favored nuclear weapons. But it was being discussed at the highest levels as often as the week's sporting events.

Mucking this up was the Director of the CIA, who saw every school crossing guard as a potential commie spy. Most thought this type of craziness went out with Joe McCarthy, or at least, with the space race.

It hadn't, and their insecurities continued to grow exponentially. The responses to the paranoia expanded. Add to this, the CIA was trying to develop insidious poisons and drugs to get the results they desired. The red scourge had to be eliminated even it if meant destroying the rest of the world. Nothing – *nothing* – was off the table.

Meetings had been going on for years at the highest levels of the American government on how best to deal with the Soviet problem. The rift between the State Department, the CIA, and the Department of Defense had been growing and it was getting testier and testier.

Then, one spring morning at the White House, the beginning of the end of the Cold War began to take shape. The names have been changed to protect the families of the stupid and crazy and not to mention, me. Let's go back and watch.

***

This meeting takes place in the White House Situation Room. The far wall is covered by maps of the world, with pins for locations of missiles, tanks and troops. A long table is set with pitchers of water and glasses as well as personalized ashtrays. Simply by having the meeting in that specific location shows that the players want to hike up the actions.

Sitting near the head of the table is Secretary of Defense General Hayden. Although he is in a civilian role, the general comes to these meetings as if he were reviewing the troops. There isn't much fabric showing below all his ribbons and medals. Nothing could ever convince him that he isn't in Korea or Nam. He misses the action. If he were a few years older, Hayden would be confused with Captain Crunch. He stretches his neck to look around the room, once, twice, three times. Then he looks under the table like he is looking for bombs. He moves the pins on the map incessantly. Then, he lights a cigarette.

CIA Director Russell Morris keeps looking around, which makes no sense as the Situation Room is completely secure. Only those with Top Secret Clearance can even get onto its floor. If this were happening in the late 90s or 00s, you'd swear he was tweaking on meth. His beady eyes keep moving. Every few seconds he scowls, points and whispers – sometimes, to himself. He gets up and looks behind the maps on the wall a few times, convinced the room has been broached. He doesn't like or trust anyone else. Occasionally, he draws his young Deputy Director Gabe Stein close and whispers something. He is constantly fidgeting. Like all the leaders in the room, he is chain smoking.

Sitting next to the head of the table, as usual, is Secretary of State Daniel Mitchell. He is annoyed to be obliged to be in their presence, believing the others in the room are dramatically beneath him both socially and politically. His attitude shows, and the others are contemptuous of everything he stands for and how he acts. Nothing they could say would ever be up to his standards. Like his hero, FDR, Mitchell smokes his cigarettes from a holder. Even his butts aren't good enough to touch his aristocratic lips.

Something is thick in the air today. Normally these meetings happen in the Oval Office or the Cabinet Room. It is also rare to have everyone together without there being a major dust-up or a detailed pre-arranged agenda. Nothing much makes sense about this meeting. The normal apprehension has been dialed up to full-blown paranoia.

The only thing thicker than the anticipation in that room is the low-hanging smoke. These guys sure can puff. It is almost like there is a contest of who can burn more cigarettes in the shortest time. Everyone has two packs of cigarettes next to his personalized ashtray, but their stashes are dwindling fast.

The door opens. Everyone puts their cigarettes out and snaps out of their seats. First, to enter the room are two Secret Service Agents, who scout out the room. The lead guy nods his head. President Thomas enters the room. Before he reaches his seat at the head of the table he waves the Secret Service out of the room.

Everyone stands and screams in unison, "Good morning, Mr. President."

"Good morning. Please sit down. We have a lot to do today."

His chair is rich brown leather with a blue and gold seal on it. The President reaches into his jacket pocket for a cigarette. He pulls out an empty pack. "Damn, no butts."

Russell, Mitchell and Hayden madly thrust their packs forward. President Thomas chooses Hayden's. The others slump like twelve-year-old girls who weren't asked to dance by the quarterback.

They all try to light the butt.

The President takes a long drag off the cigarette. He blows a couple of smoke rings and smiles as he turns to look at the Secretary of State. He looks serious as he glares at Mitchell.

"Mr. Secretary, how was your weekend in Miami with the go-go dancer? Go, go, go."

Everyone but Mitchell roars. Everyone blows smoke into Mitchell's face.

"Or was it a rendezvous with a Rockette wannabe again?" Morris jokes.

Mitchell looks ashen. "Ah, Mr. President, it was truly my secretary."

There is more laughter before Mitchell sneers at Hayden. "I cleared it with the Secret Service. At least it's not a camel in the desert somewhere."

Hayden jumps up, ready for war. "That's a totally unsubstantiated rumor that I have repeatedly denied."

Gabe Stein whispers into Morris' ear. "His daughter, the one with a hump, contradicts his denial."

They chuckle. They smoke. But they tap their fingers. No one is sure why they are in the Situation Room.

The President pounds the table. "I'm getting tired of this standoff with the Soviet Union. We need to end this god damned Cold War. We have spent hundreds of billions of dollars on it and are no further along than we were ten years ago. Why can't this group come up with a solution? How do we bring these godless Soviets to their knees? Are you that stupid? Or just a bunch of pussies?"

Hayden stands up, unbuttons his jacket. He's got grenades hooked to his belt and pulls one off. Stein jumps across the table. Hayden fakes a throw.

"There are no windows to throw that out of, you madman," the junior G-man cries.

Hayden pushes Stein away. "Sit down, sonny boy. I'm just playing with you pencil-necked geeks. It's clay. There's nothing inside. Mr. President, we can blow the Soviets off the face of the earth one hundred thirty-seven times. I can start right now. All you have to do is give me the order, sir."

Secretary Mitchell says, "You fucking idiot. They can blow us off the face of the Earth one hundred thirty-four times."

Hayden lowers his sunglasses to look at Mitchell. "See, we'd win. It's as easy as pie… American apple pie. The first launch will be in ninety minutes. Finally, I get to kill them godless Ruskis."

Everyone in the room is cringing, but they don't offer anything else up for discussion. They are waiting to hear what President Thomas says. Each takes several deep drags off their cigarettes. The cloud envelops everyone. It keeps growing.

"General, I will take that under consideration, but I don't want to start it so soon. We can always nuke them after I go to the Michigan-Ohio State game this weekend. I'm tossing the coin to start the game."

"Good idea, sir. I'm here whenever you need me."

"Does anyone have any ideas that don't include nuclear Armageddon? We spend billions every year spying on them. Is there any way we can use this intelligence?" the President asks.

Mitchell motions for Gabe Stein to move from the corner to the adults' table. "Mr. President, Stein and I…"

Hayden says, "Who the fuck is Stein? Why don't I know you? You're fucking nine years old. What could you possibly know?"

Stein glares at Hayden but starts out almost stuttering, "I'm twenty-eight. I'm, I'm, I'm Gabe Stein. I am Deputy Director of…"

Hayden interrupts him. "Some pansy-ass think tank golden boy is going to take my war away from me? What the fuck is this world coming to? Mr. President, *please* let me nuke them. Or at least let me shoot this risk-playing choirboy? Hell, he's not even smoking."

"General, no one is taking your war away from you. We can always nuke those bastards after we listen to Mr. Stein. Give him a chance to explain his idea."

Hayden leans back in his chair. He pushes his sunglasses back up higher on his nose. He leans forward for just a second to blow smoke into Stein's face. Stein is the only person in the room who isn't smoking. The President's cigarette goes out. Hayden jumps over the table to light one for him.

Stein shakes his head. "Mr. President, I have been working with Secretary Mitchell and Director Morris to coordinate the intel to come up with a more clandestine but equally as devastating a plan to eliminate the U.S.S.R."

Stein puts some charts on the easel at the end of the table. He stands straighter as he pulls out his pointer. Morris decides to stand up next to the easel and help Stein with his presentation.

In fact, Morris opens the discussion. "Mr. President, as you can see, the Ruskis are totally self-sufficient in oil, food, textiles and machinery. Initially, Stein and I thought about instigating a coup."

Hayden leans forward. He seems excited as he puts one cigarette out and lights another, "Now we're talking. Let the bastards shoot the other."

Morris continued, "We decided the resultant chaos could, and I stress *could* not *would*, lead to someone unstable leading the U.S.S.R. and having their itchy fingers on the red button."

Hayden jumps out of his seat. "Fuck that! Bring it, asshole! Let me kill them before they kill us!"

Morris cleared his throat, "Gabe and I have given serious thought to this problem. What do Russians crave? What can they not live without?"

Mitchell, "Teenage Eurasian girls?"

Hayden, "Teenage Siberian boys?"

The President furls his brow. "Gentlemen, let Director Morris continue."

Morris smiles broadly. "We plan to plant our operatives throughout the U.S.S.R. in cities that have vodka distilleries. Surprisingly, there aren't that many of them. We are working on a compound that neutralizes the alcoholic content of the vodka. It becomes potato-flavored water."

The President lights another cigarette from one that is almost out. "I love it! We give all those commie bastards the willies at once. They will lose their damn minds. Like Mitchell without his go-go girls."

Everyone cackles except Mitchell. He glares at Morris and lights a cigarette.

Stein enters the conversation. "Mr. President, this will create political upheaval in the U.S.S.R. Our operatives speak all the different languages of the Soviet Republics. We will foment unrest across Europe and Asia. The Soviets should have to use all their power to control their empire. It could take years. We'd be the least of their problems and we might be able to put some of our people in power in those republics."

"Stein, you are one conniving Jew-boy. Let's control all their vodka!"

Hayden is jumping up and down, "Gooooooooddamn! I can't wait to see those commie bastards squirm for a drink like the cockroaches they are. They aren't strong like Americans!"

The President nods. Mitchell taps the table. "OK, this is a good start.

Let's meet Wednesday to see where we are. This has real possibilities."

President Thomas nods. "Well, General, are you on board with our new war on the U.S.S.R.?"

Hayden is smiling. He gives Stein a bear hug and spins him around. "Yes Mr. President, this is frickin' *war!*"

Morris puffs out his chest and his smile covers his entire face. "Let's end the standoff and win this thing once and for all, Mr. President."

"Yes sir, Mr. Director. Good job. Let's do this. See you all on Wednesday."

***

They were on their way to starting a pseudo-war to end all wars based on a chemical no one knew would work or if it even existed. They truly believed they could bring the U.S.S.R. to its knees without a shot being fired. This would be easy. It would be surgical and go off without a hitch. Of course, we'd be able to infiltrate and neutralize 100% of their favorite beverage's production. They will welcome us with open arms. After all, we're America! We can do anything! What a country!

Chapter 15
Is Crazy Contagious?

Mid-spring in Moscow means only about two feet of snow is piled up around the Kremlin. It is an impressive, mysterious and intimidating building that represents the U.S.S.R. well. In the cold and the snow, crack Soviet troops do choreographed marches in front of the seat of Soviet power. None of the normal passers-by seem to notice them. It is the antithesis of Buckingham Palace. But this is a show of Soviet precision, of Soviet superiority.

Unlike the bunkered White House Situation Room, the Soviets hold their high-level meetings in a room with ornate thirty-foot ceilings and three-story-high bulletproof windows. Ever present are the fifteen-foot high pictures of Lenin and Marx as well as a wall with a flag that runs its entire length. There is a flag carpet under the 19th century table in the center of the room. Multiple TV screens are implanted on the wall opposite the windows, with maps of their empire next to the TVs. Next to those maps are maps of the U.S. and Europe with hammer and sickle targets on them. On the table are bottles of vodka and full glasses are all around.

Foreign Minister Yuly Davinko chugs a glass and refills it. He is a dumpy man who is wearing an ill-fitting black suit; his shirt was white once upon a time and his red tie has seen its better days. He has the appearance of a County Clerk who kept getting promoted due to seniority rather than any pretense of competence. Davinko appears more out of place here than an Outback Steakhouse in vegetarian Mumbai.

Across from Davinko is Field Marshall Petrov. Compared to Petrov, Stalin had no eyebrows. His green dress uniform is covered in ribbons and medals. He has a ribbon with a huge, dangling medal on it around his neck. He is wearing a double holster with two ornate handguns and has dozens of bullets attached to it. Seeing Davinko finish his glass, and not to be outdone by a civilian, Petrov gulps his full glass in one swig, refills it, and glares at Davinko. He finishes the second glass and slams it on the table. He is gloating. He drinks like a real man.

KGB Director Nitvik is writing on a little pad. He puts the note in his outside jacket pocket. Then he gets down on his hands and knees and starts looking under the table and the chairs. He stands with what appears to be a rotted piece of old chewing gum he took from under one of the chairs. He looks at all sides of it. Then he takes out his pen and makes some more notes. He stuffs these into his pants pockets. While under the table he finishes his glass of vodka.

"OK, who put this bug in the room?" He jumps onto the table.

Davinko sneers, "That's a piece of chewing gum, not a bug; you are a paranoid idiot."

Petrov snickers. "Who can find gum in our country? There should be an investigation. Maybe Nitvik can send the culprit to Siberia like he did with your babushka."

Davinko stares a hole through them. "You morons. How are we the most powerful nation in the world with fools like you in power?"

"Well, she did have a pair of American jeans," Nitvik bellows. "She was a capitalist sympathizer. It is the law."

Davinko replies, "You gave them to her. You brought them back from your trip to the Olympics."

Nitvik then starts taking the phone next to the big red phone apart. He looks at every piece and then can't put it back together. Davinko and Petrov see this and choke on their vodka as they snicker at Nitvik. Vodka slops onto the table.

Davinko and Petrov jump out of their seats and snap to attention while Nitvik is looking at the TV screens. Premier Boski and his guards enter the room. The guards quickly leave.

Nitvik hears the door close and turns around. All of them chant, "Welcome, Comrade Premier Boski." They do their best to stand at attention in unison but can't pull it off.

Boski moves behind the large leather chair at the head of the table. He pours himself a glass of vodka and holds it up. "Mother Russia!"

Everyone stands, toasts, and drinks. "Mother Russia!"

Boski motions for them to sit. He sits and takes another swig of vodka. He looks amused. "Yuri, I hear you have a new roof on your dacha. Do you think you should have a finer roof than I have?"

Davinko stammers. "Comrade Premier, it is one model less than you have. My wife was very upset about the snow seeping into the library. She shouldn't have been reading all those books. It is my fault, Comrade Premier."

Petrov looks at Davinko. "You let a woman rule your life. How can we defeat the Americans with you in such a position?" Petrov looks at him mockingly.

Everyone crows and drinks. They refill their glasses. Boski looks angry. "We must bring down the imperialist American dogs!! How should we proceed? Field Marshall Petrov?"

"We could use Fidel. Who cares if the Americans blow him up if he loses?"

"That's one idea. We do send him billions of rubles per year," Davinko suggests.

Nitvik is smiling. "I'll go to Havana tomorrow."

Boski bellows in laughter. "You mean like the last time you went to Cuba and embarrassed the Motherland with that shemale hooker?"

Nitvik looks sheepish. "In my defense, he or she or whatever it was, taped the Adam's apple. That won't happen again. I'll have the hookers disrobe before going to my room."

Boski, "Nyet. Who else do we have that can help us?"

Davinko was thinking and writing. "How about Arafat?"

Petrov shakes his head. "We can't trust that camel lover. How about if we use the poison umbrellas on U.S. leaders? It will slow them down until we come up with something."

Boski slams his fist on the table, chugs his vodka and screams, "What kind of people are you? The Soviet Union is the most powerful nation on Earth and you want to use a cigar-rolling, Cuban relief pitcher or umbrellas or a guy who was living in tents ten years ago! I hear Siberia is very nice this time of year."

The other others choke on their vodka. Sweat starts beading up on their faces.

Field Marshall Petrov jumps out of his seat. "We can blow them off the face of the Earth one hundred thirty-four times! Long live the Soviet Union!"

They chant. "Long live the Soviet Union!" Then they clink their glasses together and drink. At least they haven't been sent to Siberia… yet.

Davinko looks incredulous. "They could blow us off the face of the Earth one hundred thirty-two times."

Petrov is ebullient. "See, we win!!!"

Boski can't believe what he's hearing. "But we'd all be dead. What else?"

Nitvik looks over his shoulder like someone is listening to him think. He stands up. "Comrades, what do Americans need more than anything else?"

Petrov is smiling. "Farah Fawcett. Bo Derek."

Boski asks. "Who is the brunette?"

Davinko knows. "Kate Jackson."

Everyone smiles and nods. They gaze off into the distance with pictures of *Charlie's Angels* dancing though their minds.

Nitvik is irritated. "No, Comrades, they treasure oil. Those crazy capitalists don't care how much they pay. We could break them!"

Davinko sneers at Nitvik. "Did you see what happened when they had gasoline lines? They cried for a few minutes. There were fights. Their Mafia made a lot of money. Then they paid and everything returned to normal. Attacking their oil would do nothing. There must be something else."

The silence in the room becomes deafening, and sweat starts pouring down the faces of Davinko, Petrov and Nitvik. They all rock backed and forth. The players look at their watches, then up at the ceiling – everywhere but at Boski.

Finally, Davinko throws his pen and pad into the air. He refills all the glasses with fresh vodka. "Americans cannot live without cigarettes. They smoke everywhere. They smoke in restaurants, in the subway, in doctors' offices. Their star athletes smoke on television even though they know it will kill them. Pregnant women smoke."

Boski is excited. "Those weak capitalists! Nicotine is a horrible addiction. We must do something to impact this. What fun to watch them scream and then give up to their Soviet masters!"

Their glasses are empty now, as are all the bottles of vodka. Boski picks up the phone. "We need more vodka. A case should be enough. Quickly!"

Nitvik is excited. "Yuly might be onto something. Americans are weak. They can't quit smoking. When they try, their work suffers. They become irritable. Yes."

Davinko tries to bring reason. "But they grow all their tobacco in the U.S. What can we do?"

Boski taps his forehead. "I like this. We have the most creative technologies in the world. Put our top people on this project. Bring in our chemists and everyone you think may help. But do not tell them why."

Davinko looks puzzled. "What are we supposed to tell our scientists they are doing?"

A man brings in a case of vodka. Petrov rips off the top of the box. He reaches inside and pulls out a bottle. After tearing off the cap, he fills the glasses. The bottle is empty after one round.

Boski takes a long slug from his glass. He ponders Davinko's question. "We tell the scientists it is an intellectual experiment to make Russians stop smoking to strengthen our nation. Tell them to come up with their best ideas. Maybe they could work at making cigarettes horrible to the taste or kill the plants before they grow or make them too strong to smoke. Tell them whoever comes up with the best option gets a new dacha and double vodka rations!"

Petrov drinks an entire glass of vodka in one gulp. "Nothing is too strong for Russians. We are strong! Who else can drink vodka like Russians?"

Davinko snorts, drinks and refills all the glasses. "You idiot. We are attacking the Americans. They are weak and would choke on our mildest smokes. Russians are too smart to smoke."

He holds up his glass. "To Mother Russia!"

Boski says. "To Mother Russia and ending the standoff!"

Everyone toasts. "Mother Russia. Ending the standoff!"

"We will meet this time next week to see what progress we have made."

Everyone says, "Next Wednesday, Comrade Premier."

They finish another bottle of vodka and leave. What a great day in Moscow!

Chapter 16
No, Really, She Can

The famous Greenbrier Resort had subterranean tunnels and residences built in the 1940-60s to protect the POTUS, Congress and critical staff in case of a nuclear attack. Enormous stores of food have been stashed. Elaborate apartments and large dormitories were prepared to house the elite. What no one thought it would be ever used for was a combination of a CIA laboratory and an array of vodka stills.

Several large vats are in the large hall in the facility many stories below street level. A half-dozen or so men are asleep on cots around the room. On the table are several empty glasses, some of which have tipped over with clear liquid spilled onto the floor.

Two men in their late forties and a woman in her mid-late twenties are working at lab set-ups with Bunsen burners, small stills and large whiteboards scribbled with formulas. Every few seconds it seems the numbers and letters are changing. All scientists wear lab coats splattered with liquids. They are focused and fully driven.

The men are renowned research chemists Dr. Richard Blum and Dr. Del Harris. Lucy Diamond is a top doctoral student. I guess if you are going to be buried underground with unlimited supplies of booze, you've got to have at least one super-hot woman working on the project. Lucy is working calmly but very intensely.

CIA Director Morris and Gabe Stein are studying the main white board and surveying the entire lab. Stein picks up some glasses, smells them, and shakes his head. Morris and Stein shake their heads and frown. They need definitive progress to show the senior White House staff or they will be exorcized from the group. Having known about the true purpose of the program could be a lot worse than simply being fired.

Stein smells another batch. One of the men who was on the cot tries to get up. He takes a couple of steps. Then he loses his balance, stumbles and falls into a table with a still and a lot of half-full beakers of liquid, which spill all over him. He makes a slurping sound, smiles and passes out.

Morris looks concerned. "Dr. Blum, how is your research going?"

"It's going well. It's been a lot of fun. Did you bring the dry vermouth and olives?"

"We've created a formula that raises the proof of vodka to over 215. The only problem is, it seems to eat through the tubes," Dr. Harris says with a slur.

Gabe Stein is pacing and shaking his head. "What the hell are you talking about? No alcohol can have more than 199 proof. Are you drinking more than you're testing?"

Blum staggers over to Stein. "Hey man, there aren't that many variables in vodka distilling."

"Listen, we don't want to make it *better* for the Ruskis. Is there any hope here?"

"Give us time. Moscow wasn't destroyed in a day." Harris chuckles to himself.

Morris is not amused. "The President wants this project finished yesterday. This isn't some university class. We're talking about world domination here. Get your asses sober and in gear! Stein, is this the best you can do?"

"Director, I took these from your list."

"That's not what I remember, and most decidedly not what's going to be in my report."

Gabe's shoulders scrunch up. He knows he'll be the patsy if they fail. His beady eyes and weird nose make him look like a little weasel. He glares at Morris and makes a few notes.

Lucy Diamond walks to the group with several small glasses. She has perfect posture and is beyond gorgeous. "Doctors, I think I may have found something. Take a taste."

Stein takes a glass from Lucy. Blum sighs. "Ms. Diamond, this isn't the time for a frivolous student project. I know you're working hard, but this is well above your level of experience."

Harris isn't too happy either. "Hey, she barely knows the difference between a beaker and a streaker."

Blum and Harris chuckle. They are drunk, slurring and not at all interested in her work. But they do look at her ass and nod like teenage boys.

Morris taps the lab table and sneers. "If she isn't capable, she shouldn't be here. Honey, what do you think you've found?"

"My name is Ms. Diamond. It's not honey."

Stein laughs, coughs, and clears his throat. He pauses and says defiantly, "Ms. Diamond, the President of the United States is interested. Tell me what you think you might have discovered."

Harris stands up straight. "Hey she's here to spruce up the place, not to do serious research." He spanks her butt.

She throws the contents of two of the small glasses into his face. The others cackle.

"If any of you happen to be serious about successfully finishing the project at hand, you might be interested to know that I fed all the data regarding processes and chemical formulas for vodka into our central computer."

Blum speaks loudly. "You're using the computer? Isn't that cheating? Shouldn't you be using white boards and pads?"

"I've also entered everything you gave us about quality control as well as all the algorithms."

Harris slurs his speech with a dopey smile on his face. "Director Morris, see what I'm saying about her? She's talking about personal pads and the rhythm method. She's trying to bring sex into this."

All the men snicker. Lucy ignores them. "We can't put a foul taste or an alcohol inhibitor into the charcoal stage or into the vats, because taste and purity are tested before and after bottling."

Morris sneers. "I see what you mean, Blum. Ms. Diamond, honey, why are you wasting our time?"

She rips some paper off the printer. "Look, if we can make the formula time-delayed so it is operational after bottling but before consumption, it will have the desired effect. The pharmaceutical industry has developed highly effective time-release agents for their products. If we can tailor one of them to be used for vodka, we can work around the quality control. Gentlemen, please taste your samples." She smiles condescendingly at Blum and Harris.

They all drink the samples and shake their heads. What gives?

Stein looks at her, "This is vodka. What's the big deal? You guys are right. Maybe we should transfer her to the kitchen."

Lucy smiles, knowing she's got these pigs by the short hairs. "Look at the bottom of your glasses."

"It says it was made this morning," Morris reports. "So?"

Lucy smiles. "Please come over to my work station." Reluctantly they follow her. Soon they are rewarded. As they watch, she bends over to unlock a storage door below her lab desk. As she does, her lab coat and skirt move up her thighs. The dirty old men applaud as they see her perfect butt and lace panties.

"Really? It's better than you'll ever have," Morris says glibly.

Harris bellows, "Really, we've been underground for weeks, Lucy. Give a guy a break. That's a helluva lot better than looking at Blum."

The guys cackle. Lucy glares at them. She pulls out a tray of dated glasses. She pulls one out and pours half into a device.

"Gentlemen," she snipes, "as you can see, this batch was made three days ago. That's double the time from distilling to shipping in the Russian vodka industry. This machine will tell us what the proof is right now."

Everyone watches the machine. The fluid drips out the other side. There is lit space on the device. After a couple of seconds, it lights up and reads 0.1.

"As you can see, the specimen is reading that it is 0.1% alcohol. It becomes basically potato-flavored water. Please taste it."

Everyone takes a sip and spits it out. Stein immediately goes to the trash can and throws up. Blum pukes on Harris. She nods and smiles, loving to see their discomfort. She is beaming. She can't stop snickering.

"I can change the flavor component to any level you think will work best. In fact, we can change it with every batch. However, it will take some work to perfect it."

Gabe Stein eyes open wide like he just hit the lottery. "This is incredible. Ms. Diamond, you are an absolute genius!"

Harris stammers. "How do we know this isn't a scam? Science must be replicated over and over. This needs more study. It could be just one lucky attempt. She needs more work under my tutelage."

Morris' smile covers his face. "It will take more studies and trials. But they will be led by Ms. Diamond. She's your boss, now, Harris, and yours too, Blum. Ms. Diamond will be coming with me."

Harris throws his head back. "I was the Dean of Biochemistry at Johns Hopkins and at Harvard."

Stein looks at him. "It must suck to have a student as your boss, but she succeeded and you didn't. Maybe your students should get tuition rebates."

Blum was grasping for straws. "Lucy, you must be overwhelmed. I can help."

Lucy walks over to him, smiles, and kicks him in the nuts. "That's for all the times you looked at my ass. Learn to make coffee the way I like it by the time I get back."

Stein opens the door for Lucy. "That was impressive. Welcome to the big leagues. Director Morris, thanks for reminding me that it was my choice to select Ms. Diamond for the team. Remember to tell President Thomas what you told me."

"No one likes a squirrely wise-ass, Stein."

"Gabe, so young guys get shit too, huh?" Lucy said with a smile.

"Yep. Way to go Lucy!"

Lucy keeps smiling as she picks up a few beakers and continues her experiments.

Chapter 17
The Prince is a Pauper

It's a beautiful day in Luxenstein, but that's the way the nation's dashing thirtyish Prince Claude sees every day. Their central European principality is right out of a fairy tale. Its lush valleys and spectacular vineyards are surrounded by majestic mountains that allow the citizens to have wondrous skiing and a natural playground for the rest of the year.

The idyllic geography reinforces an educated, happy, satisfied population that the Prince's family has ruled for over five centuries. There is universal healthcare. The free education everyone has the right to includes free foreign studies through the doctorate level. The privacy of the banking system creates huge profits and full employment. Everyone in Europe wants to move here, but only those invited and who pass a citizens' committee are given a chance to try. Why mess with perfection?

Things couldn't be better in Luxenstein. Or could they? What doesn't the populace know?

The prince's reputation as a flamboyant playboy and gambler has been well earned. He is widely known as the Pied Piper of Panties. The only aspect of life Prince Claude enjoys more than women is gambling. What's amazing is the Pied Piper is so kind, generous and charming that supermodels and other women don't get mad at him when they hear about his newest conquests. He lives a charmed life and deserves it.

It seems every time he put the nation's finances at risk he comes up with a spectacular move to replenish the treasury before anyone knew trouble had ever existed. His large heart and love of life are only exceeded by his obsession with taking risks. Only the prince and his top aide Paleau ever knew about all these hiccups.

Prince Claude always considered himself blessed to have a fully trustworthy Chargé d'Affaires in Jacques Paleau. His family had a small dairy and cheese business, an average life by Luxenstein standards.

There is a three-year age difference. When Claude was a freshman in high school he was already a risk taker. He got himself into a big card game with a group of seniors and lost more than his entire state allowance for a year.

Paleau knew the game was rigged and that the big winner had cheated. He approached the young prince with this knowledge, plus a way to win back everything he'd lost and then some. Paleau figured out how they cheated. Alas, the prince didn't have enough money to get into the game. Paleau pawned a gold ring his grandfather had recovered after World War I to fund the game's buy-in.

Claude followed Paleau's instructions, won everything back, and proceeded to take all the cheaters' stakes. He gave Paleau all his profits. When he found out what Paleau had done to get the money, a lifelong friendship was created. Paleau could easily have allowed the spoiled rich kid be taught a lesson, but the son of a dairy farmer decided to do the honorable thing. Of course, the ring was mysteriously returned to Paleau the following week.

When Claude's father died, his first call was to ask Paleau to be his most important confidant. Although Paleau did not approve of many of the things Claude did, he supported him and never betrayed a single confidence despite being offered millions and many women to do so.

Paleau is driving the prince's '62 Rolls Royce convertible. As usual, the prince is sitting in the back trying to read a newspaper. It is blowing everywhere. Paleau looks in the rear-view mirror and sees the paper draped around the prince's face. Paleau smiles. "Smashing day, isn't it?"

The prince peels the paper from his face. "In our homeland, it is. But it seems there is a great draught in Brazil, North Carolina, China and Turkey."

"That's interesting. Why?"

"It looks like world tobacco crops are going to be crushed. If we could get a significant position in the futures market, our treasury problems would be solved."

"We don't have enough in the treasury to buy that many futures. We don't even have enough money to buy a carton of cigarettes."

The prince opens a bottle of champagne and pours himself a glass. "You always quibble over the small things, old friend. You know we'll figure this out and it will be magical."

"I beg your pardon. I should know that money is irrelevant to the purchase of commodities contracts. But, what am I thinking? And money grows on trees here in Luxenstein," Paleau says sarcastically.

"People will give us as much as we need," Prince Claude replies, chuckling.

"Even after your escapades in Las Vegas and Monte Carlo?"

"The Americans will give us millions to help repair our crumbling roads and bridges. They like doing that. It makes them feel good."

"But our highways are wonderful and most of them are new. You paid for them after you broke that casino in Asia ten years ago." Paleau tries to insert some reason.

"Our schools aren't up to date, nor are our hospitals. How can such a beautiful land as ours have any poverty? We will have a war on poverty." Prince Claude is now roaring.

"You know perfectly well we have no poverty. We are nearly self-sufficient in food and wine."

"I will hire a public relations firm to slander our beloved Luxenstein. The Belgians have always been jealous of us. I bet we can find one in Brussels," Prince Claude says with conviction.

"If we can, that won't be enough to corner the market," Paleau says, shaking his head.

"Hmm, you may be right. But aren't we going to be on the Security Council starting next month?"

"Yes, what are you thinking? You aren't thinking about..." Paleau lowers his head.

"Well, the Soviets won't want us to vote with the Americans all the time."

"Your Highness, that would be immoral." Paleau is shaking his head.

Claude is amused. "Oh my, you must be angry with me. You only use Your Highness when you're angry or disappointed with me, like when mother used my middle names."

"You know me too well... and you are correct. But you are coming up with a way to do this, aren't you? *Mon dieu*, here we go again."

"Please pull the car over, Jacques." When the car comes to a stop, Paleau turns to look at him. "Jacques, do you have a better idea?"

"Sadly, no. You've mucked it up this time."

The prince pours them both a glass of champagne. "That's what you always say."

"That's what you always do." Paleau drinks his champagne in one gulp and holds it out to be filled again.

They cackle and sip the champagne. "Old friend, this may be worse than my freshman year. I must come up with some crazy ideas. I need your support, your cunning, your ability to keep me relatively focused. What's the worst that could happen?" Prince Claude asks gleefully. "Well, if the Soviets don't take well to what I'm trying to do…"

"But they can only kill you once. Your subjects can burn you in effigy; take your name from those buildings. But they might rename the toilets and urinals for you." Paleau says with a chuckle.

"So, what you are saying is, we shouldn't fail." Claude says interrupting.

"To success."

"See, I knew you'd come around. Think of the book you'll be able to write someday."

"As if anyone would believe it." Claude offers.

They laugh and finish the bottle. Their plan was going to work. They always had in the past.

Chapter 18
Meanwhile in Madibu

If you come to Madibu, the first thing you think is, this is how the Garden of Eden must have been. It is an amazing island sitting effortlessly in the western part of the Indian Ocean, very close to Africa. Its location could control the waterways between Asia and Southern Africa. This has been critical in much of the past five hundred years of its history.

The beaches are spectacular white sand for as far as you can see. The waves softly crash onto the empty shore. There should be families, lovers and people just getting away from their daily lives all along these beaches. Warm water, beautiful fish and perfect weather is what dream getaways are made of. From the moment Mbangu had ascended to power, turning it into a world class resort was his dream for his beloved Madibu.

Inland there is a primeval rainforest. Thankfully, it is as unspoiled as the magnificent beaches. In the hills and trees, every color known to man is innocently exposed for all to see. They have thousands of species of animals living together as they have for millions of years. Many seem totally disinterested with their neighbor's existence. This is a world within a world. The indescribable beauty should be internationally renowned. If only men could live together so peacefully everywhere as all the diverse inhabitants do here.

Since the mid-1500s, the world has fought over Madibu. First the Portuguese took control. They stayed for about two hundred years until the British sent them packing. Finally, the French took over and remained until the mid-1960s, when the first Madibu Revolution put a corrupt general in charge. His rule was brutal. Finally, in the 70s, a very young, homegrown and western-educated hero led a peaceful revolution. Not a shot was fired when Mbangu took control.

In nearly every nation on the planet, he would have been well too young to be a leader. But there was something different about Mbangu. He was serene. Mbangu was Madibu.

On a continent where brutality followed colonialism's atrocities, Mbangu was the exception. He truly cared about his people. He understood that unlike his continental colleagues, Madibu's ecological magnificence could and should not be compromised.

He had risen from the poverty of family led by a heroic mother. She had little, but she had everything. In addition to scavenging to raise her own brood, his mother taught others how to read, how to raise meager crops, what to look for in the forest or at the beach. She had limitless energy, along with the optimism of a true believer, hard-scrabble pragmatism and boundless love for all whose lives she touched. This legacy was passed on to Mbangu.

His story was mythical. He lived in a hut with no running water. Somehow his story and selfless actions led to a Harvard scholarship. He was a star among stars at Harvard. He could have been a multi-millionaire before he was twenty-five, but he chose to come home to work at a government job for $150 a month. He felt he owed his country. Nothing international bankers or multi-national corporations could say would dissuade him. Then, when his country was floundering, he was called to be president.

In spite of Mbangu's best intentions and diligent and well planned projects, Madibu was slowly descending into failure. But unlike all the other players in our story, Mbangu would never lower himself to anything untoward.

Somehow, Mbangu would have to fix the disaster about to befall his country legitimately and without any hint of impropriety. If Diogenes were still alive, his quest would end the day he met Mbangu. The Greek seeker of integrity would have approved of Mbangu's upcoming actions. Hey, he would be telling the truth. Things may not unfold exactly as he planned, but hey...

He is as unassuming as he is brilliant and careful. However, don't mistake his class and generosity for being naïve or weak.

***

The capital city is near the southern tip of the island. It's another hot, humid but crystal-clear morning. Mbangu, Prime Minister Bootu, and Foreign Minister Jinare are leaving the front entrance of a decaying hotel. An old Checker cab that has been painted with the colors of the Madibu flag approaches them and stops. Jinare and Mbangu get in the back seat. Bootu joins the driver up front.

Mbangu has a smile on his face. "I wonder how many other heads of state have a 1947 Checker cab as the presidential limo."

Jinare says, "This is just one other way in which our leader is unique and more confident than the leaders of all those other nations."

Mbangu chimes in. "The Americans have the White House. The Brits have Buckingham Palace and Ten Downing Street. Look at my magnificent state home! This marvelous hotel was upgraded in 1959. Now every bedroom had its own bath with black and white televisions in every room. Ah, such progress."

They all chuckle. It is a knowing, rueful, yet truly hopeful laugh. Unlike most politicians around the world, this cadre knows the problems of their people and wants to fix them. How they plan to fix them may be a bit out of the box, but who built that box anyway?

Mbangu continues thinking out loud. "Look at these beautiful beaches, the warm sea, the soft breezes, inviting sand. Few places in the world are as majestic as Madibu. Why do we have so little tourism?"

Jinare sighs. "Our airport is in disrepair. We can't handle the newer large planes. Our harbors aren't deep enough for luxury liners. Our hotels are still stuck in the 1950s and before you came to power, our beloved Madibu had been seen as a lawless, dangerous place."

Mbangu tries to be positive. "Unfortunately, what you're saying is accurate, my friend. We need to spend what few pennies we have changing the image of Madibu around the world. The beauty is here before us. We could be the Hawaii of the Indian Ocean. Our lush rainforest is unique in the world. We must find a way to lengthen the runway, dredge the channel, and build wonderful resorts. If we do, our nation will be on the way to prosperity."

Bootu turns his head. "Yes, Your Excellency. It would happen exactly as you say."

Jinare throws the wet blank of reality onto the conversation. "Begging your pardon sir, but we haven't anywhere near the funds in our treasury to finance even one of these projects."

Mbangu looks at Jinare. "We have to spend money to make money. That's what my Harvard education taught me. Americans firmly believe this. Maybe we should, too."

Jinare tries to be positive. "If we had some money, I'd spend it all day to build our nation. Sadly, we just don't have it."

"Maybe we should do like the Americans and Soviets when they have this problem. They print money," Bootu suggests.

Everyone howls. But something in the atmosphere has changed.

Bootu says, "We don't have to tell anyone how much we are printing. I know how to work the presses."

They again laugh. Bootu is serious. "Why shouldn't it work?"

"I trust your insights, Jinare. Come up with a plan. Time is not on our side. We need to be bold. Shock me. Don't be afraid to scare me. It could be fun and could transform the lives of the people of our nation," Mbangu says hopefully.

"I will study all options and write a report for you. Be prepared for anything."

"Do it. The people are restless and are thinking about replacing me. They took a chance on a kid to lead them. Kids are like lemurs; they do crazy things and live to try again and again."

Bootu tries to lighten the discussion. "Pondering is better than plundering."

Jinare sits up straight. "I am done pondering. We can ask for money from the Americans or the Soviets."

Mbangu shakes his head. "I do not like the Americans, because they look down on our people. I do not trust the Soviets, who are crude and dishonest. How about our African brothers and sisters?"

Bootu looks sadly at Mbangu. "Unfortunately, they haven't got any money either."

"Your Excellency, you know our island is very strategically located. Both the Americans and Soviets would love to get access to our country for military reasons. Let's milk that to our advantage," Jinare says with a twinkle in his eyes.

"The Americans are also fearful of letting the Soviets get an advantage. Their country's ego is like a child's. We must remember this at all times and use it to our advantage," Mbangu adds.

Bootu brightens up. "Remember when the Soviets came to our country offering 'economic aid'? They all wanted to decide how we spent the money."

Mbangu's eyes brighten. "What if the Americans thought the Soviets were getting an edge in Madibu?"

Jinare answers, "They would want to stop it."

"Please stop the car," Mbangu tells the driver. "Let's get out and talk." He smiles at the driver "My friend, you know I trust you, but sometimes we must have privacy."

The driver speaks. "I understand, Your Excellency."

Bootu, Mbangu and Jinare get out of the car and walk. Mbangu's face is lit up like a kid who has convinced his parent to let him stay up late to do homework when he really wanted to listen to a ballgame.

"Friends, we must tell the truth and nothing but the truth to our potential American and Soviet benefactors. But that doesn't mean we have to tell them the *whole* truth."

Bootu looks confused. "What do you mean, sir?"

"Let's ask *both* countries for help."

Jinare swallows and almost chokes. "You want me to approach both countries? Both?"

"Yes. They'll find out anyway."

Jinare snickers. "Neither country could keep a secret if they tried."

Mbangu walks faster. "What if they both thought they had to outdo the other?"

Bootu offers. "They might give more."

Mbangu strokes his chin. "We should pass laws that no one may enter our country with weapons. This will keep us safer when our 'big brothers' arrive to help our, ahem, backward nation."

Jinare is about to jump out of his skin. "Yes, we must protect ourselves. The people who fix our harbor and our airport will need explosives. Our people will guard these potential bombs."

Mbangu brightens. "The Americans build great airports and hotels. Let's ask them to help with that. The Soviets need to understand how to build safe harbors due to their horrible weather. They should be excited to help rebuild our two harbors. If they think they must outdo their foe, so be it."

Everyone nods and chuckles.

Bootu asks a life-changing question. "We have ample food, fruits, vegetables, fish and meat, but what about other needs for the future visitors? Do you think we can get the Americans to refit our soda plants?"

Mbangu smiles, not knowing he's about to change history. "Maybe we should keep our guests happy and transform the bottling plants into distilleries. Our Russian friends will want to have some available for our new hotels. How about if we transform the bottling plants into vodka production facilities?"

Jinare snickers. "I'll drink to that."

Everyone cackles at a strangely logical plan. Right now, all Madibu has is a group of dedicated leaders, beautiful beaches, ancient bottling plants, two crappy harbors and a bunch of rhesus monkeys.

Mbangu stands straight up. "Gentlemen, I think we have come up with a plan to save our nation. This is an auspicious day. And how many times does a poor, backward African nation get the super powers to fix all their needs?"

They all shake hands and hug. A new day is starting in Madibu. They smile and share Mbangu's idealism; this plan is perfect in its simplicity and honesty. It will help their nation and the superpowers won't know what's going on until it's already too late.

Chapter 19
It's Post Time in Washington and Moscow

The world is starting to change. Normally, the people who initiate the change have a plan that will be built upon and succeed or fail on its own merits. Rarely is positive, epic change in the world caused by massive fuck-ups and insane plans gone wild. Rarely do parallel egos, running in diametrically opposite directions, turn into a circle rather than a line or, more appropriately, into a circle jerk.

The small countries are about to act out of purely altruistic needs. Well, almost purely; Claude, of course, can't do anything without having fun. Everyone is putting together plans that could neither be broken or shared. Nothing anyone is going to do could ever be shared with anyone. This is impossible, but it must be this way.

President Thomas is in the Oval Office as Secretary of State Mitchell enters and sits across the desk from him. Thomas takes the full ash ray and dumps it in the trash can under his desk. He picks up a pack of cigarettes and offers Mitchell one. Thomas lights the cancer sticks.

He looks at Mitchell. "How's our plan going?"

"A doctoral student named Lucy Diamond has come up with a formula that appears to have a great deal of promise. She's busy working to perfect it."

"That sounds great. How long before it's a go?"

"Not long, sir, she just wants to get a few last kinks out before we show it to you." Mitchell takes out two briefing folders from his satchel. "Mr. President, we have two curious requests for foreign aid."

"Who are the blood-suckers, grubbing for money today? Don't they know we're in a Cold War?"

"Luxenstein and Madibu."

"Who? They are pissants. Tell them to fuck off." He lights a new cigarette off his old one.

"Sir, Madibu is an African nation that is very strategically located."

"Oh, what do they want the money for?"

"They want us to help them rebuild their airport and infrastructure to create a resort industry, to create the jobs for their people that are needed to create political stability. We could put some of our people there permanently. It's a cheap way to get a strategic foothold. I recommend we move forward."

"Jesus, why don't they do it themselves and stop blaming colonialism? The French, English, Portuguese all left Africa years ago. Now they're begging from the United States, fuck 'em." Thomas is defiant as he lights another cigarette off the one in his hand.

"Agreed, but we've been trying to get a strategic partner in the Indian Ocean for decades. They are in a great location for us to spy on the Soviets and it's not a lot of money. Maybe we should send our Seabees to help with the construction."

The President takes a long thoughtful puff. "Yes, maybe you're right; having some eyes on the ground might help us. Hell, maybe we can ship assholes we don't like there to get rid of them. We can scout for spying locations while they're there. Now, what is Luxenstein whining about?"

"They say the tough economic times have led them to need assistance to rebuild roads, schools and a new hospital."

"After all these years, they're still rebuilding the roads from what those asshole Nazis did to them? Will it ever end? Can't they pull themselves up by their bootstraps?"

"It seems like a lot of money for a small country, but they'll be on the Security Council for the next two years. It might be nice to have an extra vote on our side as we go forward."

"I like the way you think. Will it be difficult to get this money through Congress?"

"No, sir. There's a bill our opposition wants passed this week. We'll tack this on and let them know it is pass this or no deal on what they want next."

"That's great. Was I going to sign their bill anyway?" He coughs and lights another cigarette.

"Yes, Mr. President."

"You are one sneaky bastard and I'm glad you're on my side. You *are* on my side, aren't you?"

"Of course, Mr. President. It's an honor to serve you." Mitchell's hands shake as he lights a cigarette.

The President picks up the phone, "Elizabeth, please get me Ambassador Nestor from Luxenstein on the phone." He waits for the phone to ring and clears his throat. "Ambassador Nestor, this is President Thomas. Please let Prince Claude know I have approved your request for aid, and the bill should pass this month. There will be no issue. Your funding should be on its way the week after passage. Our UN Ambassador would like to host a dinner for your delegate to honor Luxenstein's first year on the Security Council... No, it will be our honor. Please give my best to Prince Claude."

"Brilliant call, Mr. President. Would it be acceptable if I called the Ambassador from Madibu? Our kids go to the same school."

"Great idea, Mitchell. Making it personal will make it more difficult for them to say no when we ask for a favor," he says with a cunning smile. "And we *will* ask for that favor."

They light up cigarettes and smile. The little guys would've asked for this money years ago, if they thought it would be this easy.

"This is a great day, Mr. President." He blows a huge smoke ring. They both stop to admire it.

Many times, the world doesn't understand how closely in unison it is working. People with polar opposite desires are simply mirror images of one another. The beauty of that is no one can say anything. It's kind of like running into your brother-in-law in the VIP room of a strip joint. You'll have a pact of silence every Thanksgiving and Christmas. It works the same in international politics.

The stories from around the world are happening simultaneously on parallel tracks. They fit together, while at the same running into the other. Is this why split-screen TV was invented? Washington and Moscow are doing the much the same.

***

In Moscow, the Kremlin is abuzz with excitement and wonder. The thought of world domination abounds. Beating the Americans is too sweet to get out of their minds. The only downside to their glee is they can't share their genius with their wives or mistresses. That sucks.

The drapes are closed in the grand meeting room. Premier Boski is watching a Cheech and Chong movie projected onto the far wall when there is a loud knock on the door.

"Come in. Do you have my ice cream?" he bellows. He is laughing uncontrollably.

"Sorry, Comrade Premier, it is Davinko, not your ice cream. Is this *Up in Smoke*?"

"It's the one with the ice cream truck. That's why I ordered ice cream."

"I'm certain that was the reason. I am here because we got two rather odd requests for foreign aid today."

"Who is it? Cuba? Or is that impudent Tito groveling again?"

"No sir, one of the countries is Luxenstein; the other is Madibu."

"Was there a revolution in the United States? Did California secede?

"No comrade, Madibu is an African island nation. Malibu is in California."

"It seems odd. We never hear from them, and then suddenly, we hear from both on the same day. What the fuck do they want?"

"Madibu is trying to revive their tourism industry. They would like to repurpose their soft drink plants into vodka distilleries and would like to dredge their harbors to allow cruise ships to dock."

Boski sits up and smiles. "More vodka? They would have to send some to their favorite premier."

"Comrade, we have long desired a port in the Indian Ocean. If we have our people dredge the harbors, we could scout locations for our future needs without arousing suspicion from anyone."

"Yes, Comrade Davinko, that is an excellent idea. We must send them the money and people. Choose only our best workers and patriots. Make this assignment a bonus."

"That is a wonderful idea. My only worry is how would get them to leave the warm beaches for Moscow winters."

"We could oblige them to come back or they could be sent to enjoy *Siberian* winters."

They both snort and take slugs of vodka. They puff out their chests as they drink more.

"The Finance Minister of Luxenstein says they need emergency capital for concrete and medical supplies. It seems a bit odd to me, but in thirty days they will assume a seat on the Security Council for the next two years."

"The timing does seem odd."

"If we don't give it to them, the Americans might. "

"We can't have that. It's Christmas and the Tooth Fairy in the U.S.S.R. Let's drink to Soviet friendship with the world's downtrodden."

They both roar. Davinko finds more vodka. He pours them huge glasses. What a way to run a country!

Boski laughs. "To Mother Russia, the world's piggy bank."

Davinko takes a big gulp. "Who says capitalists are the only nice guys? To our vacations in Madibu!"

Boski drinks. "That will be much better than winter in Moscow."

Davinko thinks for a moment. "The entire world is lining up behind Mother Russia. It's like good fortune is dropping in on us from the sky."

Boski is beaming. "Yes, Comrade Minister, it's like the universe wants the U.S.S.R. to win and end the Cold War. This is almost too easy."

They snort as the bottle of vodka empties. They seem sad when they finish the last one-liter bottle in less than fifteen minutes. But it is the Americans who have an addiction problem. Yep, they don't have anything to worry about here in Moscow.

Where's the Cheshire Cat when he is needed? Life just keeps getting more and more curious. What is amazing is this is the easy part. Nothing has happened. Well, not yet. The wheels are starting in motion. The cogs are fitting perfectly. Everyone thinks they are winning. Tunnel vision and boundless egos are creating the perfect storm. They aren't thinking about having life preservers on board. They are the masters of the universe.

Chapter 20
Let the Games Begin

The world is starting to spin faster and faster. Intertwined events are creating a massive, expanding web without any knowledge from any of the corners of this imbroglio that it even exists. Some people are being totally altruistic. Another is somewhere between a good heart and bad decisions. The so-called masters of our world continue hurtling towards their shared cliffs in willful, deluded Machiavellian blindness. Nothing can or will stop their plans and momentum.

The sun reflects dutifully off the ocean onto the beaches of Madibu. The sea glistens endlessly to the horizon. It is starkly offset by the dilapidated hotel that is about to fall in on itself. So much beauty, so much promise, but what can be done? Madibu is a gem that has yet to be mined.

Mbangu is sitting on the patio at a table that has beer coasters under two legs to prop it up. Jinare comes out of the hotel. The normally sedate and measured aide is literally jumping for joy. He kisses a waitress who is going into the hotel. It's Christmas, New Year's and his birthday all in one.

"Your Excellency, Your Excellency! You must see this!"

Mbangu is openly amused. "Yes Jinare, I am the President, at least for today."

"Your Excellency, you will be President for as many years as you wish."

"Why? Have you been drinking?" He is puzzled but getting excited.

"No sir, no sir, we have responses from both the Americans and the Soviets. I don't believe it."

Mbangu takes the papers. His smile grows larger and toothier the more he reads. "This is remarkable. How could all of this happen so quickly?"

"Maybe they feared we'd go to their enemy," Mbangu gleefully gasps.

"But we already have."

"Luckily, they didn't know." Mbangu's grin has a little devious tinge to it. "My favorite part is that the superpowers think they are going to use their largesse and people to do reconnaissance in our nation and create a foothold. I think we should have them bivouac next to their enemy."

"Your Excellency, that would be cruel, but fun." Jinare can hardly contain his joy as his smile grows and grows.

"We should keep playing their egos against the other and get more than we asked. Let them think they are teaching us their specialties. They will keep trying to outdo themselves. We should look for other things that need fixing. I'm certain they will be happy to comply."

"Yes, their egos won't allow them to stop trying to do more than their enemy is doing for us. We must think of upping the bidding war."

"We have a lot of work to do to prepare to be the people they expect us to be. This is Madibu's second Independence Day." Mbangu grins and nods.

They hug. I doubt the jaws-of-life could have ripped the smiles from their faces. As they go their own way you could see both of them thinking about how to extort the superpowers for the benefit of their beloved Madibu. It was going to be *so* easy and *so* much fun.

***

At basically the same time in Luxenstein, Prince Claude is sampling cheeses, wine and fruit while sitting on his exquisite, opulent, statue-laden patio overlooking the verdant valley of his country framed by the beautiful mountains. As it has been for almost every day of his life, Prince Claude looks over the wondrous scenery with a broad and deep smile.

Paleau comes out of the villa. He is shaking his head, grinning, and waving some papers. Prince Claude chuckles at Paleau's excitement. "You must have great news to be so upset, my old friend."

"I do, Your Highness. The Soviet Foreign Ministry has asked for banking coordinates so that they may wire the funds we requested."

"Marvelous. What about the Americans?"

"They would like the same. Plus, they want to hold a party at their mission at the UN to celebrate our joining the Security Council."

"What a nice gesture! Should we ask them to invite the Soviets?" Claude wanted to explode. He wanted to push Paleau's buttons just for the pure enjoyment.

"You are enjoying this entirely too much. We'll have to buy some concrete, some medical supplies and rebuild a school or two. We'll also have to find some people to act like they are building roads that we don't really need."

"Yes, we will. It'll be fun. Don't worry, I'll keep some of the money for our nation's most immediate needs... maybe I'll just ask for more. We could play them against the other at least one more time."

Paleau grabs a bottle of champagne from the ice bucket and proceeds to empty it in two gulps. Claude crows loudly and claps.

"Well done, old friend! For a moment, I thought I'd lost your confidence and approval. I feel so much better now."

Paleau shakes his head then motions towards the villa. A beautiful woman pushes open the magnificent cut glass doors of the mansion. She walks – no, glides – gracefully towards the two men. She is about five years younger than the prince, tall and spectacularly beautiful. She has a regal air and supreme confidence with every motion. The Pied Piper of Panties is paying attention to her every move.

Claude says. "For me? You didn't have to do this."

"She will help us. Be careful, Mr. Pied Piper," Paleau warns before he has a champagne burp.

She arrives and stops. The prince stands up.

Paleau starts to introduce the young woman. "Mademoiselle Lauren van Meer, may I introduce you to His Royal Highness Prince Claude Alexander Philippe Henri."

Lauren curtsies. "Your Highness."

"Please, sit down. And please call me Claude when we are in private."

"Thank you, Claude," she says haltingly.

"Mademoiselle Van Meer, your country needs you for a critical mission."

Paleau coughs. The fact it is contrived is not lost on Mlle. van Meer.

"I am honored to be asked, and whatever my nation needs, I will gladly do."

"Paleau tells me you studied both business and acting. That is a perfect pairing for our project."

"I hope so, Your Highness."

"You will be well rewarded for this undertaking. It is of the utmost importance but the mission must never be shared with anyone other than Paleau and myself. He is my brother. I have trusted him with my life. We will trust our nation's future with you. Are you prepared to do this?"

She squints, looks down and then at the two men. Claude and Paleau chuckle. Claude keeps talking. "Don't worry. You'll have lots of fun as you help us save our country. I've had so much fun as prince that Paleau has lost most of his hair saving me from myself. Don't worry."

Paleau smiles. "I'm the one who worries, mademoiselle. I will protect you as I have the prince. It shall be my honor and duty... and I expect much easier than the past decade trying to rescue him."

Everyone roars. Claude kisses her hand. "This must be very daunting. Paleau will show you to your apartment in the villa. We will have dinner tonight at 8 p.m. I am an excellent cook, by the way."

"*You* do the cooking?" she asks in amazement.

Paleau stares into her eyes. "We are serious in saying the three of us will be the only people knowing what we are doing. It will be very dangerous to share our mission with anyone."

"In any case, no one will believe your story anyway," Claude says, chuckling openly.

"As we save our country, no one needs to know but us," she assures them, "I have seen this villa my entire life. Never did I think I'd have the privilege to set foot inside it or eat dinner here."

"For the next few months, it will be your home."

She sits up straighter with wide open eyes. "My *home?* That is far, far too much to ask." She studies them and sees they are dead serious. "May I go home and get my clothes and other necessities?"

The prince holds her hand. "Just tell us what you need and everything will be arranged. Paleau, make sure our tailor outfits Lauren with appropriate clothing. Don't worry, we believe in you. Let Paleau show you the apartment. If you need anything, please don't hesitate to ask either of us. Get some rest, and we'll see you at dinner."

"I am honored and overwhelmed." She nods and flips her hair.

Paleau motions for her to follow him. She obliges. Claude's eyes dance with joy.

***

Are we seeing four leaders, four styles, four stories acting independently, or is it one story? For the moment, each is in a world of their own. We shall see how long that lasts and how well it works. Would it have any chance to work if anyone knew anything about the others? Who cares? This is about changing history.

If ignorance were bliss, there would be a lot of people who would be very happy with how the standoff was being addressed. Yes, they would indeed.

Chapter 21
The Red Menace Meets American Rednecks

Nitvik is working on some secret plans to end the standoff with the U.S. Of course, he is so paranoid that the next meetings can't take place in Moscow. "They" might be – no – "they" *would* be watching and listening to the top secret plans. "They" were everywhere, something spooks around the world agree on regardless of the inherent insanity of such beliefs. But it must be believed to validate the massive spending on their agencies.

The Soviet Fab Four drive about sixty miles outside the capital to Nitvik's country home. In a time when most of the U.S.S.R.'s two hundred and fifty million people live in drab, walkup apartments, their leaders live like the czars they allegedly despise. It is a classic dacha with dozens of rooms, a formal garden and fountains with spouts that look like famous spies.

A caravan of cars and security winds its way to the country. The leaders ride in several old Russian limos that are ugly, noisy and bounce painfully off every pebble. When they stop in the circular driveway, soldiers dash over to open the doors, which squeak loudly with the evil sound of fingernails on blackboards. If this is what the leaders have, think of the vehicles everyday Russians drive. No wonder they want to take over America! A 1973 Pinto would be like an Aston Martin in the U.S.S.R.

Davinko fidgets in his seat. He tugs on his clothes. "Comrades, we control about half of Germany. Can't we buy a few Mercedes Benzes?"

Boski bellows, "You know we don't own that part. Well, at least not yet."

Petrov's voice is stern. "Why must we give credence to Nitvik's paranoia?"

"I'm not paranoid. I found electronic ground hogs last year. They are trying to watch our every move. We must be careful... especially now."

Davinko hesitates. "Remember the last time we didn't listen to his 'beliefs'?"

Everyone nods. Boski is stumbling and drinking vodka directly from the bottle. "Where are we? Am I being taken to be shot? I'll put the money in my wife's bank account back in the treasury. Don't shoot me. Please."

Nitvik reaches to keep Boski from falling. Boski is completely pale. "Comrade Premier, you aren't here to be shot, but I will be glad to take notes about your accounts."

"Thank you. Thank you."

"We are here to show you how our plan works. This photograph shows what used to be one hundred hectares of thriving tobacco plants. It was treated with the chemicals we developed for our attack on America. Behold, comrades, all the plants are dead."

Petrov is amazed. "How long did it take?"

"From the time the poison was put into the ground until the plants were killed took less than sixty days. This will give our agents time to get out of the country and to destroy the most possible farms' crops without getting caught."

Boski takes a swig from the bottle. "To Mother Russia!"

Petrov sucks vodka from the bottle and gulps. "Mother Russia!"

Nitvik and Davinko follow their lead. The bottle is finished and breaks on the pavement. An aide rushes over with a replacement.

Davinko drinks some more. "What about the crops we don't kill?"

Nitvik smiles. "We have developed an aerosol that will be introduced into the curing plants. We should get 80-85% of the product."

Petrov drinks a huge gulp of vodka. "80-85% is a failure! My bombs could get 100%."

"And they would immediately know it was us, you idiot."

Davinko nods. "Plus, think of the madness if there is some tobacco remaining. The Americans will kill fellow countrymen to get some. They are weak. Russians would never act like that."

Boski reaches for the bottle. It's empty. He hurls it against the wall.

"Who drank the last drop? We're out of vodka. I'll choke you for drinking the last of it, Petrov."

Nitvik motions towards the house. "Comrades, we should go inside. I have some research materials we should watch together."

He leads them into the house and they enter a big dining room. The shades are drawn. A movie screen is at the end of the room. At the other end is a projector.

Petrov smiles. "Are you showing us dirty movies from America?"

Nitvik's voice rises. "No, comrade, I am going to show all of you what our heroic KGB agents have to deal with carrying out their glorious mission in the land of imperialism."

Boski spots a refrigerator in the corner of the room. "There had better be some vodka in that ice box. Don't disappoint me."

Petrov runs to the refrigerator. Whew! It is full. He grabs a handful of bottles and passes them out.

Boski smiles and pounds the table with his shoe. "Put yourself down for another medal, Petrov."

Davinko raises a bottle. "To our heroes! May they be successful and may they return home victorious."

Everyone drinks. "To our heroes!"

The others sit down. Nitvik turns the projector on. A picture of a redneck American is on the screen. He is chewing tobacco and spitting. Nitvik stops the film.

The blood drains from Petrov's face. "What is that pig doing?"

"Americans call it chewing tobacco."

Davinko looks astonished. "They *chew cigarettes*? That's disgusting. Revolting. Then they *spit?* After we take over, we'll send anyone who does this immediately to Siberia."

Boski chuckles. "I hear New Jersey is worse."

They all laugh and drink. They watch the screen in horror and amusement.

Nitvik taps the table. "The Americans have an odd procedure where fat, basically uneducated men of questionable character called County Agents go freely to farms to check the crops and the soil."

Boski eyes bug out of his head. "The farmers *allow* this?"

"Yes. The dolts are welcomed like their best friends. They are happy to see government agents."

Petrov smiles. "So, we kill the County Agents."

"No. Americans are greedy and incredibly trusting. Some will win vacations. Others will be made too ill to work."

"The farmers let *strangers* onto their property?"

"They trust everyone, even the *government?*"

Everyone gasps. Davinko guffaws. "They won't after we take over. We'll teach them a thing or two about how civilized countries operate."

Everyone cackles again. They are swigging directly from the bottles.

Nitvik continues. "Luckily, most of their tobacco crops are in a few neighboring states – Virginia, North Carolina, Tennessee, Kentucky and Georgia. This makes our job much easier. They have such a pitifully small country."

Boski takes a swig. "How fitting! We will be hailed as heroes in two places called Georgia."

They drink and howl with laughter. Their cheers get louder with every drink, as does the level of merriment.

"We will target the massive fields and curing sheds in North Carolina. Then hit curing sheds in Virginia and Kentucky. That will devastate their market. Our agents will live in North Carolina. There is one small problem, however."

Boski asks, "What is the problem?"

"The people in this region speak a strange dialect that most Americans have trouble understanding. Plus, we must train our agents to like things like their inedible foods, brutal sports and how to walk and act in public. To that end, I am going to show you some popular television shows from this region. It will show you how difficult this will be."

Nitvik plays a film compilation of scenes from *The Andy Griffith Show*, *Green Acres*, and *the Dukes of Hazard*. There is no laughter. Everyone watches with furrowed brows. This is far too strange for them.

Davinko is the first to speak. "What language were they speaking?"

Boski blurts. "They let actors smoke on TV in the U.S.?"

"Not anymore, but only a few years ago, even doctors did cigarette commercials on U.S. TV."

Petrov is indignant. "I didn't fall off the borscht truck this morning. You are lying to us. Why?"

"No, that is so," Nitvik says defiantly.

Boski looks serious. "How can we teach loyal Soviet patriots and military men how to speak like the people on the shows? If they don't, they will fail."

"I have a great patriot who has already learned the dialect and is teaching my team everything they need to know."

Boski drinks some vodka and tries to put on a Southern accent. "Weeeelllll Gooolllllleeee. That sho nuf sounds great to me."

They all cackle and drink.

Davinko looks serious. "Do you think this plan will work?"

Nitvik smiles. "If it doesn't, we'll deny everything. In any event, who will believe we'd try anything this crazy?"

They all drink and whoop it up.

Boski looks serious for a minute. "We must give these patriotic comrades the Order of Lenin just for learning to speak this way and learning how to drink the swill Americans call beer. Not being able to drink vodka for months on end is a level of devotion few will ever show Mother Russia."

Davinko raises his bottle. "To the great service of our comrade heroes!"

Everyone raises their bottles. "To the heroes!"

Boski is plastered and happy. "To ending the gosh-darned standoff, you all!?"

They all scream, "Ending the golly gosh darned standoff!"

When the movies finish, they pass out in their seats. Davinko is the last. There is a contented smile on his face.

Chapter 22
Training or Whatever You Call It

For most of the story we have kept the parallel parts in their own chapters. This time, things will be different. The Soviets and the Americans are training their people at precisely the same time. As amazing as it sounds, both superpowers have mini-teams of four in the beginning. Although it takes longer to reach their goals, small groups are more manageable. If things go badly there is less of a mess to clean up and less to deny. These are very heady and heavy choices.

Both groups are under serious security. What's odd is that each security contingent has the same orders. If any problems occur, burn the buildings, leave no evidence; burn everything to the ground and bury the ashes. Also, security demands that they never enter the buildings nor fraternize in any way with anyone outside the group. For the entire project, they are relegated to staying on their property. Going into town is strictly forbidden.

No one knows exactly where they are. Security is tight. The trainers and the agents have been drugged and brought to their destination blindfolded. The drivers of the trucks get drugged when they returned so they can't remember where they've been. If only they knew what was going on inside the buildings, they wouldn't believe it anyway. Will any of them talk?

The Soviets and the Americans have the same idea. The training facilities are massive buildings in remote rural areas, and near a water source. Neither side is sure how long it will take to accomplish the mission.

***

Let's go inside the American plant. It's at least the size of a football field, mostly metal. It looks like a three-story-high mobile home. Fortunately, no one lives within thirty miles of this place, because it sticks out like a sore thumb. Luckily, this is before Google maps.

Inside the building is an elaborate set-up. The upper floor has comfortable, open loft apartments as well as rat-infested, dark, dank living quarters. On the main floor are about a dozen vats of varying sizes and an intricate lab. Drs. Harris and Blum are working at large tables. In front of them is a massive white board with instructions.

Blum scrunches up his face. "Can you believe it? Thirty years in the field; fifteen years as dean of a Top 20 program and now we are in a glorified mobile home taking orders from some Barbie doll bitch who hasn't finished her Ph.D.? This sucks. Big time."

"Well that Barbie doll bitch did something you couldn't do on your own," says Lucy between clenched teeth. "You'd better get used to it, Blum, or you'll get the same shot the drivers did. But don't worry, you might be able to remember high school biology. Wait a second, that may be more than you know now."

Blum grumbles but keeps working. Stein leads the infiltration team to the other side of the room and takes off their hoods. The men try to get acclimated to their surroundings, the light in the building, and get up to stretch their legs. This area is set up like a classroom. The group looks around and fumbles with papers, but nobody says a word. Lucy comes over and the men take serious notice. Stein stands up.

"OK, everyone, we're going to use first names here. I'm Gabe. This is Lucy. She developed the product we're about use to win the Cold War."

"I'm Tim. What the fuck are you talking about? Do you think four guys, a wannabe spook and a damn chick scientist can bring down the whole damned Soviet Union? I may have been born at night, but it wasn't last night."

"I'm Sol. I've done ops with small crews, but I agree with Tim. Are you shitting us?"

She ignores the comments. "You aren't going to be shooting anyone. It's more like industrial espionage. The fewer people who know, the better. You'll be seeing if my formula works," says Lucy with her chin up, looking directly into their eyes.

"I'm Mark. I'm a great conman for an intel Army Ranger, but do you think they'll just let us waltz in and blow them up and then let us waltz back out?"

Stein is sweating and pacing. Lucy notices and continues. "They won't know you are doing it until weeks later. By then it will be too late and you'll be home."

"Well Barbie, I'm Ken. What's this Impossible Mission Force's target?"

Lucy's voice gets louder and more serious. "My name is Lucy and I'm the reason you will save the world from having a nuclear war. If we fail, who knows what will happen. Your targets are the major vodka distilleries in Soviet Union."

The team laughs their brains out. Mark tries to get it together. "Wait a second," he says with a chuckle, "you're going to stop a country with nukes and a million-person army by attacking their vodka? You can't be serious!" He pauses and looks around. "Are we on Candid Camera?"

Ken can barely control himself. "This is one fucking expensive prank. Which network are you with?"

Stein is perturbed. "Enough of this crap. You were hand-picked for this mission. If you don't think you're good enough, we'll find people who are. Don't worry, you won't remember being here."

Lucy reaches into the cabinet next to her desk and pulls out a tray of glasses. "Take one and taste the beverage. Then we'll talk."

Everyone takes a glass. They take a sip and spit it out. Ken pukes on Stein and smiles. The rest of the team loves it and roars.

Tim spits and wipes his liquid with a towel from the lab bench. "What the fuck is that?"

Lucy smiles. "That's what all of the U.S.S.R.'s vodka will taste like for the next two years if you succeed with your mission."

Sol is choking and laughing. "I hate those commie bastards as much as the next guy, but that's just plain fucking mean. How the hell will it work?"

Stein wipes off his pants and puffs his chest out. "We'll train the four of you until you are virtual Russians. You will get working papers for the biggest distilleries. You'll be placed in Moscow and be able to go other places."

Lucy shows them a small vial and cough syrup-sized bottle. "The small vial will do this to an entire vat of vodka for a month. The big ones last for much longer. It is time-delayed to avoid alerting quality control. We'll get you fresh batches for the next target city."

Mark is wiping his mouth. "If we pull this off and I party with you, Lucy, do you promise not to come up with a concoction like that to get even with me?"

Everyone chuckles. Lucy looks at Mark. "Nope, I won't promise that."

Tim keeps laughing "Damn! Smart, beautiful, funny and cold as liquid nitrogen."

Sol can't help himself interrupting. "Hey Gabe, does she have your nuts in a beaker?"

Everyone but Gabe is roaring. Lucy just smiles.

Ken nods slowly. "I'm ready. Let's start training and end the fucking Cold War."

Everyone nods in agreement. Suddenly, they become serious.

The only way the plan for one group can work is if all of them are implemented at the same time. Training may be different for each one, but is happening at the same time.

***

Meanwhile, somewhere in the Russian countryside, a medium-sized dacha with a huge barn stands alone. You can see for miles in every direction and there is absolutely nothing else anywhere in sight. If this isn't the end of the world, you can certainly see it from here. There aren't any trees for miles and miles. Why anyone would ever build such a home here is a mystery.

Two huge greenhouses are behind the main house. In the dacha, the formal entry is now a classroom. A huge movie screen is on one side of the room with a projector about twenty feet away. At the back of the big open room is a table and six desks and two large refrigerators filled with essentials. Well, ninety percent of the refrigerator is vodka. The other ten percent is food: exactly the right balance.

Georgi, Sergei, Peter and Alexi are sitting quietly at their desks. Every couple of minutes one of them looks around the room. No one says anything. As opposed to the American training group, there is palpable tension here. None of them wants to be the first to speak. The spies are busy sizing up and trying to intimidate the others. Suddenly, a door slams in the distance. They all look up.

Alexi arches his neck. "Here come Field Marshal Petrov and Comrade Nitvik."

Everyone sits up straight. Sergei starts sweating. "Those two hate each other. They don't even like being in the same room. I wonder what we've done. This must be very serious."

The bosses carry big briefcases. Nitvik puts his down by the long table, then gets on his knees to look under the tables and all the desks. He searches behind the drapes and the movie screen.

Petrov shakes his head. "Comrade Nitvik, the room, the building, the entire site are secure. We're the only ones who have been here."

Nitvik stands up and goes behind his desk. "Comrades, you must be very puzzled as to why you are here."

"Yes, Comrade Nitvik, I am," Peter says.

Nitvik is glowing. "Comrades, the four of you were selected from all Soviet citizens to be the first wave in our glorious victory over the imperialist American dogs."

Sergei is perplexed. "Comrade, there are only four of us to affect over two hundred-fifty million Americans."

Alexi adds, "Comrade General, as you know, I am a military strategy expert. The Americans have more than 15,000 nuclear bombs. They also have tens of thousands of missiles and millions of troops. There are exactly four of us. How can we possibly prevail?"

Petrov stands straight as a board. "But you are four Soviet geniuses. You have great language skills, great organizational skills, and are cool under pressure."

Nitvik looks at them slyly. "What can't Americans live without?"

The team looks at each other. They are puzzled and getting visibly impatient. Peter stands up. "Comrades, I am honored that Mother Russia thinks I am worthy of playing such an important role, but why are we starting with children's guessing games?"

Nitvik's eyes close to a squint. "Peter, answer my question."

"I do not know, sir. Girls with big breasts who wear bikinis."

The team snickers, which irritates Nitvik. Petrov understands having something to dislike can create teamwork and camaraderie. He smiles, seeing that they hate Nitvik as much as he does.

Nitvik turns off the lights and turns on the projector. The first show is *Andy Griffith*. Andy, Barney and Gomer are talking at the Sheriff's Office. Petrov pauses the film.

The team is giggling quietly. Petrov is smiling wickedly. "You will need to learn to talk like this. You will be starting near Mayberry."

Sergei is the first to break the thick silence. "Well gooooooolllllleeee, y'all look at us here Ruskis. We're gonna take over the danged world talking like what the Americans call hillbillies."

Georgi breaks in. "You can't be telling us Mayberry really exists, are you?"

Petrov smiles. "It's the lead actor's hometown. Every character was a friend of his."

Everyone roars with laughter.

Nitvik turns off the projector. "You will learn this idiom. Then you will poison their fields with the serum we are making."

Petrov looks at them. "Believe it or not, Americans trust almost everyone. Your assignment is dangerous, but don't be surprised if the Americans help you poison their own fields."

He goes to the blue refrigerator, reaches in and pulls out a case of vodka. He puts it on Peter's desk. "To make it through all those films and practice your speech, you will need this vodka. Comrade Nitvik and I will return in two weeks to grade your progress. The fate of the Soviet Union is in your able hands. Learn, comrades."

Nitvik takes the hint. He turns the projector back on and the bosses leave.

The team drinks, cackles, and begins to mimic what they see on the screen. The projector starts turning around and around, out of film. The entire team has passed out drunk on and under their desks. Sergei has rolled away from the rest.

***

Things began to move at a more rapid pace on all sides. Both teams are learning their duties. The pecking order and tasks are taking form. The U.S. group is training seriously.

Tim is pretending to be walking down the street in front of a fake grocery store. He sees a hole in the line and tries to jump into the space. Then, Mark, Sol, Lucy and Gabe start punching and kicking him.

Gabe stares daggers at him. "*Never, ever, ever* try cut a line of people at a store or anywhere. If they don't kill you, you might get sent to Siberia. Use a newspaper for toilet paper if you run out rather than cut into a line."

Lucy takes the team to multiple vats. The trainees put the poison into the product in varying amounts. She and Stein leave the main room but watch from above.

Tim looks at the others. "Are we this gullible?"

Sol responds. "At this point, what choice do we have? They can lobotomize us or we can go to Russia and drive the Ruskis crazy with shit vodka."

Ken shakes his head. "So, the top levels of the U.S. believe that changing the flavor of their vodka and taking out all the alcohol won't drive jonesing, crazy Russians to start a shooting war?"

Mark smiles and talks with a British accent. "By Jove, you've got it! This is so fucking obvious. And so fucking brilliant."

Tim challenges him in a Russian accent. "Comrade Mark, Soviet workers will greet us with open arms and chocolates. They are a warm and trusting people."

Sol joins in. "*Da!* They will want to bear our children."

***

The world is coming together. The Americans' Soviet counterparts are literally getting their hands dirty.

Georgi and Sergei are carefully placing liquids into the soil in the greenhouse. Alexi and Peter are nodding their approval.

Sergei chirps in a North Carolina accent, "Weeellll neighbor, we sho' nuf seem to be ready to take off for the New World."

Alexi squints. "Are you all sure we're ready?"

Georgi is trying out his accent. "Those good old boys can't wait to meet us. Hell, they will probably offer us their daughters and welcome us into their homes."

Everyone howls.

Chapter 23
Meanwhile, Near the Equator

Things are moving faster than Mbangu or Jinare ever thought possible. They sit in the lounge of the Madibu International Airport sipping fruit drinks, looking out over the new runway. Bootu comes to join them. Where there were potholes a few weeks ago, smooth, painted pavement is evident all the way to the horizon. Now, no airport in the world has finer runways.

Outside, a crew of about twenty black Americans is working on the runway and building a structure near the terminal, a modern, multi-use building. Everything is mechanized, state of the art, and working perfectly. We see about a dozen uniformed members of the Madibu military honor guard milling around by the entrance to the terminal. What the Americans and the Russians didn't know was that these "crack troops" had been forest workers less than a month ago. Their rifles aren't even loaded.

Mbangu thinks out loud. "I wonder what the Americans will think when the Soviets start showing up."

Bootu has some doubts. "Do you think it's a good idea?"

Jinare has a sly smile on his face. "I told the leader of the American group that the Russians were coming to help us build a distillery. At first, he was visibly upset. Then I mentioned that he knew who they were, but the Soviets will think his platoon is comprised of Africans, not Americans. He liked the idea of pulling one over on the *commies*. They cheered and laughed about it."

They chuckle. Bootu says, "What will we do when the Russians find out?"

Mbangu looks like he ate the proverbial cat. "We are just dumb Africans. We forgot. We will be so sorry. I seriously doubt they will leave and give Madibu over to the Americans."

An old plane lands and rolls down the newly renovated part of the runway. The Americans have done an excellent job. It's a 60's era Russian Aeroflot Special. How is a country with crap like this competing with the U.S. in the Cold War?

The plane taxis to a stop. A staircase is rolled out to the door, and a red carpet is rolled from the staircase to the terminal as the honor guard forms. The Soviet contingent comes out of the plane and starts down the stairs. One of them is wearing a fur hat. When they see the sun and palm trees, they start hugging. This assignment will be heaven.

Two Americans hide their small cameras behind shovels and start clicking pictures of the Russians. They seem very proud of themselves. They must be taking a dozen rolls of pictures. They want to be sure they can identify everyone getting off that plane.

The honor guard snaps to attention. A lone trumpet plays the Soviet national anthem. The Soviets stop, take their hats off and put their hands over their hearts. Jinare is closest to the stairs as the first Russian reaches the tarmac. He hands the first person off the plane a Madibu flag.

"I am Foreign Minister Jinare. It is my pleasure to welcome you to Madibu. This is Finance Minister Bootu."

"Thank you, Your Excellency, I am Vladimir Alexandrov, Managing Director of the Distillers Association of the Supreme Soviet. This is my assistant Nicolai."

They exchange handshakes. Mbangu approaches. Jinare smiles and begins, "Mr. Vladimir Alexandrov, it is my distinct honor to present His Excellency, President Mbangu."

"Your Excellency, it is my honor to meet you and our pleasure to help your nation embark upon the noble art of distilling the finest vodka outside of the Soviet Union."

"It is I who would like to thank you, Mr. Alexandrov, for coming all this way to assist us. We look forward to sharing your wonderful product with our guests and letting them know how helpful the Soviet Union has been."

One of Vladimir's team approaches Mbangu with what looks to be an antique still. It is placed on the tarmac in front of him Jinare and Bootu are doing everything they can not to laugh.

"Mr. President, I'd like to offer you this present. Comrade Stalin used this device to make his own vodka during the siege of Moscow."

Mbangu smiles sportingly. "That is a most generous gift. Please thank Premier Boski for me. Unfortunately, we are a poor nation and cannot afford fancy automobiles. Please excuse the transportation to our bottling plant."

"It is perfectly acceptable. We care more about the opportunity than the vehicles."

Vladimir and Nicolai get into one old Checker cab and the other four Russians get into the others. The driver pulls off. A monkey jumps from the front seat onto Vladimir's shoulder. The driver looks in the rearview mirror. He smiles as if this is an everyday happening.

Vladimir is freaked out. "Driver, there is a monkey on my shoulder."

The driver decides to play with Vladimir. "*Je ne comprends pas.*[1]"

Vladimir has a heavy accent and slowly says. "*Mon-key.*"

The driver smiles. "*Un cadeau pour vous.*[2]"

Nicolai shakes hands with the monkey. "We should take the monkey. It is his gift to us. We don't want to insult him. We'll keep the monkey and get him drunk."

They giggle and the monkey giggles with them. Vladimir leans over to the driver. "*Merci, mon ami.*[3]"

The driver stops the car, and the others stop as well. Nicolai and Vladimir get out. The monkey gets out, walks next to Nicolai and holds his hand. The other members of his party chuckle at Nicolai and the monkey. At least, Nicolai has a new friend.

Bootu, Jinare and Mbangu get out of their car. They smile at the monkey. Bootu unlocks the door to the decaying bottling plant and everyone goes inside. The vats and bottling machines are covered in dust. A few lizards take a look at the humans and go back to what they were doing. It must have been ten years or more since this building has been opened and smells like it. They clear away cobwebs to see more of the plant.

Vladimir and his staff look around, then chat privately for a few moments. They chuckle and point. Quickly they get serious. Vladimir and

---

1   I don't understand.
2   A gift for you.
3   Thank you my friend.

Nicolai go to speak with Mbangu, Jinare and Bootu.

Mbangu sees them coming over. "This was our most efficient plant. It used to produce about one thousand cases of soft drinks per day. Can you convert it to making vodka?"

"Yes, we can indeed. Nicolai is an expert at retrofitting plants to make them into distilleries."

Nicolai smiles. "It will take some work, but shouldn't be too much of a problem."

Jinare leans closer. "How long do you think it will take?"

Nicolai looks at Vladimir, who thinks for a minute. "About three months. We will send for the parts. When we are finished, this plant should produce about 500,000 liters per day."

Bootu gulps. "That is excellent. We will be able to export the excess. We'll need to use our new state-of-the-art harbor to ship it around the world."

Mbangu is beaming. "Mr. Alexandrov, would it be a problem to refit our other five plants as well?"

The monkey jumps onto Vladimir's shoulder. "That will be no problem, Your Excellency. I will send to the Soviet Union for the parts we need and another complement of crew members. We could do two plants first and then refit the others later."

"Fantastic! We will have a state dinner for you tonight. You will enjoy our nation's best feast. You and your team will be heroes here in Madibu."

The monkey claps. Didn't we hear that monkeys were an integral part of ending the Cold War?

Chapter 24
Movie? What Movie?

The Soviet infiltration team lands in Montreal. They spend a few days relaxing before getting their new passports. Montreal has everything, great food, great clubs, beautiful women.

Georgi is getting a bit of cabin fever. "Sergei, can't we go out for even an hour?"

Sergei gets serious. "I wish we could. But we must be ghosts. There can be no traces of our ever being in Montreal."

Peter is caught between agreeing with Georgi and Sergei. "I'd love to go out, but what if we get into a car accident or a bar fight over a woman?"

Alexi scolds. "Yes, Georgi, what about a fight over a woman?"

Sergei shrugs. "He doesn't have to worry. Even a prostitute has standards, you know. Hopefully we'll leave soon."

They drink, watch television, play cards and bitch about waiting. The next morning there is a knock on the door. Peter motions for everyone to be quiet. He picks up a gun, puts it behind his back and goes to the door. He opens it, sticks his head to look around and sees a box. He picks it up and takes it inside to open. He smiles broadly.

Peter looks serious. "It is time, comrades. These are our American documents."

He hands the team passports, driver's licenses, wallets, some keys and a file. "During the drive, memorize everything in your file. We will stop in New Jersey tonight to rest and to go over our stories. Here is some cash to use on our trip."

Georgi smiles and pats everyone on their back. Sergei is the careful one. As they all pack up, he washes every counter, every appliance and everything else. There would be no evidence left to tie them to their stay. If only they could stay this organized.

As the spies go to their cars, you could see the excitement and pride. They are about to change history. They are officially on their way. The first indication of what is about to happen comes about an hour into their journey.

Sergei is the first car to reach the U.S./Canadian border. He taps on the steering wheel and adjusts the rear-view mirror as he approaches the border guard. He plays with his documents.

"Hi, did you have a good time in Canada?" the American guard asks.

"Yes, I sure did."

"Do you have anything to declare?"

"Nope, I'm just heading home to see my wife."

"Is that good or bad?"

"I guess I'll find out when I get there."

They both chuckle. "Have a safe drive."

Sergei is *amazed*. It couldn't *possibly* be this easy. The team staggers their trips so as not to draw any attention to themselves. They enjoy the freedom of traveling in America. They meet at the hotel they had chosen earlier. Because he arrives first, Sergei stops and gets two 1.75 liter bottles of vodka and three pizzas.

Alexi is the last to arrive. He goes directly to Sergei's room. Alexi is happy. "That was fun. I ate so many hamburgers. You can get whatever you want with no limits on how many you can buy."

Peter drinks an entire glass of vodka in one gulp. "I couldn't believe how lax their border person was. He apologized for asking me three whole questions."

They all cackle, eat pizza and drink. Maybe this is going to be as easy as Nitvik promised.

Sergei suddenly darkens. "This is the last time we drink like Russians. No one can see us drinking vodka like men after tonight."

They all nod. They are devouring the pizzas. It's like they have never seen so much food.

Georgi can't get enough. "Can you believe anyone can have a feast like this in America? You don't have to be important. All you need is a small amount of money."

Peter tries to get everyone to pay attention. "We must be careful.

Read your dossiers. Practice your accents. It should take about ten hours to reach our new home. We should be careful to arrive at different times."

They all agree. As the night winds down, they go to their own rooms. They start driving to North Carolina early the next morning. Once again, Sergei arrives first and Peter is last. It is a tiring forty-eight hours. They relax on the front porch.

Peter goes inside to make dinner with the food he got at a store about an hour ago. He is amazed at the choices and turns out to be a very good cook.

Alexi is growling as he drinks a beer. "This is nothing but swill. I wouldn't let my dog drink it."

Sergei takes a swig. "Drinking like Americans is going to be tough."

Georgi wipes his mouth. "I'm off to see what an American bar is like."

Peter is pissed. "Not tonight, Georgi, please."

"I've been practicing my accent for ten hours in the car." He clears his throat. "May I have a Budweiser please? Thank y'all so much. It's so nice to meet you."

Everyone roars. Alexi looks at Georgi. "Remember, it's not just your life you'll be jeopardizing out there. We could all get shot."

Sergei wants to lighten the mood. "Like anyone would believe our story."

They all howl with laughter. Georgi leaves. They keep eating and drinking.

He drives around and around for about an hour, passing the same buildings over and over. At first, he is cursing in Russian. Then he bellows. "*Nyet.* Y'all. Remember where you are, Georgi. Especially if you get drunk, you are a redneck, not a Soviet hero. Damn, there's the tavern."

Only a few cars are in the parking lot of the Stuckiville Tavern. A big smile spreads on his face as he gets out of the car. First, he locks the doors. Then remembers no one does that in North Carolina and unlocks them. He chuckles to himself and swaggers into the bar.

A handful of men are watching a football game on the small TV hanging from the wall. Georgi walks over to the bar and sits down.

The bartender walks over. "How y'all doin? Whatcha havin?

"I'll have a bourbon."

"Bourbon and what?"

"A glass."

"That's the way to do it, stranger..." The bartender brings Georgi a big shot.

As Georgi sips on his drink, a sexy young woman comes over and stands next to him. "Are you stayin' around here? Or driving through? I'm Billie Jean. Everyone calls me BJ."

"Well howdy there, my name is George, but you can call me anything you like." His accent is spotty, but it's very loud in the bar. BJ doesn't seem to notice.

"Buy me a beer, sailor?" She smiles, winks, and moves closer.

Georgi is puzzled. "Why do you think I'm a sailor?"

The bartender brings BJ a beer. She smiles at Georgi. "Because it looks like y'all are swimming towards me."

They click glasses, then sip their drinks. The music from the jukebox changes, and BJ starts dancing seductively next to Georgi. She grinds her boobs on his arm and smiles. "Come on, George, dance with me, baby."

She grabs his arm and drags him out to the dance floor. They dance a slow dance. She is rubbing herself all over him as she gropes his butt. He looks puzzled and happy all at the same time and lets out a low sigh. She licks his neck. "Let's get out of here, sweetie."

"I'm supposed to be meeting someone here." He is half-heartedly trying to resist.

"You've met her. She can't possibly be as hot or as horny as I am."

Georgi looks around the bar a couple times. She takes his hand to lead him out of the bar. He is in heaven. His mind is racing into the gutter and loving it.

"Which car is yours, baby?"

"Over yonder, BJ."

He opens the car door for her. Before she gets inside, she wraps her arms around his neck and gives him a deep passionate kiss. He shakes his head in amazement and gets in.

"Take a right out of the driveway, Georgie boy."

"Where are we going?"

"Well, I'd take you home, but my daddy is there, and well, you know. But I promise you'll have fun."

They drive for a couple of minutes and arrive at a drive-in movie theater. BJ is kissing his neck and has her hand on his thighs. She motions for him to go into the drive-in. They pull up to the ticket booth.

"Anybody in the back with y'all?"

"Nope. Just the two of us."

"Hi, BJ. How y'all doin' tonight? That'll be six dollars."

Georgi hands him some money. He drives close to the screen. He is puzzled and horny.

"No, silly, go park in the corner."

"But we won't be able to see the movie."

"Darlin', you've never been to a drive-in movie before, have you? Well, not with me, anyway."

He pulls into a spot in a dark corner. As the window comes down so he can get the speaker, BJ is undoing her jeans. She slips out of her panties and starts rubbing them on his face. With her other hand, she undoes his belt and zipper.

"I love Southern women." He is starting to breathe heavily.

She takes his pants off. Then, off comes her blouse and bra. She rubs her boobs in his face. She pulls him into the back seat of his car where the two of them make wild passionate love.

This could never happen in the U.S.S.R. Georgi smiles. Was he thinking about BJ or gloating to his friends?

Meanwhile, back at the group's house, they are sitting on the porch drinking beer. The team is shaking their heads while talking about Georgi.

Sergei shakes his head. "Why do we have to drink this garbage instead of some nice Russian vodka?"

Peter makes an awful face. "Staying in character isn't one bit fun."

Alexi looks confused. "Peter, I don't understand Americans."

They drink some beer and laugh. "None of us do, but why are you having this problem?"

"When we stopped in Washington, people there called southerners grits. This morning when I went to the diner for breakfast the waitress asked me if I wanted grits with my bacon and eggs."

Everyone scrunches up their foreheads. Peter opens another beer. "Are they cannibals? Do they eat ground-up parts of dead Americans for breakfast?"

Alexi smiles. "Well, I tried grits. It looked like a cross between rice and gruel and tasted like sawdust."

Sergei looks longingly at the moon. "I can't wait for us to finish our mission so we can go home to drink good vodka and eat real food."

Peter says, "Americans are strange, but their farmers have a lot of money. They have huge tracts of land, multiple cars and trucks, and even own their own tractors."

Just then Georgi's car pulls into the driveway. He parks it and gets out. His shirt is buttoned in the wrong holes and he has a stupid smile on his face.

Sergei looks at him. "How did your night go?"

"You won't believe it."

Peter doesn't know what to ask. "Where the hell were you?"

"I went to a drive-in movie," Georgi says with a huge smile.

Alexi plays along. "What movie did you see?"

He reaches into his pocket and pulls out BJ's panties. "I didn't see one."

Their jaws drop. Sergei's light up. "Whose are those?"

"They used to belong to a girl I met at the bar."

Peter is puzzled. "You had sex in the bar?"

"No, she took me to the drive-in movie. We had sex in the car again and again."

Alexi looks sternly at him. "She must be CIA."

Peter glares at Georgi. "Did you tell her anything?"

Everyone nods. Georgi shakes his head. "She isn't CIA. I didn't tell her anything other than thank you. If she is CIA, her sister must be too. She said I can have sex with both at the same time this weekend."

They all gasp. Sergei smiles. "Look how decadent Americans are!"

Peter sighs. "I wish Soviet women were so decadent."

They all chuckle heartily. They are amazed. They start daydreaming about tag-teaming sisters.

Sergei taps on the table. "Georgi had a mythic experience tonight. Let's not forget the real reason why we are in this land of hedonism and decadence. We start our mission tomorrow."

Georgi is still beaming. "How long will our mission take, Sergei?"

Peter can't help himself. "It depends on which head Georgi uses to think."

Everyone howls. Sergei taps the table again. "If all goes well, we should be successful in 30-45 days."

They raise their beers. "To success! To Mother Russia!"

Georgi raises his beer a second time. "To drive-in movies and horny sisters."

Chapter 25
Moscow on My Mind

As the story unwinds, remember all these events went on concurrently. What's amazing is that with so many spies in the other's country, there was no whiff of the ongoing weirdness. Someone, somewhere, had to be seeing something. Let's see what was happening in Moscow.

Workers' apartments had been built in the late 1940s, but due to consistently bad economic factors, few repairs were ever made. The paint is fading and chipping on almost every floor. From the street, you can see exposed, dangling lights in hallways. Broken windows and open-air hallways are hell in the winter that will be hanging on for a few more months.

Three members of the main American tactical team are sitting in a dimly lit, shit-hole of an apartment. It has more barren spaces than paint on the walls. The team members are all about thirty to thirty-five years old and studiously non-descript, about six-feet tall and of average weight, on the theory that blending in will help keep them alive.

They are playing cards. Ken slams his cards on the table. "God, I am fucking bored."

Tim picks up the deck. "How about some five-card stud?"

Ken shakes his head. "We've been playing cards every night in training. Undercover work is supposed to be a lot more fun and a lot sexier."

The others shuffle notes, furrow their brows and squint. They pick up their identity papers.

Tim smiles. "These are good. My work ID looks perfect."

Mark nods. "Don't mess with them. Any problem could get us busted," he continues. "Hey don't tell Sol, but I nearly fucked up today."

Ken looks quickly at his team. "What the hell did you do?"

"I stopped at a tavern on the way to get some stuff at the store. Man, I'm getting tired of drinking vodka. I had to do something to get out of here."

Ken is irritated. "What the hell did you do?"

"My head was spinning. I felt like I was going to puke. So, I went into the store to use the bathroom. Suddenly, this old woman starts hitting me with her umbrella. Then two other old women start hitting me."

Ken was incredulous. "What did you do?"

"Nothing. Then two cops come over to pull the old ladies off me. They said they could send me to Siberia for five years if I ever tried to cut in another line."

The others cackle loudly. Tim tries to soothe Mark's mind. "Hey, Siberia is a lot like Green Bay without cheese heads and the Packers."

"Right guys, that sucked. Apparently, cutting into a line if you need to pee is a felony in the U.S.S.R."

The door opens and Sol, the team leader, walks into the apartment. "You guys look like you're having a great time."

Ken smiles. "Mark almost got sent to Siberia for cutting into a food line because he got drunk and wanted to puke in the bathroom."

Sol doesn't look amused. "What the fuck, Mark? You can't be getting drunk or cutting lines. They could get all of us. We went over all that during training. You're in Alcoholics Anonymous until further notice."

Tim looks at Sol. "When are we getting started?"

Sol smiles. "Funny you should ask. Our guy finally delivered our working papers. It's a go. I'm heading to the suburbs tomorrow. Tim, Mark, and Ken stay here in Moscow. It'll take a few days to get started and accepted."

Everyone applauds. Mark looks at Tim. "Do we have enough serum?"

"We're ready for the first round and I'll get the rest in a few days. The other team is ready to go as well. Remember, less is more here. Everyone thinks everyone is a spy and they will rat you out for having extra toilet paper. Think! Be cool. Let's get some sleep."

Sol and Tim go into the bedroom. Mark and Ken sleep on the couches in the living room. If the CIA had gotten them their own apartments, it would have attracted too much attention. It can take years to get an apartment, so four guys sharing a one bedroom is pretty much routine in Moscow. Hell, you need to set appointments for using the laundry room two months in advance.

They all get up, get dressed and fix breakfast. The team checks and rechecks supplies and identification materials again. Silently they pat each other on the back and shake hands. Hugs are shared, and knowing looks are on their faces. It's like the quietest sports locker room in the world. The game is on.

Mark's eyes are picking up every move. He understands his location is the most important and has the highest levels of security. From the beginning of training, it has been crystal clear that he would be the person most at risk. The number of covert missions anyone had participated in the past is irrelevant. You are only as good as your current assignment.

It's about a thirty-minute subway and bus ride to his target. He starts on the dark and grossly overcrowded subway. Then he gets on a bus for another short ride. From the bus stop, Mark walks about five minutes to the gates of the distillery. The way it is set up makes it look more like Fort Knox than a place where cheap vodka is produced.

A line of workers is waiting to get into the plant. Guarding it are two uniformed soldiers; the female looks more intimidating. They are checking the workers as they enter the gate. About every third worker is frisked. The female chooses to frisk Mark.

As she runs her hands through his pockets, she finds a vial with a clear liquid. Mark doesn't give anything away. "What is this?" she demands.

Mark blinks and looks away knowing if he looked too calm it would give him away. "It's cough medicine. I have a prescription."

The male soldier grabs the person who walked in directly in front of Mark. "Was this man coughing?"

"Yes. He coughed several times."

The male soldier frowns. "If you're going to use medicine, you must tell us."

Mark nods. "I will be bringing some the rest of the week. I brought this small amount today, hoping not to use too much."

The female soldier looks sternly at him. "Bring only what you need. You cannot be harming the product."

"Yes, Comrade Soldier. I will do that and will come through this gate every day."

The female soldier nods. "Good idea. But if you need it next week, I'll have to take you to the doctor myself."

"Understood. May I clock in now?"

"Get to work."

This is a great first test for Mark's coolness under pressure. As the other workers punch the time clock and walk into the plant, a worker looks at Mark. "You're new here. If you ever need a drink, ask me. You don't want them watching you. They are pigs. Follow my lead and it won't be like being in jail. This can be a great job, or a quick ticket to Siberia."

"Thanks. I'll remember that." They walk through the courtyard of the distillery; the other man enters the first building. Mark smiles at him. "I'll see you tomorrow."

Mark's job allows him to deliver materials throughout the building. Being new, fellow workers give him the once-over. He must be much more careful than he ever imagined. One time he bends over to tie his shoe and puts several drops of the serum into a vat. By the end of the day, he has emptied his vial into multiple vats. He clocks out. As soon as he hits the street, he lights a cigarette. He is still chain-smoking all the way back to the apartment. He opens the door and is lighting a new cigarette off his old one. The odd thing is, before taking on this assignment, he barely smoked at all. It's amazing what seeing your life pass before your eyes can make the strongest do.

Sol squints and glares at the same time. "What's wrong?"

"I damn near got busted on the way into work."

"What? Are they onto you?

"I got frisked on the way into the plant. A female soldier found the vial."

"How did you beat that?"

"I said it was cough medicine. The guy in front of me hates the guards worse than we do and he covered for me telling them I'd been coughing. The soldiers believed him."

Tim gasps. "Damn, if they'd caught you, we'd all be dead. Now what?"

"The soldier said I could bring a bigger jar of medicine but only for this week and only if I checked in with her every day."

Tim thinks for a minute and smiles. "We'll get you the super high-test for the rest of the week. It's far more concentrated and will adhere to the vat, making it last longer. Almost getting killed may have helped us."

Sol nods. He thinks for a few moments. "I think I'll have everyone use the high-test. The person who created it says it will last for several months. It will get us all out of here a lot sooner."

"Luckily, it was only Mark," Ken says with a sigh and a grin.

Everyone grins and stares at Mark.

Sol glares and taps his fingers on the table. "We'll split up and hit the outlying locations on our way out of the country. Let's not leave anything standing."

Tim looks out the window. "I'm glad we're getting out of here sooner. Sol was starting to look good."

Everyone laughs and eyes Sol up and down.

Sol slaps him on the back. "OK, everyone do your jobs over the next few days so Tim can get laid."

Mark jokes. "Hey, getting laid is far more important than bringing down the U.S.S.R."

Ken thinks for a minute. "I'll never trust The Beatles again. I'll never think about coming back to the U.S.S.R. after this."

Everyone chortles.

Chapter 26
New York Loves Lauren

Lauren has spent the previous three months studying for her role, immersing herself in the intricacies of the commodities market. Her stunning natural beauty is far less dangerous than her intelligence. Her combination of beauty, grace and intelligence make her a formidable foe. Even without this mission, she might have been able to be a market force on her own.

With training complete, she goes to New York to get the plan started. To avoid raising questions, she checks into the Waldorf Astoria's top suite a few days early.

As she prepares to leave her suite, Lauren knows she will try to gain as many contracts for tobacco futures as possible without drawing attention. If the prince is correct, even a minimal uptick in the prices will replenish Luxenstein's dwindling treasury. The more contracts she acquires, the smaller the amount of profit on each one that will be necessary. Further, if she is completely successful, the bigger the hedge Paleau can take to buffer any possible future losses. She is truly enjoying this game. Claude's pick is the perfect woman for his plan.

Lauren takes one last look at herself in the array of full-length mirrors. These bastards never had a chance; she's way out of their league. She has greatly lightened her hair, put in blue contacts and has added two small birthmarks in strategically selected locations to semi-disguise herself. Lauren will have plenty of plausible deniability.

She leaves the magnificent suite and walks down the hall to her private elevator. This entire plan has been orchestrated to every minute detail. Every second and every action have been planned and rehearsed.

Prince Claude is more than a bit crazy, but when he focuses, he can be a wizard. Casting Lauren is a master stroke. Without her, the entire operation could easily have become a debacle.

As she reaches the ground floor, a security guard opens the private elevator. He nods to Lauren like he knows her. She strides quickly through the lobby and everyone stares at her. She smiles at many of the men, who suck in their breath and sigh as she creates a living myth. She is the big catch. Well, at least, she wants her targets to think she is. Man, she's good.

A stretch Rolls Royce waits for her at the curb, distinct from the constant stream of Lincoln town cars, because Claude wants her to stand out all the time. The doorman opens the door for her. The limo winds its way through Manhattan's crowded streets. At many traffic lights, New Yorkers gawk at this incredible ride. After about twenty minutes, it pulls over in front of the New York Commodities Exchange.

The driver gets out and opens the door. Lauren says, "Please be back here at noon."

"Yes, ma'am."

"Thank you."

As she walks across the landing and into the building she glances over her shoulder to assure herself that everyone has noticed her. She goes directly to a private room overlooking the trading floor. She opens a glass panel to see the theater going on below.

The floor is abuzz with constant motion. It's very loud, a mixture of noise, motion, signals and emotion. Trading floors at major exchanges are unlike any place else. Craps tables at a Vegas casino during a heater are as quiet as libraries compared to commodities trading floors.

Lauren is examining some paperwork.

A security guard knocks on the door and enters. "Ma'am, I was instructed to bring these gentlemen to your suite."

Lauren smiles. "Thank you." The security closes the door and leaves. Three well-dressed me are with her in the suite. "Please come in and sit down."

Lauren begins her instructions. "Gentlemen, I want to buy as many tobacco contracts as possible. You will stagger your departures so as not to bring attention to yourselves. On the floor, you will only bid against the other once at most per contract. There's no sense pushing the prices.

Each of you has a budget. Do you understand your tasks?"

In unison, they say yes. Lauren eyes them. "Stone, you will meet me at 11:15 at the coffee shop across the street on the northwest corner. Hamilton, meet me there at 11:30. Harris, I'll be back in this room at 11:45. I'll settle up with you then. Good luck."

Stone is the first to hit the floor. He is picking up contracts consistently and inconspicuously. Rather than using the tried-and-true concept of having a fistful of paper, he puts more and more into his pockets, making it appear that he is just completing a few transactions. He takes three breaks from the trading floor so as not to draw attention to himself or the volume of his purchases. He is playing it very cool. His eyes focus on the trading board and he remains very calm.

Harris isn't following procedure as diligently and gets into a bidding war with Hamilton for several contracts, which causes a temporary surge in the price. Harris realizes what he's doing and tones down his bidding. He can know nothing more than he has been told already. Harris is new to the big leagues and is likely to give away all the information he has if enough pressure is put on him. Hell, he'll give everyone up if anyone asks. Did someone make a mistake picking him?

Hamilton is positioned near the outside of the gaggle of traders. He is studying the trends and the other buyers, which leads him to believe that two Europeans have noticed what they are up to. He recognizes one of them as a runner for Count Clausen, whose family owns one of Europe's biggest tobacco businesses, but he is buying much more than he needs. The Clausen family hasn't been major players for two centuries by sitting on their hands and not taking any chances. The other person making large purchases is renowned speculator David Clerient.

What is unusual about Clerient is that he walks the floor himself, trolling for places to make quick hits to ride the market. He is an action junkie, and his mere presence can move a market. His family has had immense wealth for centuries. Playing commodities markets around the world is as much a passion as it is an addiction for him. It's not unusual for Clerient to make – or lose – tens of millions of million dollars on a single trade. The big hitters see him as a cowboy. Due to his spotty track record, the large conservative houses tend to stay away from the market segments when he makes a big play. Typically, they wait to pick up the pieces of his trades after he gets out. He dreams of being Prince Claude but has neither the panache nor the heart. Clerient is a poser whose family money buys him out of his mistakes.

As it approaches 11 a.m., Stone finishes up his paperwork. He totals his trades and prints the chart. He makes his way from the exchange onto the street. It is a very bright day. He puts on his sunglasses and walks to the coffee shop.

Lauren is waiting in the back booth. She peruses the restaurant to see if anyone is paying attention to either Stone's entrance or to her. No one is interested. As gorgeous and as perfectly dressed as she is, this is remarkable. She motions for him to come over and join her.

Stone sits down. His voice is strong and direct. "I've been able to buy about 31% of the contracts that were available today. Here's the list, the prices, and the total. I tried to spread out my buys."

"Excellent. The money will be in your account within the hour as will your commissions." She writes out a check, puts it in an envelope and hands it to him. "This is a bonus for your performance. Your company doesn't need to know about this or about what you did."

"They won't. Will the money be coming in one lump sum?"

"Of course not. We have dozens of accounts at your bank. They would lead any investigator on a legendary wild goose chase. You have nothing to worry about, Mr. Stone. Thank you."

"Let me know when you want to sell. I'd be honored to help."

"We'll be in touch. Thank you so much."

Stone looks at Lauren, and understands that her "thank you" means get the hell out of here. So, he leaves quickly, quietly, and without looking back.

A few minutes later, Harris arrives. He looks over his shoulders and is sweating profusely. Lauren expected this and has his check already made out.

"Hello, Mr. Harris. How was your morning?"

"I think it went well. Here are my purchases." He slides her a piece of yellow paper.

Lauren studies it. "The money will be in your account within the hour and will come from many different accounts. You need not worry about any problems. Accounts are aged and vetted."

"There's no chance for any trouble?" His voice is breaking. He is still looking around the diner for bad guys.

"What trouble? You made perfectly legitimate purchases. Thank you, Mr. Harris. Good day." Lauren has a funny feeling and writes herself a note that Harris needs to be watched. Lauren needs to cover her tracks to avoid possible problems he could create.

Harris leaves. Every few feet he looks over his shoulder. Lauren takes her bill to the cashier and pays. She walks over to the exchange building and goes directly to her meeting room. A few moments later Hamilton arrives.

"How was your morning, Mr. Hamilton?"

"I think we did pretty well. It would have been better if Harris hadn't bid me up about half a dozen times."

"He did seem a bit nervous." She looks over the paper he handed her. "You did very well. You'll be able to close the sales within the next two hours."

She slips him an envelope. He understands what's inside but doesn't open it.

"Thank you, ma'am." He hesitates. "There's something you should know."

"What's that?"

"I think two people caught on to what we were doing."

"Let me guess, Count Clausen and David Clerient."

"How did you know?" Her knowledge of the market impresses Hamilton.

"It's my business to know, but I greatly appreciate your expertise and awareness. My group rewards such professionalism and confidentiality. We are very private and very loyal. I look forward to working with you many times in the future."

"Thank you, ma'am. I hope this turns out to be very profitable for you and your group. It's been my pleasure to help. Let me know if there is anything else I can do."

"Thank you, Mr. Hamilton. I must take care of a few details. If you will excuse me, I must go."

"Absolutely, have a wonderful stay in New York. If there is anything at all you need, please give me a call."

"Thank you for your service and for your extremely generous offer. You'll be hearing from us soon."

Hamilton leaves, smiling broadly. Lauren puts the papers into her briefcase, looks around the room to make sure she isn't leaving anything behind. She then takes a new handkerchief from a package and wipes down her chair, Hamilton's chair, the table and the door knob before she leaves for good. If, God forbid, Harris freaks out, there will be no traces left behind.

The limo is waiting for her at the curb. The driver opens the door and takes her back to the hotel. She puts her hat on before getting out of the car. She doesn't want to make as grand an entrance as she made an exit this morning; she wants to be a myth.

As she gets out of the elevator, she takes off the hat and looks in amazement at the spectacular view from the suite's middle level. Because the staircase is in a corner, people on any of the three floors may not know the floors are internally connected. It looks almost like the staircase is decorative rather than utilitarian.

She enters the main sitting room, opens a bottle of wine, pours herself a glass, and dials the phone. "Your Highness."

"I thought we were beyond Your Highness. How did it go?" Claude asks.

"Better than expected, but in many ways just as we planned."

"*Et alors?*" Claude wants to know where the strengths and weaknesses are.

"Stone and Hamilton did extremely well. Harris was a nervous school boy. In total, we acquired about 72% of the contracts that were available for this year's crop."

"Excellent!" His voice is stronger.

"Almost all of the rest is currently owned by Count Clausen and your baccarat sucker David Clerient."

Claude chuckles. "Just as we thought.'"

"I have dinner with Clerient tonight and then drinks with Clausen later."

"Those poor horny bastards won't know what hit them." Claude's howl belies his attempts to be diplomatic. For the moment, he's still the Pied Piper of Panties.

"Claude, I know you will want to rub Clerient's nose in this event, but you mustn't."

"You're taking away all the fun," he says with a chuckle.

"And your jail sentence." She is laughing with him.

"Would there be conjugal visits?" Claude bellows loudly.

"Not from me." She knows this will push his buttons. "Oh my, Clerient is early. There is a knock at my door. *Bon soir,* Claude."

There is another knock. "It is I, David."

"*Un petit moment,* David."

She looks at herself in the mirror and smiles as she walks to the door. She slowly opens the door, allowing Clerient to feast on the sight of her long legs first. "You're early."

"Shall I come back later?" His eyes nearly pop out of his head.

"No, please come in. I've taken the liberty to order champagne with our dinner to celebrate our successful agreement."

"But we haven't…" Lauren's kiss on his cheeks stops David mid-sentence. "We haven't yet solidified our deal. "

Lauren kisses his lips. "But I'm sure we will. Please sit, make yourself a drink. I'm going to get into something more comfortable."

David sits on the sofa. He gets up to pour himself a drink. Through the slightly open bedroom door, he can see Lauren getting out of her dress and into a slinky very low-cut evening dress. He smiles, gulps his drink, pours another and sits down.

"You look gorgeous." He is almost stammering.

"Thank you." She smiles.

There's a knock at the door. "Room service."

Lauren opens the door and the waiter sucks in his breath. "Over by the couch, please."

He places the tray and opens the champagne. He is staring at Lauren's cleavage as she signs the bill. David pours the champagne and all but pushes the waiter out the door. The waiter looks back at Lauren and winks at Clerient. As the door closes, the smile on David's face broadens.

A serious look comes across his face as Lauren hands him a piece of paper. "Is this the contract? Is this the right time? Shouldn't we wait until after dinner?"

"We'll be drunk and, ahem, otherwise occupied by then. You wouldn't want to stop our momentum then, would you?" Lauren kisses him on the neck and slips her hand inside his shirt. He glances at the contract. She tongues his ear and hands him a pen. He gasps and signs. She licks his neck, pulls away and hands him a glass of champagne.

"Let's toast our success in both business and pleasure."

He hesitates. She reaches for his hand as she raises the volume of the music, pulls him closer to her and starts grinding her body on his as they sway to the music. He is sighing with pleasure.

They sit and make out. She starts taking his shirt off and points to the contract. He scribbles. She slips something into his freshly poured glass of champagne. As she takes his hand, she lets her dress fall to the floor. He smiles broadly.

They finish their champagne while standing. Lauren is gloriously naked as she leads him towards the bedroom. He has a huge smile on face. Immediately, he starts to stagger. After a couple of steps, he falls onto the bed. She pulls off his pants, lays down on the bed naked and smiles at the camera in the ceiling. She kisses the unconscious man a few more times, then straddles him as the camera clicks a few more times.

She gets up and goes to the dressing room to fix her make-up and hair. Lauren thumbs through several dresses and settles on a provocative red one. She puts it on, makes sure it looks great, runs her fingers though her hair. She checks to see that her cleavage is clear and distracting. Everything is perfect.

Upon reaching the table in the sitting room, Lauren picks up the contract and puts it into the safe, which is hidden behind a picture. She matches red lipstick to her dress, spritzes perfume, and puts her hair into place. The drugs will keep David out for hours.

As she goes to the living room, Lauren turns to look one last time at the mess. She smiles knowingly. The internal elevator opens. She checks herself out in the mirror as the door opens again. She strides quickly into the other floor of the suite. The second act is about to begin.

She reaches for a bottle of champagne and a silver bucket. Once the bottle is in she puts some ice in the bucket. Lauren looks and finds a tray of cheese and fruit. It is placed on the table in front of the overstuffed couch next to the champagne.

The doorbell rings. "Who is it?"

"It is I, Count Clausen." He seems as excited as a school boy.

She gets up and opens the door. "Please come in, my dear Count. How are you?"

"I am wonderful, now." His eyes nearly pop out of his head.

He enters the suite and closes the door. He's about to explode with horniness.

Lauren smiles. "Champagne?"

Both reach for the bottle. Clausen gets it and pops the cork. A small amount dribbles out. Lauren holds the glasses up for him to fill. He joyously fills both.

She smiles and gives him one. "To success."

He looks puzzled. "What kind of success?"

Lauren is slightly bothered. "The success of our business and our pleasure."

"I can concur about this evening, but I'm not sure about the business, mademoiselle. You are magnificent, but that won't cloud my judgment."

"Of course not."

Lauren had planned for this. Clausen is not a weak-willed playboy like Clerient or, for that matter, Prince Claude. A challenge is more fun. Lauren turns on some music and sways seductively in front of Clausen.

"Let's dance, dear Count." Her plan is falling into place.

They dance. Lauren motions for him to spin and dip her. She looks up at him. Her cleavage spreads and the dress opens to show up to mid-thigh. "If we do business together, I'll be able to see you much more often."

"Miss Van Meer, you are the devil incarnate. What would my wife say?"

"I won't tell, if you don't." She kisses him on the neck and licks his ear.

She pulls away from him. "It's getting warm. Let me get into something more comfortable."

She leans in and kisses him, then leaves the room, keeping the door to her bedroom ajar. He positions himself so he can see her changing into a see-through nightie while he plays with the contract to give the illusion of reading it. Lauren comes back. She smiles hugs and kisses Clausen deeply. He gropes her butt. Her tongue plays in his mouth.

They sit down and she rubs the top of an exposed breast on his arm. Somehow the Count is signing the contract. He fondles her breasts. She purrs. She uses her free hand to place the contract under a lamp on the side table.

The phone rings. Clausen is kissing her neck and rubbing her shoulders as she picks up the phone. "*Mon dieu!* How did you find me?" Lauren is in full-scale panic. She jumps to her feet and adjusts her negligee to get her breasts back inside.

"What? Who is that?" The Count is terrified.

Lauren is ashen and shaking. "It's my ex-boyfriend, Rock. I don't know how on earth he found me. He must have bullied his way through the security guard. He's a former rugby player from New Zealand. Rock got suspended for punching a ref during a test match. He hasn't ever accepted that I broke up with him."

Clausen jumps up. "He beat up a referee and bullied the security guard and is on his way up here?" The color leaves his face.

"I'm afraid so. Rock is huge. One time he threw six men through the window of a bar, because they wouldn't tell him which one of them bought me a drink. I'm sorry, but for your own well-being, you should take the private elevator. I'll meet you tomorrow at your place."

There is a pounding at the door. "I know there's someone in there with you, and I'm going to kill the bastard."

As the next thunderous knock at the door echoes, Count Clausen grabs his coat and his shirt.

The voice is getting louder. "I'm going to knock this God-damned door down if you don't open it right now!"

The in-room elevator is hidden behind a false door. Clausen dashes inside it. The door closes. She kisses him and smiles widely. "I'll see you tomorrow, darling. Sorry about the interruption, but you're making a wise choice." She pushes a button in the elevator and the door closes. Her smile is broad and lights up the room.

She puts on a robe and opens the front door. A hulking man enters and makes sure she's alone. "How did I do?"

She reaches for her purse and takes out several hundred dollar bills. "You were perfect. Your timing was absolutely exquisite. Thanks so much."

He leaves and she starts cleaning up. She picks up the contract, glances over it, and nods and smiles broadly. After putting it in the safe, she changes back in to the negligee she was wearing earlier and rushes back to the other suite.

After about ninety minutes, she goes into the bathroom and comes out wearing only a towel. Clerient is still passed out naked on the bed. She shakes him. "Wake up, tiger."

Clerient is so groggy he tries to get up but falls back to the bed. "What? Huh?"

"I've got to go, lover, and you need to get dressed."

"I feel like I've been hit by a truck."

Lauren feigns insult. "You told me I was the best lover you ever had. That you cared about me."

"I do care. I just can't remember much." David's eyes are moving in opposite directions.

"That's even worse. I guess I'm nothing to you after all. How could you? Please get dressed."

"I'm sorry. You are incredible. Please forgive me. I will never forget this night."

She leans over and kisses him. "OK, I'll forgive you this time, but I do have to get to the airport. My flight leaves in an hour and a half. I'm sure you won't forget, tiger."

"Oh. When will I see you again?" He is barely able to stand up.

She helps him get dressed. She kisses him on the cheek. "Soon, baby. I'll be counting the days. But I've got to get changed and go to the airport."

"My car can take you. It's no trouble at all for you, darling."

"One is already waiting for me. Thank you for an amazing night, one I'll always remember."

This brings a smile to Clerient's face. They kiss. *"Adieu* until next time."

He leaves. Lauren waits about a minute, falls back against the door and bursts into laughter. She goes to the bedroom to put on a nightgown and a robe. She sits on the bed to make a call.

"Your Highness, I'm sorry to call you so late."

"You've had a very long day. How did we do?" His voice is excited and playful.

"I got David drunk. I told him he had the greatest night of his life. He signed the contract before he passed out. Clausen succumbed a bit. As expected, he only sold us his excess."

"That's wonderful. It's a day that will go down in the glorious history of our nation."

"I thought no one would ever know about today," Lauren says half-jokingly.

"I had to say the glorious part for you. Unfortunately, no one will ever know how you helped save the nation of Luxenstein. At least the three of us will; I hope that is enough."

"It is, Your Highness." She realizes how momentous the day has really been. She takes a deep breath and nods with pride.

"If we weren't Claude and Lauren, equals, before tonight, from today on we certainly are." His tone has changed. The Pied Piper has met his match. This is a day of change.

"I am honored, Claude." The importance of what she has done is truly sinking in now.

"Lauren, you have had a long, intense, exciting and remarkable day. It is time for you to relax and ready yourself for your trip home the day after tomorrow. Thank you."

"Amazingly, the adrenalin is still flowing. Maybe a long bath will help me get to sleep easier."

Claude can't help himself. "That lucky tub!"

"Claude, you scoundrel, you haven't changed at all, but yes, the tub and the bed will be lucky."

He has met more than his match. It's almost like he has accepted the fact that the Pied Piper has played his last tune.

Chapter 27
Planting Some Seeds in North Carolina

It's hard to believe so much is happening in so many places around the world at the same time without anyone knowing about what else is going on. What is more astonishing is all the plans are succeeding beyond any possible projections and without any hiccups. None of them makes any sense. They are impossible. Or, to a sane person, they certainly seem that way.

Things are starting to swing into full gear in North Carolina. The Soviet plan has fewer moving parts but far more personal interaction between the assets and their enemies. Add to this, the Russian spies must change their speech and physical actions much more dramatically than the Americans. Of course, the enemies don't know they are in a game.

This morning, the Russians split up to visit multiple farms. Each must be perfect. These farmers may be trusting people, but they aren't stupid. Would the script work? Would they fall out of character? The Russians would have to be more Andy than Gomer to have a shot and the odds are against them.

Peter pulls into the Smith farm. Tobacco plants stretch as far as you can see. A large home with a circular driveway sits about a half mile off the road. Richard Smith is riding a tractor looking over his land near the barn when Peter stops his car in front of the house. Smith drives over.

Peter has a perfect North Carolina accent as he begins. "Hey, Mr. Smith, I'm Peter Jones. Your regular County Agent ain't feeling so hot. So, they asked me come check up on y'all."

"What did you say your name was?"

"Peter Jones."

Smith holds his out. "Nice to meet y'all. Just call me Richie. How long will Harry be takin' off pretending he's sick?"

"Nice to meet you, Richie. He should be up and at 'em next week. You know tough Harry is."

"You're right, my friend. What can I help you with today?"

"Well I'd like to take a few samples of your soil. See how the crops are growing?"

"Sure, sure. How many do you need?"

"You have five hundred acres. The big boss says I need to bring him back five samples for every hundred acres."

"Big boss? More like big pain in y'all's ass."

"You got that right!"

They both chuckle, but are laughing for completely different reasons.

"Listen, my boys and me gotta work for a livin'. Why don't you take the old tractor to get what you need?" Richie tosses Peter the keys.

"That's mighty nice of you. Thanks, Richie." Peter is so stunned by the openness and friendliness of Richie that he nearly falls out of character. Americans were very nice people, not the rabid dogs he was led to believe.

"Go over to the house and Annie will make you some sweet tea. It's powerful hot out there."

Peter dutifully goes to the house where Annie Smith gives him a big bottle of sweet tea. Peter smiles and thanks her. He goes over to get on the tractor. Although he trained to do this in the U.S.S.R., Peter is far more of a city boy. Richie and his son snicker at how awkward Peter is at driving the tractor.

"Hey Petey, you been behind that desk too long." Richie is enjoying the show.

"If I'm not back in an hour, y'all should send out the dogs to look for me," he says with a chuckle.

Peter drives deep into the fields. He is meticulous about injecting and planting the toxin into the ground and into stems of tobacco plants. The process is so easy that he does it many more times than he planned. It works like a dream.

Meanwhile, Alexi is approaching a farm on the North Carolina/Virginia border. What's important here is that the waterway feeds farms for miles in every direction. He pulls off to the side of the road. Billy Ray Johnson is working in his tobacco field.

"Hey stranger, are you lost? Can I help you?" Billy Ray seems larger than life.

"Yes sir, you sure can. I'm Alex. Jimbo ain't feelin so good this week." Alexi's accent is almost comical. His Gomer-like accent could do him in. He tries to slow himself down to fix it.

"That's too bad. Whatcha y'all doing all the way out here, Alex? I'm Billy Ray."

"Billie Ray, the County wants me to take some soil samples. We want to see what is so good that y'all do out here. Your yields are off the charts. Maybe you can help others expand their crops."

"I'd love to help those other fellers who ain't doing so good. That's how we always are up in here. It's hot as a witch's tittie out in my field. Let me give you a couple beers to cut the heat."

"That's might neighborly of you, Billy Ray." Alexi is amazed at Billy Ray's hospitality.

Billy Ray hands Alexi a cooler. "Get yer stuff, I'll drive you over to get my pickup. Your city car won't get you through them fields."

"That's mighty kind of you, Billy Ray." Alexi is smiling broadly.

Alexi gets his back pack from the car and hops up on the tractor. They ride back to the barn. Billy Ray gets the keys for the truck. He smiles as he hands him a mason jar filled with clear liquid.

"When you finish your work, we'll take a couple of slugs of my aged-overnight-in-the-barrel shine."

"Thank you, Billy Ray. I'll be back in about an hour." To fit in, he cracks open a beer and drinks. Billy Ray smiles and nods.

The pickup doesn't seem to have any shock absorbers and he is bouncing all over the place. Several times he needs to save his sternum from hitting the floor. He goes directly to the creek/small river at the back of the property. Looking very pleased at the speed of the water, he carefully drips a large amount of the fluid into the current. He proceeds one hundred yards in every direction and repeats this. He drives around the property injecting the ground and plants. To make his cover story work, he puts soil into several labeled tubes.

Billy Ray is waiting for Alexi when he returns. "Get everything you need, buddy?"

Alexi gets out of the truck, hands Billy Ray the keys and the empty cooler. "I sure did, Billy Ray. You've got great soil."

"I sure enough do. I brought you some of my good stuff. It's been aged for a month… smooth."

Billy Ray takes a sip and hands it to Alexi. Then Russian takes a long swig. His eyes open wide. "Wow, that's strong and smooth."

"You know your shine. Where does your kin live, Alex?"

"I'm from Georgia."

"They make some good shine down Stone Mountain way."

"I better not sip too much more of that. Wouldn't want to show up drunk at the office. Thanks for all your help." He sneaks a short drink and smiles.

"Any time, Alex. Next time bring the missus and sit a while."

"I'll do that. Thanks, Billy Ray."

Alexi drives away as the sun sets. It's been a long day for the Soviet operatives. Alexi pulls up to their home. Georgi and Peter are sitting on the porch. They have their feet up and have beers in hand. Alexi gets out of his car. He is staggering a bit and taking a swig from the large Mason jar Billy Ray gave him. The others start laughing at him.

"Hey Alexi, did you go to bars hoping to get as lucky as Georgi?" Peter shouts.

Georgi bellows, "Did you get chased away from a farm?"

Alexi reaches the porch and plops down in a seat. He speaks in an over-the-top-accent. "Hell no! I even got invited to a pig roast with my missus. Why don't y'all take a swig of this? If you're man enough take a gulp like it's vodka." He hands them the jar.

They take a sip and almost gag while Alexi howls with laughter. Peter comes out of the house. "Comrades, I have good news. Our work over the past weeks puts us near our goals. Soon we may be out of this horrible place. Maybe only another month."

Georgi takes another drink and hands the jar to Peter. "Try this, Peter. It's locally made."

Peter takes a big drink and nearly gags. Everyone cackles. They pass the jar around a couple of times. For the first time in a long while, they are letting their hair down a bit. The banter and sharing don't stop.

Alexi is getting drunker. "How do these Americans stay alive? No one asked me for my credentials. No one called the office to see if I was lying. They didn't follow me around the farms. I could do anything I wanted. They are like children."

Georgi smiles. "BJ ain't no child and she checked out all of me."

Everyone snorts and drinks. They are slipping out of character. Sometimes they tell jokes in Russian. But it is late and they are almost a quarter mile from their nearest neighbor.

Sergei shakes his head. "And one of the people I spoke with said he had gotten up at 3 a.m. to get cigarettes! How weak and addicted Americans are!"

Peter makes a face as he swigs more moonshine. "They are weak. Russians don't have such weaknesses. We are strong. Maybe we should bring some of this moonshine back with us. It would punch up our vodka."

Georgi's eyes get bigger. "Yes! Moonshine vodka would be great at lunch or dinner, or any time." He looks at his watch. "Oh no, I must leave. BJ and her sister are waiting for me. I don't want them to worry their pretty little heads."

Sergei giggles. "That's not the head you're worried about, Georgi."

Everyone hoots as Georgi staggers toward his car.

Peter shakes his head. "Decadent, perverted American women."

Sergei passes the moonshine to Peter. "But you'd change places with Georgi in a heartbeat."

Peter takes a sip and thinks. "You're probably right. I wonder if they have cousins."

Everyone howls. Then, Peter passes out. Sergei and Alexi pick him up to carry him inside the house. As much fun as it would be to leave him there, they are too close to finishing their mission to take such big a chance.

Chapter 28
Two Little Guys Look Ahead

In a short few months, the changes in Madibu are nothing short of miraculous. Considering how few people are involved, the rehab of the beachfront hotels, airports, and bottling plants are months ahead of schedule. This might have something to do with how little there was to do for the American and Soviet workers besides work.

Mbangu sits on the newly renovated veranda sipping a drink. "Where are we?"

Jinare looks at a sheaf of paper. "The airport is almost finished. I'd say the terminal will be done next week. The second runway is finished. And in about four more months, we will have over two thousand hotel rooms suitable for western visitors."

"You are doing remarkably well, my friend. How about the bottling plants?"

Jinare smiles. "We have two choices. Either we need to build massive storehouses or start switching vodka for water in our homes. We will have so much that the people may have to shower with it. We could fill the hotel pools with it."

"Are we producing that much?" Mbangu can't decide if he should laugh or be concerned.

"These Russians just can't stop. We are already at almost 25,000 cases a day and they say we can be at 500,000 cases a day by adding more workers and converting all ten of the plants."

"Are there that many potatoes in all of Africa?" Mbangu asks with a huge smile on his face.

They both chuckle. Jinare writes something down. "We could become one of the world's largest vodka producers in six months. You are truly a visionary."

"Yes, Madibu and vodka, what will the rhesus monkeys think about losing their status as the #1 product of our nation? At least we can export vodka to more places than monkeys for pets of pop singers."

"We should make tens of millions of dollars from the vodka exports. We can build everyone villas."

"We, ahem, poor, backward Africans can't compete with our big brothers." Mbangu is beaming.

They both chuckle again. Their smiles cover their entire faces.

"Jinare, we need to start winding down their presence. If we don't watch out, the two groups could start interacting. There's no sense getting greedy."

Jinare pauses for a moment. He smiles. "Your Excellency, wait a second, would that be such a bad idea?"

"Why?"

"They'd work faster. They could take great stories of Madibu to their homelands."

Mbangu chortles deeply. "We could use that to get more money if we need it. Since they brought some Russian women, who knows, there might be some babies who should call Madibu their true homeland."

They share a deep laugh. "What should I do?"

"What if we have a big party on the beach near the port for the Americans?"

"There are some strapping young men there. What if they have fights?"

"Have the 'servers' be off-duty police and military."

"Excellent idea. It's a shame we are so stupid and backward. Such a shame."

"We were told that over and over at Harvard and Cambridge, my friend, but we do need to keep them here long enough to train our people to run everything."

"You are correct, Excellency. But are we bright enough to understand these complex issues?"

"If we aren't, our riches will allow us to bring in Europeans to be our lackeys."

Jinare is howling with laughter. "Ah, they did teach us turnabout is fair play."

They smile, snicker, and sip their drinks as they peruse all the construction going on around them. They are ready to have Madibu take its rightful place in the world. It is a wonderful day in Madibu.

***

Meanwhile, in the hills of Luxenstein, Prince Claude and Paleau are driving towards an old estate. It is expansive with a huge main house, several barns and other large houses that are visible from the country lane. They pull into the long driveway, built during the times when horse-drawn carriages brought noblemen here.

It's much more of a castle than a home. Many of the second-floor rooms have fifteen-foot-high windows and patios large enough to accommodate tables. As they enter the foyer, it is obvious that the ground floor has been turned into a factory. The massive rolling and packing machines are in incongruous juxtaposition with the 17th-19th century portraits and murals that adorn the massive walls.

"Excellent, excellent. How much production can we expect, Paleau?"

"Thank you, Your Highness. The machines can produce about one million cigarettes per day. We currently have fifteen machines. We will have three hundred machines in a month."

"That's fantastic. How's the upstairs coming?" The Pied Piper is now a boss and he has employees. He is becoming an adult. The horror... this *can't* be... it's not worth it. Or is it?

"There were thirty-seven suites. We kept the five biggest for the senior staff and their families. We have turned the others into very comfortable living quarters for about one hundred workers."

"Will we need more? Remember, they deserve absolute comfort," says Claude.

"We might, but they can be housed in other buildings. Per the manufacturer, we need about five support staff for each machine. This leaves us with space for about thirty others in the curing facility and the shipping crew."

"That hardly seems like enough."

"That's enough to do 75,000 cartons per day at this location." Paleau is serious but raises an eyebrow and smiles as he finishes.

"We bought a lot more tobacco from Turkey than that." Once again Claude realizes he has bitten off more than he can chew. (That's a bad pun.)

"We have access to 75-100 more such homes. Your father seemed to like to overpay his friends for their properties before their families chopped them up."

"Papa wanted to keep the grandeur of Luxenstein intact. It's our duty to bring it back."

"It was easier than divorces for all the women."

"Papa had good taste and a large treasury."

They chortle. "Your Highness, we can easily produce over 2,000,000 cartons of high quality cigarettes a day and much more if we do three shifts."

"Good. It's amazing how many people are addicted to cigarettes."

"As opposed to Louis XIII cognac, women and baccarat."

"You are right, my friend. The latter is far better and more fun. But that is changing."

"Do you think the Soviets or the Americans have caught on to your plan?"

"What if they do? They don't want to lose my vote or let the public know they tried to buy it."

"Why can't you play poker this well?" Paleau says, smiling and prodding his old friend.

"Would it be half as much fun?" Claude strikes back with a smile.

"It would be considerably less stressful, Your Highness."

"Paleau, after all these years, why do you still insist on calling me Your Highness when we are alone?"

"Would you prefer if I called you the Pied Piper?" Paleau jibes before Claude finishes his sentence. They roar.

"As a matter of fact, yes."

Claude slaps Paleau on the back as they enjoy a belly laugh. Maybe Claude sees the days of the Pied Piper coming to an end. All good things do end.

Luxenstein is a beautiful country. Around every corner is a new postcard picture to take. After the third stop, Prince Claude is getting bored and restless. It's been a good day but it's time for them to head back to the castle.

"Jacques, there have been too much commerce and not enough fun today. I'm not sure I would have made this play if I knew how much work was involved."

"Now *that's* my old friend Claude. Let's try to fool someone and think about what may happen later. Please, never grow up. I couldn't take it."

"Your sarcasm belies how much fun you're having." They chuckle knowingly.

Paleau parks the car. They get out and go to the library. After a few moments, the butler enters the room. Van Meer is with him.

"Your Highness, Mademoiselle Lauren Van Meer." The butler seats her across the desk from Claude.

Paleau is standing near the massive bookcase. He smiles at Claude as the Prince can't take his eyes off Lauren.

"Mademoiselle, this is a great day in the history of Luxenstein and you are a primary reason we have been successful. Our nation owes you a debt of gratitude and we like to pay our debts."

Paleau chuckles. "Well, most of the time, anyway."

"Be kind."

"Thank you, Your Highness. I did it for my love of our nation." Lauren beams proudly and the twinkle in Claude's eyes is not lost on her.

"That is appreciated, but we have started to make the arrangements."

"The new prosperity for our nation is enough for me."

"Jacques, listen to her altruism. I guess we should cancel the manor house, servants, and stipend."

Paleau smiles and shrugs. "Possibly. She is so unlike you."

"Maybe she doesn't want to be a Countess either."

"And you ordered all those plates and silverware. Well, we can always melt them down." Paleau is having fun.

"Countess? Manor?" Her smile broadens, realizing she has become the third musketeer.

Claude nods at Paleau, who reaches under the bar. He pulls out three glasses and a bottle of champagne. The bottle is very, very old.

Paleau hands both a glass. He pulls the foil off the bottle and carefully pops the cork. Not a precious drop is wasted. He pours. Lauren looks puzzled.

"Countess, only three people in our country who know what's going on. The three of us are bound together forever. There is no one I trust more than Jacques, and now you. Shall we toast to the success of our venture?"

"To success."

Small talk is exchanged as they finish two bottles of champagne. They are telling stories and laughing. Inhibitions are lessened as the stories get bawdier.

Claude stands up with a full glass is in his hand. "Henceforth and forever shall you and your descendants have the rank of Countess Lauren van Meer."

Claude then pours the champagne over Paleau's head. "You didn't expect me to ruin the Countess' hair, did you?"

Claude hands Paleau a towel and they all chuckle.

"Your Highness, I hope I can live up to this honor."

"Countess, your limousine will take you to your new home. If there is anything you need to make your manor more comfortable, please don't hesitate to ask. It will be our pleasure."

Lauren gets up. She almost loses her balance as she tries to curtsy. Everyone howls. "Thank you for everything."

"Have a wonderful evening. It is I who is in your debt."

As she leaves, Paleau hands Claude some newspapers. "There is something wrong with vodka production in the U.S.S.R. There seems to be some unrest."

"Maybe they should drink champagne and smoke our cigarettes."

Paleau and Claude light cigars. "Just keep them away from our cigars."

They snicker, smoke and drink some more. Claude's face can barely contain his smile. Paleau shakes his head. "She's different, Claude. Don't let the Pied Piper out with her."

The Prince roars in laughter. "It's not about her. There's a story that some sort of virus is infecting tobacco crops in the United States. Our product is going up in value by the minute."

"Wonderful." Paleau shakes his head. "You are the unluckiest person in the world. Then the luckiest. Wow!"

Little do they know how those two five-paragraph stories would change world history. After all, this was simply a game to Claude, one he had won in unimaginable ways.

"Jacques, I think it may be time for the Pied Piper to stop playing his tune."

"It's about time, my friend."

"We had some good times, didn't we?"

"Great nights! Hell, great months, Claude! She is what you were looking for on all those continents and in all of those clubs."

.He takes his last sip of champagne. "I hope I know what to do with just one."

"Don't worry, she'll tell you what to do..."

They howl. "I think she will. How else would I have found her?"

"All it took was losing countless millions in Las Vegas and Monte Carlo, then selling our vote on the Security Council, and planning to use the money to corner the tobacco market. On top of all of that you had to find the perfect woman to carry out the plan."

"Over all these years, I have seen many tribulations. There have only been two constants. You have always been by my side cleaning up after me, and I have always found a way not to get even but to make things better."

"We're not nearly done yet."

"I've got the same feeling. We aren't *close* to being done yet."

"That's the champagne talking... and love."

"Always the cynic."

"Usually the crash test dummy. If the Pied Piper is no more, shall we have a wake?"

"Of course, we should. Poor Mick will be crushed. I hope we don't break up The Rolling Stones."

"I think he'll do okay on his own, Claude."

Claude smiles. "I have taught him well. What about the casinos? And airlines?"

"They will find other suckers, but none as grand as The Pied Piper."

They cackle and embrace. Then, Claude pats Paleau on the back before leaving. Claude turns to look at his old friend. They smile and nod.

Chapter 29
Success! Back to Mother Russia

The team is watching TV, eating BBQ, and drinking a lot of vodka. A festive yet serious and semi-sad feeling envelops the group. They will miss the freedom they have had here. The reality of their infiltration being over and returning to the Soviet Union is setting in and they drink more.

"Do you have your money, license plates from different states and identification papers ready?" Alexi asks.

Sergei is the first to reply. "I'm ready. Are we returning at different times to different places?"

Peter coughs. "Doesn't that make any of you nervous?"

Georgi takes a long swig from the bottle of vodka. "Are we sure everything we did is working? I could stay and redo whatever needs to be fixed."

Sergei guffaws. "You just want to stay so you can fuck BJ and her sister more."

Peter slaps Sergei on the back. "Like that's a bad thing? I understand his motives."

Alexi sighs impatiently. "We've all got to leave at the same time and go in our planned directions. Georgi, they don't know anything, do they?"

"All they know is they want me, *bad*." Georgi's new-found pride echoes in his voice.

Everyone roars and drinks. The party goes late into the night before everyone passes out on the couches. Sergei awakens first and makes everyone a huge breakfast.

Peter shovels down eggs, grits and bacon like there is no tomorrow.

"I wish I could bring bacon and ham home with me. Hell, I wish I could bring home a case of toilet paper."

Everyone nods and chuckles.

Alexi says, "Don't worry. Our leaders say we will be heroes like Gagarin. We will have dachas and German cars."

Sergei snorts cynically. "They also said the Five-Year Plan would work."

Everyone eats and chuckles nervously.

Alexi stands up. "We'll be leaving tomorrow. Everyone knows what needs to be done today."

He pours them all a vodka. "To the greatest team ever and to Mother Russia."

"Mother Russia."

Sergei gives them envelopes. "None of these are the same. If any of you are feeling nervous about not being received as heroes, I've arranged for alternate routes and identities. I wouldn't want to lose my brothers after everything we've been through."

Everyone reluctantly takes their envelope. Somehow, Sergei has made sure they all have a lot of cash, just in case. Everyone looks surprised, but no one says anything.

One by one, they drive around the state finishing up and saying their goodbyes. Georgi stops often and then goes around corners to see if anyone is following him, as he has a strong sense that someone is. It isn't unusual for the KGB to kill the weakest link as a warning.

He diverts from his planned route and heads instead for a small diner. He grabs a bite to eat and goes to the bathroom. "Darlin', I was getting worried. This is so hot."

It's BJ and she starts kissing and undressing Georgi. They get naked and have wild sex right there in the bathroom.

Georgi is almost dressed. "Do you love me?"

"Yes, baby."

"Today is my last day in town. Do you know the payphone at the Dairy Queen?"

"Yes."

"Go there tomorrow at 6:30 p.m. I will call you."

"Ooh, this sounds kinky. I'll be there."

"Good. Maybe you'll come see me for the weekend."

"You bet I will."

"Don't tell anyone, not even your sister."

She sticks her hand into his pants. "I love secrets, sweetie."

She gets dressed, puts on sunglasses and a brown wig. Georgi leans over and kisses her. "I'll call you tomorrow. Please be there."

At this point in history it is easy to move back and forth between the U.S. and Canada, which makes movement seamless and tracking nearly impossible. Team members are planning to leave from Montreal, Toronto, Vancouver and Boston.

Peter drives east. About every fifty miles he pulls off the road to dump some of the liquid into streams and rivers. He is very careful not to be spotted. By sundown, he is around Washington and stays the night in Virginia.

Alexi heads west towards Tennessee, land that have not been targeted. His mission takes him an extra three days. To be safe, he does many of his insertions at night. He can be cautious without being obvious. He is thinking a lot about what Sergei said. He might take advantage of the alternate identity. He is already dispensable.

Sergei adheres to his orders until about noon, then he doubles back towards their home base. He pulls off the Interstate into a Stuckey's. After loading up on pecan rolls and Dr. Pepper, he sits in his car and waits. It looks like he knows something important is about to happen.

About an hour later, Georgi pulls into the parking lot. He looks in every direction and goes to the pay phone. This was one of Georgi's weaknesses. Sergei moved around the lot a second time to be sure they weren't being followed.

"Hi, honey." Georgi is on the phone.

"Hey baby, what's up?" BJ says to him.

"Were you followed?" Georgi asks.

"Why would anyone follow me?"

"Do you love me?"

"Forever and ever, baby."

"Do you trust me?"

"With all my heart."

"Go to the bank and get your money. Pack some clothes and meet me at the Roadway Motor Inn in Bristol, Virginia. I'll be there waiting for you. You'll see my car."

"This is weird, but I like weird."

"If anyone asks, you're meeting me at the beach."

"OK, baby."

"I love you."

"I love you."

Georgi hangs up the phone. He smiles. He looks around to see if anyone is paying attention. He goes inside the Stuckey's, goes to the bathroom, gets some snacks and walks towards his car. He's about two steps away when he spots Sergei. His eyes open wide and he starts sweating.

"Are you here to kill me?" Georgi asks.

"No, my friend, I'm here to say goodbye, good luck, and warn you to be more careful than you have ever been."

"You aren't going to try to stop me?"

Sergei smiles knowingly. "Stop you from doing what?"

They hug. "We'll never see each other again." Georgi's voice trails off.

"No, we won't."

"Will they come for me?"

"Probably, but you can hide. I'm more worried about what will happen to me when I get home."

Georgi reaches into his pocket and hands Sergei some money. "Use this to change your plans."

"But you need it," Sergei says haltingly.

"I'll be fine. Use what you have and this money to buy a ticket to Helsinki. When you get there, go to Nurmi Place, Apartment 33. Here's the key. You will find a passport that will get you back into the U.S.S.R. as Fyodor. They won't have a clue where you are."

Sergei is tearing up. "I thought my envelopes were the only ones. How can I ever thank you?"

"By being who you really are, not who you are told to be."

Sergei smiles and nods, "So, you know?

"Yes, and don't worry. Just get a good picture for the passport."

"You and I have learned a lot in America and we've both changed."

"You bet I have. I'm not horny anymore," Georgi says, laughing and crying at the same time.

They hug, chuckle, get in their cars and leave in different directions. Georgi starts driving south. He pulls off the road into a rest stop and changes his license plates. He opens the trunk and takes it apart a bit. He finds what looks like microphones. He starts tearing them apart and keeps looking.

He finds more. He throws some into a trash can. Then, he throws a few into the back of a pick-up truck and some into the cab of an eighteen-wheeler.

"That should confuse them!" He also tears his passports up and throws them into the trash can. He takes one last look around before getting on the road and heading back north towards Virginia. Freedom and wild sex are awaiting him. What a country!

Georgi checks into the motel. He sits with the shade open, and smoking a cigarette. As he reaches for another butt, BJ pulls into the lot. He immediately goes outside.

"You made it."

"I wouldn't let you down, sweetie," BJ says, running toward him.

They hug and kiss. Georgi looks around, gets her bags and they go to the room. BJ puts her things in the drawers and sits on the bed with him. He is beaming yet still looks serious.

"Is your wife just horrible?" BJ asks.

Georgi sits up straight. "How did you know?"

"I saw the discoloration on your ring finger. You don't have any babies, do you? I'd feel terrible if I took someone's daddy away."

"No kids, just a low-down cheating, money-grubbing wife."

"Why would anyone cheat on *you*, darlin'?"

"I don't know. We can change our names so no one will find us."

"Well, if we get married I'll change my last name anyway. I could change my first name, too."

"You are amazing, baby." Georgi is in heaven. He can't believe how great his life is about to become.

"Where are we going to go? What do you want to do?"

"First, we'll sell both cars and buy another one. That way it'll be harder to trace our movements. You know how I like those drive-in movie theaters. Maybe we can get jobs, save money and buy one for us to run ourselves after a while."

"That's a great idea. I'd love to do that with you. I love you. Just think of all the fun we'll have."

They start kissing and making love. They are wild and loud. Finally, they fall into a peaceful sleep only two people completely in love and about to be completely free can share.

Chapter 30
Trying to Get out of Dodge or Russia

Tim, Mark and Ken are sitting in their dimly lit apartment. Not much is being said. They share a bottle of vodka as Ken picks up what looks to be a big loaf of rye bread. He takes out a big knife and can barely cut it, because the crust is as hard as granite.

Tim shakes his head. "I can't believe I waited in line for three hours to get this. I'll be happy to get home and have some day old-doughnuts."

Mark grabs some bread and a hunk of moldy cheese. "Is Russian cheese supposed to be this color and texture?"

Tim guffaws. "The woman in front of me in line cried when she got hers, she was so happy."

Ken takes a gulp of vodka. The bottle glugs like he's drinking a soda. Mark's eyes almost pop out of his head. He laughs. "Man, we've got to get Ken back to the States. He's starting to drink vodka like a Ruski."

They all snicker, drink and try to eat. The door creaks and Sol enters. He is disheveled, haggard and sweating. The frivolity halts immediately. Everyone's face drops. The room is silent as Sol picks up a chair. He turns it around and sits down.

Sol clears his throat. "We did much more than we planned, boys. I've got some contacts. People are starting to lose their minds, and it's going to get worse."

Tim is usually the cool one, but not this time. "Whoa!?"

Mark is freaking out. He starts speaking Russian.

Sol chimes in. "Calm down, Mark."

"Calm down? Right. We're public enemy #1. Hell, Benedict Arnold was a Boy Scout compared to us. I thought the time delay would give us time to get out of here."

Ken shakes his head. "Fuck the Russians. What will our people do to us to keep us quiet?"

Sol smiles. "Mark, you're the poker player."

"Are you thinking what I'm thinking?"

Tim grabs the bottle of vodka and takes two huge gulps. Those two gulps empty almost a third of the bottle. He wipes his dripping mouth with his sleeve. "Let me get this straight. The formula reacts sooner in big quantities? This will happen before we're supposed to leave? We need to get out of the country. If we don't get caught by the KGB, you want us to keep some to blackmail the CIA and the POTUS as 'protection'? You are one crazy bastard."

Sol roars. "I think you've got it."

Ken grabs the vodka and tries to empty it. "That sounds doable. Hell, a year ago, 'Nyet' was all the Russian I knew."

Mark opens a new bottle. "So, we have to split up and not use our original exit strategy."

Sol nods. "You've got it. Luckily I know a couple of black-market guys."

Tim shakes his head. "I was wondering why they picked all single guys for this."

Sol's eyes twinkle. "Now it's going to bite them on their asses. That weasel Stein is going to be chum for the big boys. But if we say anything, it'll be our own asses, you know."

Mark puts the vodka down. "Can we have new pictures for the new passports?"

Sol nods. "I'll get a cable to him telling him we're simply moving up the exit plan."

"Great! Remember they brought me along to do costumes and make-up. I bet they never thought we'd need disguises," Mark says.

Ken drinks some more. "Who the hell thought that fucking with all of Russia's vodka all at once would be a good idea? And they haven't completed testing yet. They just threw us in here to see what would happen."

Sol snickers. "Maybe it was either this or nuke them."

Tim drinks some more. "This is a lot meaner, but what fools thought they would get away with it? They were going to blame us while we were in country."

"We have to leave separately. Then meet someplace they'd never think to look," Sol says soberly.

Ken looks puzzled. "It can't be England, France or Germany."

Mark thinks for a second, "Monaco is too expensive. How about going to Luxenstein?"

Sol nods. "Perfect. They have a crazy prince, there. They call him the Pied Piper of Panties."

Tim snorts so hard that he almost pukes. "That's got to be our place."

Sol nods. "Maybe we can get some of his castoffs."

"Sounds like a plan and he is my brand-new hero," Ken says.

Chapter 31
Happy Days in DC

Since ignorance is bliss, this is becoming one of the happiest months America's senior power structure has seen in decades. On the surface, things couldn't be going better. The only hiccup is that the incursion team hasn't returned to the U.S. Where are they? Who will believe them anyway? Hell, the economy is going well. Americans are fat and happy and not asking why.

The Soviets have been quiet for several months. The saber-rattling, expansionist threats and crackdowns on dissidents have stopped. To some, it is almost too quiet. Whatever is going on is building a deep sense of security on the Potomac. Boy, these guys were easy.

The sense of wellbeing and having the world on a string is permeating the WH as the POTUS is having a meeting in the Oval Office. It's a small group this morning. The President is sitting behind his desk with the CIA Director Morris, the Secretary of State, and General Hayden on the couch.

Morris' chest is puffed out and his voice is stronger than ever. "Mr. President, it appears our initiative in Russia is working out much better than we had hoped. Our team started in Moscow and then fanned out across the satellite states before exiting the U.S.S.R."

President Thomas looks pleased. "Nobody was caught or detained?"

Hayden is making paper airplanes and throwing them around the room, trying to hit one with another. It looks like he is having a war of his own.

"Our onsite assets throughout the U.S.S.R. are reporting widespread instances of fights at plants, soccer games and schools. There has been a growing number of people calling in sick, complaining of nausea and the shakes."

The general picks up his airplanes, wads them up, and throws them at Morris. There's a knock at the door. A secretary comes in with a pot of coffee and hands everyone packs of cigarettes. As she leaves, they light up, sigh contentedly, and take sips of coffee. They are all smiling.

General Hayden glares at Morris. "Your pansy vodka attack makes them suffer. That's good. Do you know what will make them suffer more?"

The Secretary of State shakes his head as he exhales a huge hit off his cancer stick. "We know, General, a bomb would make them hurt more, but they'd bomb us right back. Right now, we're punching them every day and they don't realize it."

The President nods his head. "That's great news, Director! How much longer before we have them where we want them?"

"I'd say in a month there will be widespread chaos. It will probably hit in the remote areas first, as they don't have much inventory or ability to get replacement product."

The Secretary of State cackles so hard he coughs up years of smoking. "That's just cruel. Ruskis living in bumfuck nowhere and they can't even get drunk."

"Good." President Thomas smiles broadly.

"Mr. President, we may have hit a major snag."

"What's that?" President Thomas' smile leaves his faith.

They light new cigarettes and blow out their puff of smoke in unison. The room is enveloped in smoke.

"It seems Madibu has just started producing vodka in massive quantities."

Hayden jumps to his feet indignantly. "Those damn hippies in California. Ain't beautiful women and sun all year enough for those bastards in Malibu? I'll get them for you, Mr. President. That's treason!"

Morris glares at Hayden. "You idiot! Madibu is an island off Africa – not Malibu, California."

"Let's sink the damn island. Nobody will miss it. How many people know it exists, anyway?"

"Wait a second, Mr. President, we just funded their economic development plan and helped rebuild their airport... They owe us big-time."

Director Morris shakes his head. "It seems like the Soviets sent a team to turn their outdated soda plants into distilleries at the same time we were rebuilding the airport. Plus, the commies were dredging them a new deep-water port. That was going on while we were rehabbing their airport and hotels. It was right under our goddamned noses."

The President blows smoke in Hayden's face and shrugs. "Looks like we got played. Didn't their president go to Harvard?"

Morris jumps in. "Yes sir, it seems like we taught him how to take advantage of us."

Hayden throws a paper airplane. "Before I sink the island, I'll send the Green Berets to shoot his ass. That'll teach him to fuck with America."

"We could drive up the price if the Soviets try to buy it. We could convince our people that Madibu vodka is an aphrodisiac," Stein interjects.

"Good idea, whoever the fuck you are. Is he on the list?" the President says, not remembering Stein or why he is there.

Morris thinks for a minute. "Yes, we could strain their hard currency and make life difficult for them to fund anything else. This could work out extremely well for us."

The President crumples up his cigarette pack, and so does Hayden. The Secretary of State reaches into his pocket, brings out a new pack, opens it and offers everybody a smoke.

Morris shakes his head, "You know, prices on butts have skyrocketed in the past couple of weeks. I've never seen anything like it."

Hayden takes a drag. "And the 7-11 by my house ran out completely over the weekend. I've never seen that happen. But I can be tough. I'll find 'em or start some other habit."

At that moment, there is a knock at the door. The Secretary of Agriculture comes into the Oval Office. There is sweat on his forehead and his hands are shaking.

Morris barks at him. "Do you know why the hell has the price of cigarettes been going up so much?"

"That's why I came to the meeting, Director." He hands out a report.

"Well, what's the problem?" President Thomas demands.

"Mr. President, there is a strange virus infecting the crops in North Carolina and Virginia with smaller infestations in Georgia, Kentucky, and Tennessee. It seems to be getting worse every day. We have reason to believe that it's in the water too."

"Why haven't I heard of this?" President Thomas is now barking.

"Mr. President, we've kept it hush-hush until we got more data. We wanted to be sure and not panic the public. I've got scientists trying to develop an antidote."

"Are you even close?" Thomas' fingers are tapping on his desk.

"It's been so widespread and so damaging that it's almost like our lands were poisoned. Hundreds of farms were affected at the same time. We suspect foul play. This many all at once could be the result of covert foreign activity."

Everyone gasps and reaches for another cigarette. They glare at the other.

The Secretary of State shakes his head. "Morris, how could you let people infiltrate our country and do this? Is it the Soviets?"

"How do we know it's them or anyone else? The CIA isn't allowed to operate in the U.S. It's not our fault... asshole."

Hayden howls. "See, we are being pansy attacked. This is frickin' rich."

They all put their butts out, think for a minute, and reach for the pack that was on the President's desk. It's empty. Everyone stands up and surrounds the Secretary of Agriculture. They are glaring at him. He starts sweating, adjusting his collar.

Morris bumps him. "Where are you hiding your cigarettes?"

"I don't have any."

"Your President is asking you to fork over your cigarettes."

Hayden throws the Secretary of Agriculture onto the desk. He starts ripping at his pockets. "We can do it the easy way or the hard way."

"General, two years ago, my doctor made me quit smoking. My wife works for him. I had no choice."

"Pansy, I bet he smokes," Hayden belches.

The President is pale and his eyes are drooping. "You've got to work on the antidote. We can't let this get out of hand. Our nation is begging you... begging you. You must succeed, and the sooner, the better."

The Secretary of State taps the desk with his hands. "Shit, we'll have to set an example. We'll all probably gain thirty pounds. "

"You need to quadruple your staff to solve this. Keep everything secret, it's a need-to-know situation. This news never leaves the White House. It is now classified Top Secret. We're the only ones who need to know."

The Secretary of Agriculture is almost running for the door as he turns and says, "Yes, Mr. President. All our resources will be used. We will not fail you."

As the President flops back down behind his desk, everyone moves chairs right in front of him. He breaks a pencil. Hayden pretends he is smoking his pen and bites the cap off. Ink splatters on his face and uniform. Everyone guffaws.

"Next time, I might bite your neck off, Morris. Watch it, you think-tank wuss."

The President leans back in his chair. "There's going to be panic in the streets as soon as the public finds out. No leaks. It'll be considered treason if any of you spills the beans."

Hayden snaps to attention. "Maybe we should legalize mary-ju-auna. You can smoke that and there's plenty available. People will forget they don't have Marlboros."

The Secretary of State mocks Hayden. "Are you sure you haven't started smoking it already?" He furrows his brow. "You know, I seem to remember a small story about a woman who somehow nearly cornered the market on tobacco futures. She was supposed to be some foreign supermodel or something."

The President's voice rises. "Find her. We'll pay whatever she wants."

Morris looks serious. "Was she a Soviet spy?"

"No, I heard she was from central Europe, which is known for beautiful women. They said she had great legs and fabulous boobs. She wasn't, um, exactly opposed to using her body to snag the contracts."

Morris smiles. "Wouldn't you use your boobs to make money if you could?"

"From Sweden?" the President asks.

"That's not it," Stein says. "Doesn't sound right."

Hayden jumps up. "How about Uganda?"

Morris slaps Hayden. "Uganda is in Africa. All the politicians are black. I hear she has light brown hair and blue eyes. Maybe she was from Belgium?

"No. Hold on. Luxenstein." Mitchell nods.

Morris is puzzled. "Where did she get that kind of money? Didn't their idiot playboy prince lose the entire national treasury in Vegas and Monte Carlo?"

The Secretary of State puts his head in his hands. "We gave about 50% of what they needed to buy the futures as a bribe to get their vote on the Security Council. That crazy prince played us."

The President leans forward. "I thought it was for schools, roads and a hospital. That bastard scammed us. Let's get him to sell us our cigarettes."

"I'll blow them back all the way to the Middle Ages. Small country, one well-placed bomb could do the trick."

The Secretary of State is aghast. "You idiot, how the hell would that help us? The whole world would hate us."

"They wouldn't be a threat. You should have listened to me when I told you to nuke the Ruskis." Hayden looks at Mitchell with derision.

Morris cackles loudly. "I bet they got the other 50% from the Soviets to buy their vote. Their prince is a gambler. He's just ballsy enough to use our money as blackmail against Moscow."

The Secretary of State stands up. "We'll simply try to buy them back at a profit. The prince always needs money."

Morris snickers. "If you were called the Pied Piper of Panties, you'd always need money, too."

The President shakes his head. "The Soviets will bid us up. This is going to be expensive. Damn, I miss the old days when we'd lob a bomb or two and that would be that."

"I'll try to outbid them, Mr. President," Mitchell promises.

Hayden takes his gun from his holster and puts the barrel on the Secretary's forehead. "You'll do better than try, bucko."

Everyone gasps. "I'll do better than try. Anyone sandbagging a cigarette?"

They all turn their pockets inside out to show they have none. They are almost ripping their pockets off their shirts and jackets. No one finds a single butt. Hayden gets on his knees to look under a table. His eyes tear up.

Damn, this is getting bad.

Chapter 32
Moscow Madness

As we start to see what happened in the U.S.S.R. and U.S., you may ask, if this really happened, how come no one has heard about it before? Well, Area 51 has been in existence for over half a century and what do we know? Did you think *Men In Black's* neutralizer was fictitious?

It is another gray day in Moscow. The clouds couldn't be more than a couple of thousand feet off the ground. The sun never seems to come out while the constant mixture of snow and freezing rain makes it feel even worse. This seems to be the only weather that exists. Day after day, this mess shrouds the ancient buildings in the capitol of socialism. One can argue that for thousands of years Russians/Soviets have been among the world's most pessimistic people. The weather contributes, in a big way, to their disposition. How could it not?

The drab exteriors of massive office buildings and rows of apartment complexes meld together. The people may wear parkas or old cloth coats, as gray as the rest of their environment. Due to ever-present shortages, people wear mismatched clothing, because that is all that is ever available.

Somehow, this winter is different from the past sixty-plus years of communism. It's almost as if the Soviets live American country music themes like hating their jobs and their wives are sleeping with their daddies. The aura is more ominous. There is an omnipresent tension and feeling of doom. Somehow, they are trying to accept it as their lot in life as they have for centuries, whether under the czars or under the comrades.

The huge velvet curtains in the Kremlin meeting room are drawn. The interior lights are flickering. Foreign Minister Davinko, Field Marshal Petrov and Prime Minister Boski are sitting at the seemingly never-ending table. Their fingers are playing a cacophony of notes on the table as their toes tap to another beat. Silent glares are mixed in with turning of their heads to see what else is going on in the room.

Nitvik stealthily enters the conference room. First, he puts his head inside the door. Suddenly, he pulls back. He gets about half of his body into the room and stops, plunges all the way inside, slams and locks the massive door behind him. He puts two briefcases on the table. Then, he sprints over to the drapes. He goes behind them. We can see his hands rubbing all over them. He jumps to explore more. After a couple of moments, he emerges.

He looks around the room. "Did anyone follow me? I know for sure someone did. Who was it?"

Davinko taps his fingers angrily. "Even more paranoid than usual, Comrade?"

Boski looks sternly at every person in the room. "How are things going in the United States?"

Nitvik smiles proudly, "I see reports of tobacco crops failing and puzzling shortages of cigarettes in many places. It looks like our plan is succeeding beyond our wildest dreams."

Boski beams. "Excellent. Comrade Petrov, please fetch some vodka for our celebration."

Petrov goes to a cabinet and brings back three bottles. He opens one and empties it pouring one round. Everyone is smiling.

Boski stands. "Success and Mother Russia."

All join with him. "To success and Mother Russia!"

Each takes a big gulp of vodka and immediately spits it out. Davinko spits his in Nitvik's face. Nitvik tries to lick it up.

Boski is sputtering. "Field Marshal, what the fuck vodka is this? It is worse than that undrinkable American swill."

"It's the same as we've been drinking for years. We only get the best. It's made at the Moscow distillery in special vats like it always has been."

Nitvik speaks. "The same thing happened to me last night at home. It was so bad that I spat it on my dog. When he tasted it, he bit my arm!"

Petrov wipes his mouth. "I'm sure that's why he bit you."

Everyone snorts. But they are still trying to get the terrible taste out of their mouths.

Boski's eyes narrow. "Davinko, is this just a bad batch, or is something more sinister going on?"

"Yes, Comrade Premier. I will have an answer for you tomorrow."

Boski smiles. "Do that. If our project works, do the Americans have any options to buy tobacco?"

Davinko opens a pad. "It seems a woman from Luxenstein has cornered the market on tobacco futures and they are now building cigarette plants all over their country."

Petrov shakes his head. "I wish to hell they were producing vodka."

Everyone chuckles.

Boski leans back in his chair. "How the hell did this happen?"

Nitvik gets on his hands and knees to check under the table for listening devices. Then he leaves the room. "Let's kill her and all of her family for the glory of the Soviet Union."

Davinko almost stutters. "Comrade Premier, it may be partially our fault."

"What?" Boski demands to know.

"We gave them over a billion U.S. dollars as a bribe, uh, incentive, to vote our way on the Security Council. We spoke of this and thought it to be a good idea. It seems their Prince Claude used the money for this reason rather than for the building projects he'd told us about."

Petrov slams the table. "You idiot! Comrade Premier, I can bomb Luxenstein within twenty-four hours and have an invasion from the south and the east rolling in three days. It will all be ours."

Davinko starts choking Petrov. "You idiot. We'd have to invade West Germany and Belgium to get there. You'd be starting another World War, you fool!"

Boski puts his hand on Petrov's shoulder. "Comrades, calm down. Let us pay more for the cigarettes than the Americans. The Prince appreciates profits and he will owe us more than ever."

Davinko reflects for a moment. "If they scammed us, they probably scammed the U.S., too. The imperialists will try the same thing."

"We are Russians," Petrov says hotly. "We held out for three years against Hitler. We can beat this pissant and the Americans."

"Yes, we are stronger," Boski says with pride and defiance.

Nitvik blasts back into the room. He locks the door behind him, picks up two chairs and puts them against the bottom of the curtains so they won't move. He looks like he is in a horror movie. His hair is standing on end and his eyes are bulging out of their sockets.

"Comrades, I have terrible news."

Everyone gasps. They open the second bottle of vodka, pour it, take gulps and spit out the vile liquid. They gag. Petrov runs to the trash can and vomits. He wipes his face with his uniform arm, then smells it.

Boski stands. "Tell us."

"With the help of despicable unpatriotic dissidents, American operatives have embedded a disgraceful product into our vodka distilleries that create this awful taste and eliminate all alcoholic content of our beloved nectar. What's worse is, we don't know how to stop it."

Petrov pounds the table. "This means war!!!! Our nukes will be in the air in ninety minutes."

Davinko grabs him. "Shut up, you moron!"

Boski is beside himself. "This can't be, Davinko. Nitvik, what do you suggest we do?"

Nitvik smiles slyly. "We turn all our farms into distilleries. Fuck the American act of war!"

Davinko is shaking. "That will take years, you moron. We need something *now*."

Boski looks them all in the eyes. "Who produces enough vodka for us to use as a bridge? We must get as much as we can to pacify the people."

The others gasp and sigh. Davinko speaks first, "That will show unacceptable weakness. We cannot lower ourselves to ever showing such weakness."

Petrov pounds the table. "No one can make vodka like Russians. The people won't accept it. It's more beloved than mother's milk."

A smile crosses Davinko's face. "Wait a second, we just built several vodka distilleries in Africa. It will taste just like ours. They have Soviet vats and an eighteenth-century formula." He sighs longingly.

Nitvik snarls. "Finally, that rat bastard Fidel did something right in Angola."

Davinko makes a face. "Not Fidel. We sent people to Madibu. They are producing real Russian vodka. Vats and vats and vats of it. We will buy it all. They are making millions of liters every day. The insurrection can be avoided."

Boski shakes his head. "Didn't we get intelligence that the Americans were there at the same time we were doing that?"

"Yes, but they have no idea about the capacity. We can blindside them."

"Since they're the ones who did this to our plants, they are sure to bid up the prices and try to bankrupt us."

Petrov pounds the table again and harder. "Then I will sink the island of ingrates. It will only take a couple of days."

Davinko is dumbfounded. "Then how the fuck will we get our vodka?"

"Shit!" Petrov frowns and sinks back into his seat.

"Davinko, please call the leader of Madibu and bid 300% of whatever price he is asking. Then remind him why he is going to be so rich."

"Yes, Comrade Premier. I will execute your orders."

"Petrov, Nitvik quietly bring the ancient vodka of the czars to the Kremlin. We are going to need it. No one can know it exists. This is super top secret. It doesn't leave this room."

The Russians are on their way to save the socialist dream. They will get their wondrous vodka and stick it to the American imperialist pigs at the same time. Out of what could have been the worst few months since Stalingrad could come unimaginable glory... Or not.

Chapter 33
Two Old Friends Talk

Every day seems to be brighter and more hopeful than the day before in Luxenstein. The mountains reflect the never-ending sunlight. The valleys are filled with flowers, calm cows, and happy people. If you walk down the streets, people stop and chat. They sit in cafes basking in their fairy-tale lives in magnificent ignorance. They have no idea how this golden age was begun and don't care. In a world where governments are routinely overthrown and people mistrust everything their regimes do, the people of Luxenstein love the royal family and revel in their idiosyncrasies and quirkiness. It has seemingly always been this way.

Prince Claude is riding in his normal place in the back of an open Rolls Royce. He and Paleau are checking out the villas, manors and other production facilities throughout their nation. The old friends smile as they peruse the countryside.

"How is the production ramping up, my friend?"

"We are well ahead of our initial goals. Things couldn't be going better, Your Highness."

Prince Claude opens an envelope and reads two cables. He rereads them. Then looks at them again. For the first-time, Prince Claude seems truly befuddled.

"Paleau, would you mind pulling over for a moment? I would like your input on these cables. They make no sense to me whatsoever."

Paleau stops the car. "What is this? Why are Russians and Americans begging to buy our vodka? Are you doing something crazy again without telling me? Please, don't do that. Everything is going so well. Don't mess it up."

"Don't worry, Jacques. I'm way over my head with our tobacco project. We couldn't find enough people to do anything else right now. I'm crazy, not stupid. Why would the Russians, of all people, want to buy vodka? They make it by the trainload. This is very strange."

"I have no idea. Why would the American State Department be interested in buying vodka? Do Americans like vodka that much?"

As they sit and ponder this curious event, the car phone rings and Paleau picks it up. "May I help you? One moment please, Your Highness, President Mbangu from Madibu is calling. Would you like to speak with him?"

"Of course; he's a friend of mine." Claude's smile covers his whole face as he grabs the phone from Paleau.

The prince is so excited he nearly pulls the cord out of the box. "My old friend, Mbangu. How long has it been?"

"Much too long. It must be close to fifteen years," says Mbangu.

"Are you going to our twentieth reunion at Harvard? Is that why you're calling?"

"I'll try, but my life is pretty hectic these days. Madibu is having an historic economic expansion."

"It couldn't happen to a more deserving person. Luxenstein is experiencing the same. This is great. What can I help you with?"

"It seems like I have received cables that should have been sent to you. They involve tobacco, and I've been reading reports about your booming tobacco products industry."

"That's curious. Very curious indeed. Have you by any chance recently built giant vodka distilleries?"

"Yes, we have become a resort destination and will be a major port for cruise ships. We turned our out-of-date soda plants into state-of-the-art vodka distilleries. Why do you ask?"

"I just received cables wanting to buy large quantities of vodka. It seems that they were meant for you."

"Are yours from the Americans and Soviets, offering astronomical prices?"

"Yes, they say they will pay anything for the vodka. The offers are indeed astronomical."

"They are saying the same thing about your tobacco. Luxenstein doesn't grow tobacco. Claude, my dear friend, what on earth did you do this time?" Mbangu couldn't stop himself from laughing.

"Between old friends, I had some, uh, budget problems," Claude says quietly.

"Was it a woman, or a casino this time?" Mbangu giggles knowingly.

"How about some casinos, then some women? By the way, how is your lovely wife?"

"She is as beautiful and wonderful as ever. So, tell me, what did you do?" His laughter grows.

"We are on the Security Council for the next two years."

Mbangu pauses and chuckles. "After you sold your vote to both superpowers, what else did you do?" Mbangu truly knows his friend.

The two old friends share a laugh. Mbangu's gets louder. Then, Claude's grows louder.

"Me? You think I'd ever think of doing such a thing as selling my votes? I'm terribly insulted," he says with a smile.

"Claude, you are a scoundrel through and through... and I love you for it." He laughs and laughs.

"It wasn't all me. I did it with the help of a beautiful woman. We bought and leveraged tobacco futures from the U.S. and countries around the world. It was my money and her wisdom mixed with using her, um, assets, um, very wisely."

"A womanizer and a gambler. You will never change."

"I hope not. Whatever is going on is putting us both in an excellent position. They don't know that we know."

"Nor should they. After all, I am only a backward African and, what do they call you?"

"That's not fair... the Pied Piper of Panties."

They both chuckle.

"We must keep in touch," Mbangu says seriously. "Let's set up a secure line. No telling who might be listening to us." Mbangu shows his rationality again.

"That's an excellent idea. It's too bad that a playboy and a poor African were taught so well at Harvard. We shall have a great story to tell."

"Not until many years from now. Speaking for myself, I'd like to be around for a few more years to enjoy all of this."

Claude chuckles. "You're right. It's one thing to rob them blind in private. They can live with that. If we embarrass them in public, we could be in big trouble. Maybe we should have a decoy line just for them to listen in on."

"Exactly. Do you have a secure place to keep copies of all of the documents as insurance?"

"Yes, and you be sure to do the same. Let's chat again in a few days."

Claude gives Paleau the phone to hang up, a big smile on his face. Paleau looks at Claude quizzically. Claude pauses. Paleau sneers.

"You went to Harvard with Mbangu?" Paleau has learned something he didn't know, but that's not what he wanted to know.

"Yes. Do you want to know what's happening?" He is chuckling wickedly.

"You enjoy torturing me, aren't you?"

"*Mais oui*, it appears we are going to be successful beyond our wildest dreams!"

"Why?"

"Neither of us is entirely certain, but somehow the Americans and the Soviets are attacking the other's vices and we just happen to have precisely the products they need. And, of course, they're willing to pay any price for them."

"Don't push them too far. Listen to your friend. Don't upset the superpowers. We are just a tiny nation. We don't need much."

"When will we ever have such a chance again?"

"This isn't a hot streak in Monte Carlo."

"No, no, it's much bigger than that."

"And, much more dangerous."

"Don't worry, my friend. This is going to be glorious. It will make up for all the headaches I've caused you over all these years. You may even grow your hair back when we're done." The Prince's face is glowing.

Paleau nods and smiles, knowing this time is different. The gods are living in Luxenstein and smiling on every citizen. He looks to the mountains and crosses himself.

Chapter 34
America Loses Its Mind

It has been only two months since the Soviet plan had begun working. At first, it is only a trickle of worry about a temporary lessening availability of cigarettes. Those who dare to say something serious is going on are thought to be crazy. As the rumors of shortages and crop problems grow, panic becomes widespread. People are taking their kids to shooting ranges due to the rise in home invasions.

There have been countless robberies of distribution centers. RJ Reynolds, Phillip Morris and American Tobacco now have 24/7 guards armed with machine guns at their plants. Gun turrets are on top of the executive building, as there have been constant death threats. Shipping companies have had to turn tankers around in the middle of the Atlantic and Pacific if their cargos included containers of cigarettes. Some are taking containers out of shipping rotation if they have a tiny tobacco residue smell, not wanting to put their staff at risk.

The consumption of beer, wine, pot, booze and prescription drugs has gone through the roof. People have taken to rolling grass from their lawns in bamboo pot papers. If there's even a rumor that you can smoke it, you can name a price for sale. Some have transitioned from smoker to non-smoker without many issues. Millions of others are virtual zombies. The country is quickly descending into deep chaos.

In Iowa, a group of senior citizens is at the state fair when one blue-haired granny stops dead in her tracks. "I smell someone smoking."

"Where?"

"Over there, that young man with the cap."

The three drop their canes. Two push away their walkers and miraculously start sprinting towards this twentyish young man. Innocent bystanders run away, seeing multiple grandmas going on an uncontrollable rampage.

"Give it up, kid. We know you have cigarettes."

They don't give the young man a chance to turn around. They pummel him to the ground and strip him naked, looking for one half-smoked cancer stick. A single, tiny butt would make them happy.

Alas, he has none, but that doesn't stop one old lady from kicking him in the nuts before leaving, "It's not nice to tease the elderly, sonny."

***

Meanwhile, a small crowd waiting outside of a DC hotel is hoping that the government meeting inside will lead to a solution. A TV crew has its lights on and the newscaster is beginning her story. They have taken the precaution of having armed guards.

"Good evening, today is the ninth consecutive day that cigarettes have been all but unavailable through legal channels here in the Washington area. The same is happening across the nation. Tension and panic are spreading like the black plague in Europe or the flu if the 1910s. We don't know how much longer this will go on. Here is Secretary of Defense, General Hayden. General, do you have any news?"

The general shoves a couple of people out of his path. "What kind of half-assed pansy question is that? Give me a god-damned cigarette or I'll shove that mic right up your ass."

Hayden lunges at the reporter. A security guard pushes him off. The reporter keeps talking to the camera but her voice is breaking.

"The entire country is on edge. We need to know more from our leaders. What are you doing to get some cigarettes for the public?"

The general's eyes glaze over. He snaps to attention as he pulls his side arm from its holster. He shoots three shots into the air. "I've had enough of the whiney bitches begging me to do something. I smoked three packs a day for fifty years. I haven't had a drag in a week. It's time for me to get even with all of you who have been clawing at me."

The reporter motions to the cameraman to cut. The cameraman reaches into his pocket and pulls out a flask. He's chugging the booze and smiling narrowly. His hands are shaking so much that he spills liquor on the camera as he passes the flask to the reporter.

Hayden points his gun at the reporter. "Aren't you forgetting something?"

"You want some?" she asks.

"You bet. Too bad the damn Ruskis can't see us drinking this beautiful booze. They'd storm the Kremlin."

Hayden finishes the flask and throws it on the ground before storming off. He turns around, aims and shoots. He hoots with pride when he sees the flask explode.

This is virtually the only story being covered by national networks and local newscasts. With less than half of the public being smokers, the rest are mesmerized and frightened by how crazy their neighbors are acting. If you saw the attack of the Iowa grannies on Monday, by Thursday, there were ten more that were worse. The media adage, "If it bleeds, it leads," is how almost every news station organizes their shows during the cigarette shortage.

Stories pop up on all media.

***

Raul Gomez has been making a name for himself on TV in Amarillo but is taking his act on the road, hoping to make the big time. He is in a seedy part of Dallas trying to find a story. Before starting, he studies himself in the mirror and approves of what he sees. He practices his sexiest grin.

As he walks in the dark, a man bumps into him. They both are startled but say nothing. The game of checking the other out is progressing. Gomez has no idea what he's doing. It's more likely that he gets killed than finds a story.

Gomez has a wire and a button camera on his shirt as he winds his way through alleys and seemingly empty streets. He is about as subtle as a sledgehammer.

"This is Raul Gomez. There is a bustling, dangerous black market in cigarettes. It's almost barbaric. Bugsy Siegel and Lucky Luciano were choir boys compared to some of these gangs. I'm hoping to meet a myth called Nate Newport – and buy some cigarettes."

He keeps going. He turns a corner and is dragged into a doorway. The thug pats him down. "What the fuck are you doin' here?"

"I'm looking for Nate Newport. Frenchy said if I came around here he'd find me."

"What does Frenchy look like?"

"He's Creole and hit every branch of the ugly tree. Even his momma thinks the dog is cuter."

"OK, put this hood on your head and come with me."

Raul is so vain that he tries to get the hood to sit correctly. The man leads Raul in circles and through a couple of buildings. Finally, they stop in a closed dry cleaning plant that has no windows. Two lights are behind Nate Newport sitting behind a table, which makes seeing him very difficult. Three armed men are in the room. They are huge and cock their guns as Gomez enters. This is a fortress.

The hood is pulled off Gomez's head. He shakes his head and looks around the room. The bright light makes everything look blurry.

Nate pounds the table. "Look here. Nothing else matters. You wanted to see me?"

"I wanted to see Nate Newport."

"That's me."

"You're white."

"Just because I'm called Nate Newport, I have to be black? Put the mother-fucking hood back on him. Get his prissy ass out of here"

"I'm sorry, man. I *really* need to score. How much?"

"First rule, no smoking until we drop you off. We don't want anyone doing a Hansel and Gretel on us. If you take a cigarette out to suck on, our man will beat you and take back whatever you bought. Got it?"

"Got it. No problem." Gomez is fidgeting with his coat, and sweat is beading up on his brow.

"Low tars are $6 each, $100 a pack, $850 a carton. Marlboros are $10, $175, $1500 a carton."

"I'll take three packs of low tar."

Raul hands the money to the guy who led him there. One of the armed goons hands Gomez three packs of cigarettes. He puts the cigarettes in Gomez's inside pocket to hide them.

"Thanks, how do I get more?"

"If you have money, you can come back again. If you tell anyone, you're dead. Got that?"

"Got it."

They put the hood back on Raul's head. One of the goons opens the door to let the two of them out to the alleyway. They take him out a different door than the one they brought him in. The route they start on feels different.

"Thanks. Think you could take the hood off?"

"Not yet."

They take about five steps before a crowd appears with all sorts of people – some in suits, a couple of hippies and some old people. They storm over Nate's lookout and throw him to the ground.

Two people push Raul to the ground and rip through his clothes to find the cigarettes. His hood comes off. A man ties Raul's hands together.

"He's got three packs!" A middle-aged man screams. He takes one and passes the pack around. People start lighting up, exhaling smoke, smiling and crying. This lasts until the smokes are gone.

Raul is groggy as he frees his hands. "How did you know I had cigarettes? How did you know where I was?"

A man takes a big drag off his cigarette. "Remember when I bumped into you?"

"That was you?"

"Yep, I work for the FBI. I put a bug in your pocket. We followed you. You are such a sucker. It's amazing you've lived this long."

People's cigarettes start going out. Two little old ladies are sitting on the lookout. One shakes her cane at him. "OK, sonny, take us to Nate Newport."

"He'll shoot you."

"He won't dare shoot three little old ladies."

Raul stands up. "He's got three goons with him. They very well might."

A huge man puts his arm around Raul. "I think my twin brother and I can hold our own."

The crowd starts chanting, "We need cigarettes! We need cigarettes! And we need them now!"

The giant man puts his arm around the lookout's shoulder. "You were just about to take us to Nate's hideout, weren't you?"

The lookout's voice quivers. "I'll tell you where to go but if I take you, I'm dead."

"Just to make sure you're not fibbing my cousin will stay right here with you. Okay?"

His cousin is a six-foot tall, three hundred-pound woman with tattoos and bulging arm muscles. The lookout gasps. She smiles a toothless smile and puts one of those massive arms around his shoulder.

The group gets very quiet during their approach to Nate's office. The two little old ladies knock on the door. "Hello, is anyone in there?"

One of the goons opens a slit. "What's up, grandma?"

"My friend and I are lost and need to use the restroom."

"I'm sorry, ma'am, we don't have a bathroom."

The other little old lady raps on the door. "Would you lie to your own grandma like that?"

The goon opens the door. All the cigarettes are covered and the lights are on. Nate Newport stands up. "I'm sorry for my assistant's behavior, ladies, the bathroom is the door over there."

The second old lady enters. Then the twins kick open the door and the mob enters. Five or six people grab Nate Newport and sit him down behind his desk. They see his safe but keep looking around. One person throws off the towel covering boxes of cases of cigarettes. Everyone stops and gasps. It's like they have found the leprechaun's pot of gold.

Seeing that turns the wild mob into civilized human beings, as if just beholding the stash had become a religious experience. One of the larger people passes out cartons. A couple people are crying. They start lighting up and hugging.

A twentyish girl is laughing. "Hey, look, the great Nate Newport is Mr. Givens, the eighth-grade health teacher. He taught us about VD."

One of the giant twins blurts, "I bet he never got laid without paying until he became a gangster."

One of the old ladies kisses Nate on the cheek. "Thanks, sweetie, you made an old lady very happy tonight."

***

The next morning several of these stories make their way onto the *Today Show* and other morning news programs around the country. The FBI guy sends his video to every network. Raul Gomez is now a national laughingstock. The grannies are getting hundreds of wedding proposals.

This is a nice diversion, but most of the country is still smokeless. Fear and near chaos are growing by the minute. Could a revolution be far behind?

This is not lost on the White House, where the normal 10 a.m. meeting is moved up to 7 a.m. The senior staff is waiting for President Thomas in the Cabinet Room. Hayden is pacing and spinning a hand gun on his finger. CIA Director Morris is looking out the window and taking apart every phone looking for bugs. The Secretary of State is zoning out and pretending he is smoking a cigarette.

The door opens and President Thomas enters. Everyone stands up. He motions for them to sit down. He sits across from them. For a few moments, everybody is silent. The President starts, "Did you see that story about the gangster known as Nate Newport?"

Morris crows. "Gangster my eye, he's a junior high school health teacher whose brother-in-law stole some cigarettes in Mexico and smuggled them into the U.S. with a homemade sub."

Hayden snickers. "I liked the pictures of grandma stepping on Nate's head and blowing smoke in his face. What a wuss! Does he have any more that weren't taken?"

The Secretary of State speaks up. "This is spreading across the country. It's getting worse by the hour, Mr. President. We need to act before they storm the White House."

Hayden shoots his gun into the air. Everyone ducks for cover. "Let's blast those commie bastards off the face of the Earth."

"Calm down, Hayden," the President says. He takes Hayden's gun.

Morris smiles broadly. "The commies are falling apart. Their top two newscasters had a hissy fit in prime time last night. Babushkas are attacking cops and soldiers trying to find vodka. I love it. They won't last more than a couple of weeks. We've got them right where we want them."

The Secretary of State looks amused. "The great Russian resolve is weakening. We've got to figure a way to tough it out until they totally fall apart."

Hayden points his finger like a gun. "Just a few bombs will make them quit like little girls."

"That's what the Germans thought in WWII. There must be another way. Hell, we made it through Valley Forge with no food or heat," the President reminds them.

Hayden smiles and jumps on the table. "And Little Big Horn."

The Secretary of State is incredulous. "Hey dumbass, we lost that one."

The President sits up straight. "Americans are tough. We can win. What if we bought all the vodka in Madibu? Let's take all the money from trying to buy cigs from Luxenstein and put into one bid to Madibu."

Morris nods his head. "We should do that. The Ruskis will fold and then we can use our troops in Germany to control the cigarettes in Luxenstein."

The President looks ebullient. "Then we are agreed. We will buy the vodka regardless of cost."

Everyone cheers and starts singing the National Anthem. Tears flow when they finish. They all hug. Finally, the standoff will be ended! America will win!

Chapter 35
Moscow Melts, Soviets Sizzle

From the borders with Finland and West Germany to the Siberian tundra and the coast of Kamchatka, comrades are finding new levels of crazy. Waiting in line for food is OK; having to wear six sweaters to stay warm in your two-room apartment where you live with the eight other members of your family is to be expected, but every day with undrinkable vodka leads to a new level of hell. This cannot be accepted. This *will not* be accepted.

If it goes on much longer, damn the nukes and machine guns, there will be a revolt in the U.S.S.R. It will be bloody and could last until they march into Western Europe to find liquor. This could be the start of World War III. We could see farmers with pitchforks become marauding hordes.

Every part of life is being impacted. Teachers are trying to fly in class. Potato farmers have military protection. People are ripping up water pipes so they can use the copper tubing to build homemade stills. The problem is, there aren't any potatoes to make vodka with or berries to make liqueurs this late in the year. There isn't even any wine or beer anywhere in the U.S.S.R.

Is the end of the world nearing? When will the people find out what is happening in Kiev or Vladivostok? In an empire with a dozen time zones, almost anything can be swept under the rug. The last thing Boski and his crew need is the insanity being seen in public. The KGB and Red Army are jamming every ham radio signal and frequency they can find. The depth of this problem must never be known. It must be suppressed. No cost is too high.

This desire was about to be shattered on their national nightly news. Ivana and Boris are the nation's most trusted people. Ever since they were paired together fifteen years ago, every Russian has believed in them. Ivana and Boris have gotten the people through cold, hungry winters, empty grocery stores, and international scares. The comrades love them.

Behind Boris is a news tape of a man becoming enraged after trying the "new vodka." He is flailing away at anyone who moves near him. Boski is being burned in effigy.

Boris shakes his head. "Friends and comrades, do not let this be you. Mothers and fathers of the Soviet Union are better than this. We are strong people. Vodka doesn't rule us."

Another tape of Americans attacking an old lady to get her cigarettes is showing on television. It is the grannies who kicked the innocent naked guy in the nuts.

"Look at these weak imperialists. Their babushkas are maiming innocent people over their lack of cigarettes that has only lasted nine days. We are better than that. Have a good night, comrades."

Ivana smiles. "Yes, comrades, we have been without vodka for two weeks and nothing like that has ever happened in Mother Russia."

"You are so holy. You aren't a man. You don't understand what we need. You sip your vodka, bitch." Boris is lecturing her.

"You are a sexist pig. I drink a bottle a day. I'm just not a sloppy drunk like you."

"Just like you don't show your period."

"I don't have to take this!" She pushes away her microphone and jumps across the desk at Boris. "Are you going to run away again?"

The weather girl is standing on the set. "Without vodka, I've lost my interest in sex."

Ivana hits Boris with her script. "Of course you have, look at these ugly men. If Russian women aren't drunk, why would we ever demean ourselves by having sex with these pigs? Maybe I'll become a lesbian."

Boris picks Ivana up and puts her over his shoulders. "Let's get you out of here."

***

A group of people are standing in front of an appliance store in Moscow watching this on the TV in the window. Some are laughing. Some are cheering. Some are open-mouthed in disbelief.

A woman strikes a man. "She's right. I'd never fuck you unless I was drunk."

"If I didn't drink three bottles a day, I'd never be able to look at you naked. You and your mother need cranes to lift your boobs above your waists."

All the couples on the sidewalk start fighting. One man and woman stop. They act like they smell something at the same time. "That little man over there smells like real vodka. He's got some. Get him."

The crowd chases the man. He falls. He looks up at the throng, frightened for his life. "Yes, I had a little vodka, but it's all gone. I swear."

Then throng strips him naked looking for vodka. They don't find any. The man shivers on the cold pavement.

An old woman leans over and kisses him. "I'll even kiss you for a taste of that vodka..."

She closes her eyes and inhales deeply. She seems content for a moment, but soon she slaps him and starts pursuing other prey.

***

It's not just people watching Ivana and Boris through plate glass windows on the street, or ten people huddled in a flat in Leningrad to learn the day's news. Somehow, they have news of what is happening in other cities. This is not good. Boski, Nitvik, Davinko and Petrov are glued to the TV at the Kremlin. They fear an imminent coup. Nitvik picks up a spider and looks at it. He talks into it.

Petrov is tapping his fingers on the table while watching the screen. Boski has his head in his hands. Nitvik looks under the table for something. He looks behind the drapes and out through the window. Then he goes to the door, opens it, sticks his head through the gap to look around, closes and locks it.

Davinko's eyes narrow and smiles at the same time. "Can we find a sip of real Soviet vodka for Nitvik?"

Petrov chuckles. "How can you tell it's the vodka? That's how he always acts."

Boski pounds the table. "This is what you are worried about? We've lost Ivana and Boris? The nation trusts them more than us. What's next?"

Petrov stands at attention. "Let's bomb Washington. They did this to us. It's an act of war! We have no choice!"

Davinko shakes his fist. "Then they bomb us and everyone loses. Drunk or sober, you are still a moron."

Boski looks around the room at the pictures of Lenin, Stalin and workers. "What would they do? Comrade Stalin, please come to me. Speak to me. Tell me what I can do."

Nitvik jumps on the table. "They would drink vodka and attack. Stalin would send the weak to Siberia in railway cars."

Boski is annoyed. "You are an idiot. We don't have any vodka. That's the problem. In World War II, Stalin refused to let the Soviet Union be taken. He knew Germany couldn't handle our winters. To hell with the vodka, let's bring the Americans to their knees. We should only buy cigarettes. Russians are much tougher than those pansies!"

Davinko nods. "Yes, cigarettes could calm the craving for vodka and we could have them delivered very quickly."

Petrov is confused. "But people smoke when they drink. Won't they miss drinking?"

Boski thinks for a moment. "Let's have Luxenstein make the cigarettes much stronger."

Nitvik is dancing on the table. "You are a traitor, comrade. How could we dance like this without vodka?"

Davinko jumps to his feet. "I'm with Comrade Premier Boski. Russians are tougher than Americans. If we take their cigarettes, they will crumble like Nitvik's sanity. We will win. Mother Russia will be victorious! That was our plan all along."

Nitvik picks up a glass. "Let's toast to victory!"

Boski snorts. "Toast with what? Davinko, double our offer to Luxenstein."

"Yes, Comrade Premier. I will call right now. Nitvik, you moron, get down from there."

Nitvik jumps off the conference table and runs around the room, looking under every table and chair. Finally, he slides under Boski's chair. Davinko runs over and drags him from between Boski's legs.

Boski shakes his head. "I have to rely on *you two*? Please end this standoff before I end up *like them*."

Nitvik and Davinko stop fighting, become quiet and sit at the table. Davinko writes some notes. Boski glares.

Everyone stands and makes a motion of toasting. "Mother Russia and victory."

It is a weak and quiet effort. It's all they can muster.

Chapter 36
Madness, Madness, Madness

The streets of Washington, Philadelphia, Moscow, Leningrad and all the towns and villages in the U.S. and U.S.S.R. are descending into total chaos. Gangs of people jonesing for their vice are growing, roaming the streets, looking in trash cans and starting fights. Even those who didn't smoke or drink are in jeopardy. They're getting beaten up for not being in pain. Life is truly out of control.

The shades in Gabe Stein's office are constantly drawn. A knock on the door causes him to jump up from his chair. As he does, he dumps papers, credit cards and his passport on the floor. It makes some noise. He tries to cough to cover it.

This startles Dr. Lucy Diamond. She pushes the door open to see Gabe gathering his mess up from the floor. "Sorry, I didn't mean to scare you, Gabe."

"It's alright, Dr. Diamond. How can I help you?"

"I've seen stories about people in the Soviet Union detoxing and roaming the streets. Is that what my formula was used to do?"

"I'm sorry. I can't discuss that matter. It's on a need-to-know basis."

"I can't decide if I should laugh or cry. By the way, it looks like you might be going on a vacation. Where are you heading?"

"I've got some time coming. Who asked you to ask me that? Was it Morris? Hayden?"

"No one asked me. I haven't seen any of them. I saw your passport on the floor and a bunch of maps."

"I like to be ready before I leave. It can be a lot of trouble if you aren't."

She glances at the maps. "Wow, it's a wide variety of places... Rio, Bhutan, Andorra, and France. They don't have much in common."

"Who wants to know? CIA? State? Who do you work for, Diamond?"

"I just saw them lying on the floor. You need to calm down, Gabe."

Lucy is freaked out and leaves. As she does, Gabe locks the door behind her. He gets on his hands and knees and looks under his desk. He tries to get up quickly and bumps his head on the desk.

"No bugs in my desk, good."

He starts throwing books off his shelves looking for bugs. He doesn't find any. Books are everywhere. He doesn't care. It looks like he's not coming back to his office any time soon. Gabe moves frantically around the room.

"I've got to get my ass out of here. I know too much. They're going to kill me," he says to himself.

He starts shoving papers into a shredder and puts others into a file. Then he puts both the shredded paper and files into his oversized, accordion briefcase and locks it. He reaches for another briefcase but it's locked and papers fall to the floor.

He quickly leaves his office, hugging his briefcase to his chest. He winds his way out of the building and to his car. He turns at nearly every corner. Stein goes in and out of multiple parking lots. The sweat is dripping through his shirt.

***

Meanwhile, at a bar in the international terminal at Charles de Gaulle Airport in Paris, Mark is on his third scotch and munching on roasted hazelnuts. A couple of seats over from him is Sergei (now Fyodor) drinking his double bourbon. They both reach for the nuts at the same time.

Sergei stops. "I am sorry. Please, you go first."

"Thanks, you speak English. Where are you from?"

"Helsinki. My name is Fyodor."

"Hi, Fyodor, I'm Mark. I would've guessed that accent was Russian."

"Nope, I'm Finnish. Many people get those accents confused."

"Sorry, where did you get a taste for bourbon?"

"I visited the Kentucky Derby once and loved it. I wish it was easier to see at home."

"I'm an American and I've never been to the Derby." They touch glasses. "It looks like you've had a long trip, too."

"You don't know the half of it. How about you?"

"Six months away from home. It's been tough."

"I understand. It will be nice to see familiar faces again."

"I wish it was over." Mark's voice is unusually weak.

Sergei hears his flight called and gulps down his drink. "Me, too Mark. Me too. Be safe, my friend…"

Mark is a little puzzled but more buzzed. "Have a safe trip, Fyodor."

Sergei/Fyodor leaves. Mark motions to the bartender for another drink. He looks at the TV. The news shows near rioting in the streets of Moscow. Broken windows in liquor stores are commonplace. Under his breath, he says, "Holy shit, what have we done?"

The TV news then shows Chicago. The story is about how there are no cigarettes in the U.S. Mark shakes his head and mutters. He chuckles at the epiphany he has just had. "No fucking way. They're screwing with us, too." He looks around to see if anyone has heard him.

He picks up his drink and casually walks to a bank of pay phones. He dials a number. Then, he puts a lot of change into the slots. He's drinking and tapping his fingers on the phone. "Sol, have you seen the news?"

"Yeah, what did we do? It's a lot bigger than we were told."

"It's not just us. All the cigarettes at home have disappeared. How did they do it?"

"Shit, we've got to get to the drop and then run. I hope that cigarette shit is true."

"Why?"

"I found out my girlfriend has been banging my cousin and both smoke two packs a day. No butts will fuck them up. They deserve it."

They both cackle. Mark doesn't realize how close he came to knowing half the story. He is now in a much higher state of alert, feeling the team may have hits out on them.

This is the perfect four-card monte game, except two of the cards are taking some power soon. Imagine what the Russian and American spooks would be thinking if they knew all the other parts of the story.

Chapter 37
Old Friends, New Power and Wealth

Prince Claude and Paleau are sitting on the deck of a yacht the size of Manhattan that is moving slowly through the Mediterranean. We can see both Africa and Spain. The beauty is mythic with a continuum of centuries-old buildings on each side of the sea. The Prince and Paleau are smiling but appear to be deep in thought.

"My friend, what are we going to do?" Claude asks, taking another sip of wine.

"Your Highness, you want me to make a decision? So far, every insane idea you've come up with has, to my utter disbelief, worked perfectly. We've been friends for so long that I don't want to mess this up. For once you are on the heater. My only suggestion is not to get too greedy. There is an American saying – 'Pigs get fat. Hogs get slaughtered.' There is plenty to be piggy about for us." He is laughing but his eyes are dead serious.

"That is a great phrase. If I become a hog, there will be a price to pay, but I do like pig. I love ribs and pulled pork."

They chuckle heartily as the prince pours more wine. A very loud noise interrupts the temporary silence, and a helicopter appears. The yacht comes to a stop to allow the chopper to slow down, hover, and land on the aft deck.

Jinare and Mbangu get out. The helicopter takes off again as they walk towards the Prince and Paleau. Claude cannot control himself. He starts running to greet his old friend.

Their hug lasts for almost a minute. As they part, the smiles on their faces are huge and a few tears are rolling down their cheeks. They walk to the table with their arms around each other. Paleau and Jinare shake hands and sit with their bosses.

Claude has tears on his cheek but recovers first. "How long has it been, my friend?"

"Since that month after graduation when you took us to Monte Carlo and Las Vegas."

Jinare snickers. "Las Vegas? I finally figured out that you sent three women over to keep me away from the two of you. But it sure was fun."

"He was already the Pied Piper of Panties." Mbangu shakes his head fondly. "Where are my manners? Prince Claude of Luxenstein, may I present my friend and brother, Jinare. You never truly met him, but he sure did like those party favors."

"What an odd family picture we are about to have! President Mbangu of Madibu and Mr. Jinare, may I present my protector and brother, Jacques Paleau. I have known him since my first week of boarding school. He protected me then. He protected the Pied Piper, and now he protects the crazy Prince Claude. I'd probably be dead without him."

They all embrace. Claude opens more champagne. They sit together at the table on the forward deck.

Mbangu clears his throat. "To old friends, new friends, and ahem, ahem, being too backward to compete with the mighty United States and the all-powerful Soviet Union."

They touch glasses, drink, chuckle and sit quietly for a moment.

Claude smiles broadly. "Isn't it fun for us to have the ultimate power? It is at the same time too formal for conversation. Having someone to share it with is priceless."

Paleau suddenly sits up. "Wait a second, how well do you know the helicopter pilot?"

Jinare answers. "He is married to my sister and she knows nothing. How about the ship's captain?"

Paleau smiles. "He somehow got the impression that I am a Greek prince and Claude is my lackey. You two are friends trying to buy Greek citizenship. We paid cash. He didn't ask any more questions."

Everyone howls and drinks. Claude reaches under his chair for some papers. "There is more odd news today. The Americans said they are no longer interested in my cigarettes, but the Soviets more than doubled their previous bid. It was already double the going rate."

Mbangu giggles loudly. "Oh my, we are truly changing the world. The Soviets withdrew their bid for vodka to me and the Americans asked me to name my price."

Everyone looks at the other in disbelief. Reality is setting in.

Paleau finishes his glass of champagne and then chugs the bottle. "No, you can't do this. Don't be the *hog… again.* For once in your life, my dear friend, be the pig."

Claude chortles and slaps Paleau on the back. "You know, I'd never get greedy."

Mbangu is amused. "We hold all the cards. The superpowers each think they are tougher than the other. They are trying to bring their enemy to their knees."

Claude brings out a bottle of cognac. "Who are we to deny them this? It is very hot in Madibu, is it not?"

Jinare is puzzled. "Yes, but so what?"

"Colorado has marvelous mountains and great snow for skiing in the winter. Why not ask for Colorado as part of your price?"

"My friend, you have always loved the beach and Cuban cigars. That's a small price for the Soviets to pay," Mbangu adds.

Paleau and Jinare are sharing full-throated gulps of cognac. Mbangu and Claude are laughing loudly. Paleau starts to wander off. Claude is serious.

"Mbangu, let's not get greedy. How about buying a few thousand acres there and have them build you a hotel and some homes for citizens to use?"

"That sounds good. You should think about just a few hectares of beachfront property. You could build a casino. Instead of trying to beat the house, you could *be* the house."

Paleau pauses for a moment then drinks some more. Claude owning a casino is the twilight zone.

"Let's do it, Mbangu."

"Yes, my friend, but don't forget, we are far too backward and frivolous to hold our own with the big boys."

Soon everyone is drunk and passed out on the deck. The exhaustion is likely more the primary cause of everyone passing out than the booze. For the first time in a few months, they could let their guard down and discuss the future without worrying about being discovered. The pressure gauge had been opened slightly. Here we go! The next few days will change the world. Too bad no one will know the story.

Chapter 38
Great Countries, Great Power, Great Decisions

Life in the Soviet Union will never be confused with a day at Disneyland, but now the people are experiencing a new level of despair. They had survived a revolution. They lasted through the siege of Stalingrad. They put up with no food, no heat and no toilet paper, but no vodka? This was too much to ask.

Twenty thousand nukes, three million troops and thousands of tanks couldn't do this much damage to the psyche of the nation. The streets looked like the remnants of a bad frat party. Men and women were staggering but weren't drunk. People would hold bottles upside down praying there would be one last drop. Then we'd hear the inevitable sad shrieks of failure. It was like everyone was in their own little world. Loud cries from ten meters away don't rate a glance to see what's wrong. Everybody knows what's wrong.

Oh, to be stumbling drunk just one more time. They are dreaming of puking on the other's shoes again. Finding a drop of rotgut vodka that blinds them for a week will be as welcome as no snow in January in St. Petersburg. Alas, this seems as likely as seeing a leprechaun riding a unicorn in Red Square.

This despair is not confined to the streets and alleys, the villages and towns of the Soviet Union. The satellite republics are nearing open revolt. Soviet troops value their lives more than their positions. They can't be counted on any longer. The concept of national security is secondary to survival.

The madness is exploding in the inner sanctums of the Soviet power structure in the Kremlin. Our fearless team of communists is meeting to come to a decision regarding their next move. Nitvik is smelling an empty bottle of vodka and sighing like a teenaged girl staring at the most recent heartthrob. He seems lost in the moment when a lit Molotov cocktail bounces off the window. Then a brick hits it. Everyone jumps.

Twenty years ago, those actions would have led to execution. Hell, such insurrection was unthinkable even three months ago. The old crew is sitting at the long table tapping their fingers, looking sadder than a funeral dirge. Finally, Nitvik starts shouting, "The people are right to revolt. This country was built on revolution. Mother Russia! Mother Russia!"

Petrov's voice gets louder. "Shut up, you paranoid drunk. How can we fight a war without vodka? Who would be crazy enough to follow us into battle sober?"

Davinko clears his throat. "Comrade Premier, I have some important news."

Boski sits up straight in his chair. He looks excited, but his voice almost cracks. "Is it good news?"

Davinko starts haltingly. "It's good and bad."

Nitvik pounds the table. "Tell us! I need a drink."

Petrov takes his gun and points it at Nitvik. "We all need a drink, you fool. Maybe if I shoot him, there will still be vodka in his blood."

"Well, the nutty prince has agreed to our undoubled price."

Boski looks puzzled. "That's fantastic! What's the bad news?"

"He wants us to give Cuba to him."

Petrov takes his hat off and scratches his head. "But we don't own Cuba. The Americans would never allow this."

Boski shakes his head. "What if we say no to Cuba?"

"He'll give the tobacco to the Americans for free."

"Offer him four times our offer. He's a gambler. He'll lose it back. If he says no, give him some beachfront property and a casino license in Cuba."

Petrov pounds the table. "If we pay him that much, we won't have enough money left to buy any vodka. I can kill that pig Fidel. The Cubans will love the Pied Piper of Panties."

Nitvik smiles. "Hell, the Cubans hate Fidel more than they hate us."

They all instinctively reach for vodka. They lift their glasses and shout "Mother Russia!" before realizing there is no vodka. They throw the antique crystal glasses at the pictures of the U.S.S.R.'s Founding Fathers. Then they gasp in despair.

Three Molotov cocktails explode against the windows. The Soviet leadership dives under the meeting table. Time is running out.

***

Meanwhile in Washington, a few people are watching televisions through the window of an appliance store – pictures of rioting and mayhem around the U.S. The POTUS is being burned in effigy in nearly every state. People are shrieking and crying on the streets.

A man shakes his head. "What is wrong with our country?"

A well-dressed woman glares at the man. "I bet you never smoked."

"Nope," he says with an arrogant smirk.

A long-haired man screams, "Get him!"

Six people jump the man. They punch and kick him. He staggers away. His clothes are falling off as he starts running away. Every few strides, he falls to the ground. The mob claps and cackles. They push him forward.

The woman swings the man's tie over her head. Cheers erupt. She snarls, "I bet he wishes he had a cigarette about now!"

More cheers echo down the street. A few blocks away, the White House is under siege. Throngs of people are moving like zombies. Platoons of heavily armed military personnel and tanks are guarding America's House.

The senior staff is huddled in the Situation Room. General Hayden is sucking on a grenade. CIA Director Morris is trying to light an empty cigar tube. The tension is palpable. Something needs to be done and done *now*.

The Secretary of State is beside himself. "Mr. President, we could suffer the first coup in U.S. history."

President Thomas is looking randomly from side to side. "Huh? What makes you think that? Zombies in the street? Grannies attacking mobsters? Are you sure? That sounds like a perfectly normal day to me."

Morris speaks up. "There's a surge in marijuana imports. But it never gets off the docks. All the drug tunnels in Texas and Arizona have people waiting for the mules."

Hayden perks up. "Well, let's start smoking that."

The Secretary of State looks at a cable. "Mr. President, President Mbangu is willing to sell us all the vodka they can produce at a lower price than we offered."

Thomas is puzzled. "What's the catch?"

"They want us to give them title to the entire State of Colorado."

Hayden jumps from his seat. "Holy shit, we've got the Ruskis right where we want them! Fuck Colorado. I'll retake it in three days after this shit settles down."

Thomas pauses. "Offer him three times our top offer, but no Colorado. We'll bring the Soviets to their knees. Then we'll go get the tobacco."

Morris claps loudly. "That's a great idea. I'll start getting my guys to sell some pot. If everyone is stoned for a month, they won't miss their cigarettes. Maybe I'll buy some Pizza Hut franchises."

Everyone roars. The President stands up. "It's settled. Call President Mbangu and tell him our offer is take it or leave it."

Chapter 39
The End is Near

It's another perfect day in the idyllic land of Luxenstein. The people are going about their daily lives with a confidence, pride and contentment the world envies. They trust their prince implicitly. They find his wild lifestyle and rollercoaster handling of their country endearing. He will always find a way to protect them and have the country prosper. They aren't bothered by the news from the outside world. Why should they be? Luxenstein, their beloved home, has never been happier or wealthier.

It's not like the Pied Piper of Panties is unique in his family lineage. His great-great-great-great grandfather was given the beautiful countryside that is Luxenstein to keep him quiet about his numerous dalliances with Napoleon's Josephine. His grandfather held markers from Kaiser Wilhelm that could have brought down their government. This protected the beautiful nation during WWI. The populace knew there were reasons throughout that defended them from the cold realities of the world, but they never cared to know what those reasons were.

Why should the Luxensteiners be worried about Prince Claude? Everyone knew he had many close calls, but their pacific, glorious lifestyle had never been interrupted. So what if the tabloids had pictures of him naked with the wives and daughters of world leaders? The women were of age and Prince Claude was single. Let him have his fun.

The Prince is sitting on the back porch. He is beaming, eating strawberries and sipping champagne as he reads some cables. His chuckle echoes across the porch.

Paleau doesn't know what's going on, but chuckles anyway. "Okay, Your Highness, what trouble are you in this time?"

"Sadly, we won't be taking over Cuba. However, the Soviets are willing to quadruple our asking price if we don't sell any tobacco to the Americans."

As he finishes, Lauren walks out onto the porch. Paleau hands her a glass of champagne.

"Wasn't your plan not to sell to both sides?" Paleau asks.

"Of course it was, but they don't know that. Now this is working out better for us. We won't have to build container ships to deliver product to the United States."

"Your Highness, please don't lose all the excess profits in Monte Carlo this time."

"I'll try not to, old friend. I'll go to Las Vegas instead. Could you bring me the secure line and call our old friend Mbangu?"

"Of course. Be right back." Paleau leaves to get the phone.

Lauren flirts with Claude. He loves it.

"Lauren, I am truly sorry that you won't be the Empress of Cuba."

She smiles and shrugs. "I guess you're stuck with me here, then."

"That's for sure. After the news of what we did comes out, I'll have to protect you."

"As a loyal subject, I might have to allow you to do that." Her eyes twinkle as she looks at him. She furtively moves some hair from her face.

Has she tamed The Pied Piper of Panties? This could be bigger news than scamming the superpowers.

Paleau returns to the patio with a phone and hands it to Prince Claude. He puts it on a speaker box. "Mbangu, my old friend, how are you?"

"I am well. And you?"

"I think I'm supposed to feel inferior to the Soviets and the Americans, but for some strange reason, I just don't."

They share a loud guffaw.

"Claude, the strangest thing has happened. The Americans have multiplied my offer by three but refuse to include Colorado. Can you believe it?"

The Prince laughs. "Cheapskates! The Soviets have quadrupled their offer to me if I don't sell to the Americans, but I don't get Cuba."

"Don't worry. I'll call Fidel. I'm sure he'll give me a great estate on the beach for causing all these problems for the Americans."

"And Mbangu, you should be able to buy up lots of land in Colorado with your bounty. I'm not sure they are prepared for an influx of African skiers, though."

They laugh heartily again. Claude gets up and pretends to be skiing.

"Claude, I'm so happy they brought us back together."

"Me, too. It's sad that we are so backward. Sooo very backward."

"What do you think will happen?"

Paleau rolls his eyes. "I'll have to pay off a boatload of bets and quite a few pissed-off mothers."

Lauren looks at both. "Maybe not so many mothers."

Claude smiles. "I'm not sure what will happen, but it'll sure will be fun to watch."

Mbangu roars with laughter. "I think you will be more fun to watch."

"And you will change your country's history. I am the sinner. You are the saint."

"Thank you. Come to Madibu and watch the new forms of madness evolve. Please bring Paleau and Mademoiselle van Meer."

"How long do you think it will take to get the deals done?"

"Neither country can last much longer. You'll be on our beaches in a matter of weeks."

Lauren smiles. "I'll have to bring lots of Coppertone."

Everyone howls.

"Paleau will set up a network of accounts in our banks, in Switzerland and other safe places. He's excellent at it. He's had a lot of practice."

"Mr. President, I'll work with Jinare to set it in motion."

Jinare grins. "It will be my pleasure. I think I'll send all the Russians home with their own personal Rhesus monkey to remind them of their stay in Madibu."

Everyone snickers. Claude jokes. "You've got to watch out for the quiet ones. They can be brutally mean."

Lauren laughs. "I like the quiet ones, too."

Everyone howls.

"Claude, I'll see you soon."

"I'm looking forward to it. Goodbye." Claude hangs up. Lauren gives Paleau a kiss on the cheek. Then she kisses Claude right on the lips and quickly pulls away.

Chapter 40
The More Things Change

The sun is shining over the White House for the first time in months. Armed soldiers guard a small truck as it enters the grounds and winds its way around to the loading dock. The driver and three armed guards go to the back of the truck and pound on the sliding door. The armed person inside hands one of his colleagues a small box. The person who receives it is escorted inside the White House. He hands it to the CIA Director Morris, who takes it to the Situation Room and places the box on the main table. He pulls the top off and smiles. He pulls out a bottle that says "Madibu Premium Vodka."

Morris beams. "Gentlemen, this is how we brought down the Soviet Union."

Everyone in the room claps and hollers. They are slapping each other on the back. Everyone is smiling. Could they have won the Cold War after all?

Hayden finally barks, "Let's try it."

President Thomas opens a bottle and pours everyone a drink. He lifts his glass, "We have ended the Cold War, boys. And we won. Big time!"

They all whoop and holler.

General Hayden shrugs. "But we didn't kill any commies."

The Secretary of State shakes his head and takes a big gulp of vodka. "Jesus, you are a piece of work. This stuff actually tastes good." He reflects for a moment. "Almost great."

Morris takes a gulp. "This is the best vodka I've ever tasted. But people are still without cigarettes. What should we do?"

Hayden pours everyone another drink and opens a second bottle. "I could bomb Luxenstein's cigarette factories."

President Thomas empties his glass and wipes his mouth. "No bombing!"

Hayden picks up a bottle and drinks directly from it. "Damn, I haven't felt this good since Nam. I'm almost forgetting about not having any butts."

Thomas takes another drink. "How much vodka are we getting?"

Secretary of State pauses. "About 7-10,000,000 cases a week."

President Thomas stands, takes another drink. "That's 84-120 million bottles a week. That's one bottle for about every three people in our nation. People might forget about smoking."

Morris belches. "Yeah, they'll be too drunk."

Thomas chortles. "I can live with that until we get our tobacco growing again. Let's figure out distribution. It could work."

The Secretary of State takes a drink. "I can't believe we can turn smokers into alcoholics."

Hayden glares at him. "You're a pansy! This will win the Cold War. So, what if we have a few more drunks? We beat the damn commies!"

People may wear different clothes, speak different languages, have different economies, but power and crazy know no borders. Once you have true power, it's nearly impossible to give it up.

***

The Soviet leadership drives through the Moscow suburbs to a massive warehouse. Boski gets out of a Russian limo, while the rest get out of the next one. Nitvik is pushing the others to beat them to the door, like a school child trying to get the best seat.

A guard tower is about fifty yards away and soldiers are everywhere. Several have their rifles drawn as the crew enters the building. Large containers of cigarettes with the Luxenstein flag on them are piled to the ceiling as far you can see. A table is about thirty feet inside the door. A Soviet flag is suspended from the ceiling. An opened carton is on the table. Gilded lighters are next to spectacular ashtrays.

Boski shakes his head. "What are we going to do with all these cigarettes?"

Davinko looks around. "Could we make vodka from the tobacco?"

Nitvik jumps over the table, hugs and kisses Davinko. "I always knew I liked you, Comrade."

Boski lights up a cigarette. "You know, those old American TV shows had doctors doing cigarette advertisements saying they calmed your nerves. I am feeling very calm, very calm indeed."

Nitvik puts two cigarettes in his mouth and lights them both. After a couple of deep drags, he coughs. He smiles, still choking.

Davinko holds up a pack of cigarettes. "The package says smoking can cause cancer."

Petrov blows smoke into Davinko's face. "And no vodka can cause us to be sent to Siberia."

Nitvik blows smoke rings. "I'll take cancer over Siberia any day."

Boski nods. "Me too. Plus, when the Americans weaken and we win the Cold War, we can get our people their vodka."

They all clap and scream "Mother Russia!" with cigarettes dangling out of their mouths, coughing like crazy.

Nitvik smiles triumphantly. "If they don't, I will have the KGB send them to Siberia."

The senior staff is sitting in over-stuffed leather chairs smoking like there is no tomorrow. Davinko is blowing smoke rings around Nitvik's head. Nitvik punches at the smoke rings.

They aren't yelling at the others like they always had done. Petrov slides back into his chair. He sighs in contentment and admires the spectacular paintings.

In unison, the entire group sings, "Mother Russia! The great, the grand, Mother Russia!"

Chapter 41
Peace Breaks Out?

Much like the government set up cheese distribution during a recent recession in the U.S., they are using schools, subway terminals, VFW halls and churches to hand out free vodka. They are trying to get every smoker hooked on vodka and it seems to be working. Tour companies develop weekend getaways to vodka distribution centers. America is partying again.

In less than three weeks, the marauding gangs of jonesing addicts have disappeared. Unfortunately, there has been a spike in traffic accidents and DUI tickets, but peace seems to be coming to cities, towns and villages. Not an unreasonable price to pay.

The good news is, those town and cities are making so much money from the traffic-tickets that parks, schools and roads are being fixed at a record rate. Many downtrodden places look so good that the crime rate is going down. The very last thing on anyone's mind is cigarettes.

Farmers in North Carolina are looking for other crops to grow. They are thinking about growing grapes and making wine. Hell, they could become the eastern Napa Valley. Several farmers are thinking about opening ostrich ranches.

Meanwhile in the Soviet Union, the people seem skinnier and calmer. The contentiousness of the bread lines is a thing of the past. From Vladivostok to St. Petersburg, the lack of vodka isn't discussed. In Moscow, the stench of cigarettes is omnipresent but no one seems to care. The entire city smells like a dive bar. As much as you can expect in a gray, cold land that is run as a dictatorship, contentment reigns. There must be something besides tobacco in those cigarettes.

For over a third of a century, the world has been told the U.S. and Soviet Union are polar opposites. The Cold War was about trying to impose the other's way of life on the other. A military solution was inevitable. Or was it?

The expected bellicosity that had endured multiple POTUS and Premiers of the U.S.S.R. had all but evaporated. In three months, no one had banged a shoe threatening to bury the other. No one had called anyone an "evil empire." No one was thinking about a tactical nuclear strike. Something had to be going on behind the scenes. This new standoff wasn't natural.

Nitvik wasn't looking under tables any more. Hayden wasn't arbitrarily lobbing live grenades in the White House. But cruise ships were landing in Madibu Harbor. As usual, the people in Luxenstein didn't care what was going on in the outside world. They were happy and had graciously welcomed all the new tobacco workers as their friends and neighbors.

The most dramatic occurrence of the first six months of the new status quo was the royal wedding of Prince Claude and Lauren van Meer. This war did have one victim: the Pied Piper of Panties, he was no more, but he was too happy to care.

In America, a new industry was born: rehab centers. They were popping up like McDonald's franchises. Every county could have its own place to cure you from any vice. They named the first celebrity facility after Betty Ford. The first ones were for alcohol, but soon you could be cured for everything. It quickly became a multi-billion-dollar industry. If you had too much fun, your friends would have an "intervention" and take you directly to a rehab that "cured" your addiction.

They created sex addiction rehabs. I tried to get my friends to send me to one, but no one believed my stories.

For the next couple of years, there were occasional "confrontations" between the superpowers. They seemed a little less intense than the previous one. They just didn't want to fight any more. The Russians kept sending over hockey players. We sent them rock and roll bands. The leaders were getting older. They were tired. Their grandkids didn't know anything about shooting wars.

Finally, the superpowers got together and allowed people to tear down the Berlin Wall. Someone called Pink Floyd and they did a concert. It was over. There was no more standoff.

The so-called experts, the historians, started writing how the Cold War was won. It was Lech Walesa. It was the Pope. It was a progressive Soviet leader. It was the POTUS. It was military spending gone wild. It was just time.

BULLSHIT!

It was a leader who loved his country so much that he came up with a plan to maximize his poor nation's attributes and create a positive future. It was a crazy man who lost his nation's bounty at the baccarat tables and by partying too much and had to create a scam to save himself. It was two batshit crazy groups of leaders who wanted to go to war but didn't want to clean up the mess it would cause. It was about human weakness and addiction.

It was how all these things came together at a moment in time and how two friends saw how they could bring peace to the world and become rich doing it.

Mostly, it was about everyone keeping their mouths shut and willful blindness in not wanting to know what happened. It was burying the past as soon as it became the present. It was shredding and burning every piece of paper that could tie any of them to this "event." Remember it wouldn't have worked if both hadn't missed obvious problems. If they hadn't had their blinders on, one of the superpowers could have won.

Like so often happens, the greatest changes in world history happen without anyone knowing or why until much later. Nuking Hiroshima and Nagasaki were the exceptions. All too often, the change comes quietly and sometimes quickly.

This is how the Cold War *really* ended. Now the world knows. Deal with it!

Chapter 42
Old Friends and Foes Finally Meet

I made my way back to Luxenstein. Claude gave me complete control of the editing and printing process. But Claude was Claude. It had to be a party. The Pied Piper of Panties had been gloriously tamed, but he hadn't ever grown up. Lauren knew she couldn't stop him from having the most incredible party of his life. This was not about debauchery (well, at least, not entirely). It was about celebrating how multiple bands of people had worked independently to change the world without realizing they were doing it. Details. Just details.

Other than Claude and Mbangu, none of the living senior members knew what was about to happen. They were about to get blindsided by history once again. For once, I got to tell the story. They had to listen to me. I hoped I got most of it right.

***

The palace is massive. It has about a dozen entry points. Claude is being Claude and keeping everyone apart. No one fully knows why they are in Luxenstein or who else has been brought to this event.

Claude clears out the state dining room. He has his help bring in a dozen or so beautiful over-stuffed leather chairs. Each has its own table, light, book, cognac, vodka, caviar and cigars. Hey, the Pied Piper might be dead, but not totally. He can still throw a helluva party.

He claps and all the doors to the state dining room open. Claude beams as he holds Lauren's hand. Mbangu and Jinare have their arms around the other. Paleau is hugging me. The guests enter the room. At first there is hesitancy. Then, the old friends see familiar faces. Hugs and tears flow as freely as the champagne.

At first Sergei/Fyodor and Georgi run to the other. They are crying. "Sergei, I never thought I'd see you again."

Sergei laughs and cries. "You made me into Fyodor and saved my life."

Alexi finally breaks a smile. "BJ, you made a man out of our Georgi."

They laugh and cry and hug. Their embrace could only be shared by people drawn together by something much bigger than themselves. It's usually a war or natural disaster. This is a little of both.

Mark is looking at Sol. "I think you're about thirty years late for our meeting."

"I am." Sol laughs loudly. The years have changed him, but he is still a leader.

Mark looks at Sergei/Fyodor. "Wait a second, didn't we meet at an airport bar?"

Sergei/Fyodor roars. "You? It's you? We sure did. I was on my way home from America. Did you ever get to the Kentucky Derby?"

"Not yet, but you sure do have a great memory. I was trying to avoid going home from Russia. We went to Luxenstein to hide. I'm Mark."

"That's perfect. My real name is Sergei, but I've been Fyodor for many years. I can't believe I'm finally meeting our counterparts."

They hug. Sergei guffaws

. Mark realizes Sergei is gay. "Did the KGB know?"

"Nope."

They smile and hug again.

Ken looks at Lucy. "Lucy, an old lady almost beat me to death with her umbrella because I had to take a leak in Moscow."

Lucy chuckles. "If I'd known that, I would never have finished my experiment."

Claude comes over to me. "Look at what you've done. You have brought all these old friends back together."

"It wasn't me. It was Mbangu and you. By the way, I'm guessing that Gabe is hiding in the bushes somewhere. Shouldn't we send someone to get him?"

Marci snickers. "Nah, I think he's more comfortable with branches tied to his ears."

Lauren kisses Marci on both cheeks. "Do you think we should leave a book on the patio table for him to 'steal'?"

Claude can't control himself and cackles loudly. "And you say that I'm the plotter in our family."

Marci looks at me. I look at her. We are starting to communicate with looks – not just words – like Claude and Lauren. We know what must be done. I go around the room, excusing myself as I collect Sergei, Georgi, BJ and Alexi. Marci scopes out the party to find Natasha and Anton. We bring the group together in the far corner of the room.

Sergei looks truly puzzled. "You two look Russian, but you are too young to have been involved in our story. You would have barely been school children at the time."

Natasha's smile is so big that her face is almost cracking. I am feeling like Claude must feel almost every day of his life.

"Sergei, Georgi, BJ, Alexi, let me introduce you to Natasha and Anton Petrov."

The Russians gasp. Alexi blurts out. "You are Petrov's son?"

Anton smiles. "Guilty, as charged."

Natasha can't control her glee. "And I am Nitvik's daughter."

You could have heard Sergei's laugh all the way back to Moscow. "But you look so normal. How could this be? Are you adopted?"

The group roars, hugs and cries. Then, the stories start coming out. Marci and I realize this is their time and move away. From the other side of the room, we see the animated joy and boisterous freedom. Finally, they are sharing their stories. But these are their stories, not ours.

The servants pass out champagne. Claude taps on his glass. "Friends, tonight we learn about our shared history. Mark circled the globe bringing all the pieces together. It's something none of us could have done. To Mark!"

Everyone clinks their glasses and shouts, "To Mark!"

I am shaking. Marci holds me. "It's been my pleasure. Not that some of you haven't had some fun at my expense!" There is laughter. "You know who you are. Yes, you, Sergei. You had me convinced those were real bugs in my hotel room." Everyone cackles. "I had no idea where it was going, but here it is. This is your story."

Lucy walks over to Lauren. "I've heard a beautiful woman was involved, but you are way beyond what I expected."

Lauren seems touched. "That is so kind, but you are beautiful as well. Your intelligence will be inspirational to girls around the world. Remember, our home will always be yours."

Tears are streaming down Lucy's face. The women hug.

I had one last surprise. I lead Claude, Lauren and Marci to the far corner of the room. An old man is sitting at a table. As we approach, Claude recognizes Petey, and a huge smile explodes onto his face.

"Mark, how the hell did you find Petey?"

Petey gets up and hugs Claude. "Piper, you picked a stand-up guy in Mark. I can't wait to read the story." His happiness is infectious.

Marci is a little concerned. "Who is Petey?"

Claude has his arm around Petey's shoulders to give him some stability. "Petey took care of the Pied Piper and his merry band of fools in Vegas."

"It was my pleasure. Never was and never will be another Pied Piper. You must be the lady who did the impossible and tamed him. You made this old man so happy."

Lauren smiles and kisses Petey.

Marci whispers to Mark. "Can he be trusted?"

Mark smiles. "I'd love to know all the secrets Petey has kept under wraps for the past sixty years."

Claude walks with Petey and stands in the middle of the room. "Ladies and gentlemen, please find a seat and start reading our story. If there is anything at all that you'd like, please don't hesitate to ask. Our boy Mark has kept this so secret that I haven't seen the book myself. Read for a while and the real party will be tomorrow."

Sergei holds up his glass. "To secrets and those who kept them!"

Everyone crows and exclaims, "To secrets!"

Claude is beaming. "To no more secrets!"

I wasn't sure what I should do when I went to the center of the great hall. I cleared my throat and was feeling less secure than I had while traipsing around the world. But I knew I had to do this. Marci put her arm around me reassuringly.

"What are you thinking about doing?" She couldn't wipe the smile off her face. "I can't stop you, can I?"

I shake my head and start. "I hate to stop your reading, but tomorrow it's your choice. It's your stories and your lives. We can burn all the copies tomorrow at dinner, or we can publish it as is. It's up to you all."

Sergei is cracking up. "Aw, come on, the world deserves to know that a gay KGB agent was involved in super-secret espionage."

Sol is semi-serious. "Who the fuck is going to believe us anyway?"

Claude can't help himself. "My life is a testament to the premise that the crazier a story is, the more likely it to be true."

Mbangu joins the party. His wife doesn't know what to expect. "Even my old friend Claude used the word "saint" to describe me. That is way too boring. For a change, I want to be fun."

The biggest laugh of the evening erupts.

No one is moving an inch. Readers sigh and slap their knees. More drinking and more giggles. Claude gets up and walks to the patio. He carries a bottle of champagne and a blanket. I am puzzled and follow at a distance.

"Oh Gabe, Gabe Stein, you can come in or stay outside. It's your choice. Here's some champagne and a blanket. You needn't be worried."

Claude turns around and sees me. In the moonlight, he truly appears regal. "One must always be a good host."

As he finishes, Mbangu comes out for some air. "Mark, thank you."

He and Claude hug. They are more than brothers. They are Yin and Yang in real life. Claude pulls away. "True artists are supposed to suffer. I think Mark got away with something here."

For the first time Mbangu let down his guard. "And he got the girl."

Claude smiles and laughs as only he can. "Yes, he did. Plus, he's going to be rich and famous. I think we need to get something out of this."

"We already have," Mbangu says, putting his arm around Claude's shoulder.

The more things change, the more they stay the same. Two friends are working together to change a life, but this time it's mine.

This is their story, and I'm sticking to it.

THE END